It Is Morning

Also by Vernon Bargainer

At the Feet of Angels

It Is Morning

Vernon Bargainer

iUniverse, Inc.
New York   Bloomington

It Is Morning

iUniverse books may be ordered through booksellers or by contacting:

iUniverse
1663 Liberty Drive
Bloomington, IN 47403
www.iuniverse.com
1-800-Authors (1-800-288-4677)

ISBN: 978-1-4502-2872-5 (sc)
ISBN: 978-1-4502-2873-2 (dj)
ISBN: 978-1-4502-2874-9 (ebk)

Library of Congress Control Number: 2010906296

Printed in the United States of America

iUniverse rev. date: 06/01/2010

In Memory Of

David G. Burnet Elementary School
Wooster, Texas

Preface

Grade school may very well be the single most dramatic crisis in our lives, certainly the most decisive. Some things happen there that are never repeated. There are so many firsts in this so-called transition from childhood to adolescence: events that shape the course of our lives. Relationships pop up, innocent and seemingly transient, yet they set in motion the beginning of social personality and the building of character. Some find it easy to dismiss these early encounters as superficial passage—a mere bridge to maturity. On the contrary, these early instinctive interactions stand on their own. They are not a token bridge.

Then there's that first blush of romance. Mind you, it may not be very sophisticated, but it's no less real than all the love affairs that will ever follow. It is often presumed that there can be no significant relationships among prepubescent little people. Some say these don't count because, after all, we were just kids. This then leads to the claim that elementary school puppy love is meaningless. Tell that to the scores of people who've married their childhood sweethearts and found enduring and everlasting love.

So it is that in the rush to grow up we don't really undertake to identify which little things in our early living have taken control and shaped our character and our social behavior. Memories fade, some are chased away by the maturing process, and some just go into hiding, never to be searched for again. In light of all that takes place in this early life, whatever we forget or outgrow, one thing is inescapable: nothing in all of life, no happening in all the world, can ever take grade school out of our lives. Ask the man of our story, Andy Boone. He'll say these are the class reunions we should have.

1

He was mindless, his gaze locked hypnotically on two red spots glimmering faintly in the distance, drawing him like magnets down a flat East Texas highway. There was no physical sense at all, neither of his own body nor of the mighty vehicle that carried it above the road. He was years away from that rainy April morning.

Andy Boone trailed on through the drizzle without will, barely conscious that the two red lights were growing brighter. Suddenly, the distance collapsed and the lights burst on his windshield like fire. In the next instant, he was pushing stiff-armed against the steering wheel, his leg jammed hard against the brake. The engine was strangely aroar, the tires screaming at the sudden rampage.

He released the brake and steered hard to the left, but the car whipped around and started hurtling sideways and then backward and on across to the far side of the highway. It was dead quiet for an instant while the big machine sailed over a ditch. Then it plowed backward up an embankment and wedged its rear into a barbed-wire fence. And there, creaking and wobbling, it grudgingly came to rest.

"Shit!" Andy squinted through the driver's window at the ground, which seemed closer to his face than it should be. His hand quivered as he reached out to turn off the engine. For a moment, he sat frozen, his fingers still gripping the ignition key, staring blankly straight ahead. Finally, he sank back against the seat and dropped his head as though to drain from it the reverie that moments before had lulled him close to disaster. It was an unshakable vision of something he'd seen in a little town miles behind, an afterimage that would not burn out. But now it was fading, and the recovered dreamer, his car hooked safely on a ditch bank, peered through the windows and watched the real world fill in around him.

The rain had stopped. Andy shifted in his seat. When he tried to open the driver's door, it struck the ground only a few inches out. He tried to lower the window but it wouldn't budge. He pushed on the controls with both thumbs, bearing down with full weight. Still no luck. He started to slap at the window but stopped short as a picture flashed in his mind of that nervous moment when he had turned off the ignition.

As he started to slide across the seat toward the passenger side, Andy heard the rumbling of a vehicle somewhere in the field behind him. He strained to see out the rear window. An old pickup truck was bumping down a long, dirt driveway that ran slightly uphill to a ranch house set far back in a little clump of trees. He crawled on out and stood at the hood of his car. The truck stopped just across the ditch in front of him. The driver got out and looked toward Andy.

"You aw right, son?"

"Yessir." Son? The man couldn't have been more than forty-five years old. Andy was thirty-two. He grinned at the old man. Actually, the fellow sounded polite enough, and it was clear somehow that he hadn't intended his greeting as a put-down. For that matter, son was probably just a common expression among cattlemen for nonranchers, regular civilians. Anyway, Andy answered instinctively with yessir, which, if not said in reverence, at least showed he understood the system.

Andy shrugged, tried to look pleasant in spite of his circumstances, and waited for the next remark, which was bound to be "what happened?"

"Looks like we got work to do," said the man.

"Uh, yeah. I think you're right. Probably gonna be a little harder to get out of this than it was to get in."

The man sloshed through the ditch and headed for the wreckage, bending down from time to time as he moseyed along to see under the stranded car. Clearly, he was in no hurry even though he'd left the motor running in his truck. As Andy walked over to meet him halfway, he held out his hand. "I'm Dub Grimes," the man said.

"Andy Boone. Good to know you. Thanks for stopping."

"Nothin' to it," said Dub. Then he leaned back and eyed the front of Andy's car. "Comin' or goin'?" he asked.

"Sir?"

"You comin' from Virginia or headin' there?"

"Oh, yeah. Excuse me, I didn't know what you meant. Uh, I'm on my way to Dallas—Las Colinas, actually. I work for Clay Cutter Industries. Our headquarters are in McLean, Virginia, and we have a main branch there in, ah … there in Las Colinas. I've been transferred."

Dub Grimes glanced toward the highway. Then he looked back at Andy and frowned.

Andy laughed and held a finger in the air as though checking a point. "I know what you're thinking—that out there is not the highway from Virginia to Dallas. Too bad it isn't, I guess." He looked at his car and then back at the man. "But this is home," said Andy. "Texas is my home. I just veered off course to visit my mom and dad in Diboll for a couple of days."

"I didn't think you sounded Virginian," said Dub. They both walked toward the back of Andy's car, studying the situation as they talked.

"No, I'm not Virginian, all right," said Andy, "though that is great country. I was really raised in Baytown, Texas, down on the Gulf Coast, and … "

"Yeah, I know where that is."

"And my parents moved inland to Diboll in 1983 after a hurricane chased us out of Baytown. Actually, I was already working in McLean by then."

"And now here you are stuck in the mud, straddle a bobwire fence."

Andy swallowed hard and looked from Dub to the beached vehicle. It had broken the top three strands of fence wire, and its rear wheels were hooked over the bottom wire. The left side of the car was sunk in the soft ground about a foot. He cleared his throat and started to speak. "I'm sorry, Mr. Grimes—I mean, I really screwed up your fence."

"Dub."

"Uh, Dub. Anyway, this is stupid. Worse than that, it's made a hell of a lot of trouble for you. But I'll get the fence fixed for you right away and … and pay you for any trouble."

"Shoot, ain't no trouble to me. I been fixin' bobwire fences just 'bout all my life. But I still need the practice—know what I mean?" He smiled and rapped Andy's shoulder, like men do, and said, "You the one needs help. Let's get goin'!"

The two men stood for a moment, grinning together, pondering each other as though gauging that last measure of credibility that's necessary before sealing acceptance. Dub Grimes had the air of a totally unassuming, well-adjusted, hard-life man of the land. The brown denim pants and matching long-sleeved shirt looked home-starched, and they fitted neatly over his tall, lank frame. He wore fishing boots, not riding boots, and on his head was a blocked bib cap, not a wide-brimmed Western.

No stereotypical cowboy, this guy, but clearly a practiced rancher. His cap was set precisely straight and pulled down low over his forehead, and his hair was trimmed close around his neck right up to the edge of the cap. He had small ears, and that helped to keep his lean face from looking quite so gaunt. His complexion was ruddy and hard—probably toughened by the range winds—but his eyes softened when he talked, and he had the countenance of a man who, though he would take no bullshit from anybody, would always take care of things and see after his family and neighbors.

Watching Dub Grimes get around, Andy thought he seemed not to hustle at all, though he did move efficiently and deliberately. But when he got in his truck, it was a different story. He wheeled around on the shoulder of the road, scattering mud and grass, and then shot backward across the ditch and spun up to the front of the disabled car in the time it would take Andy to crank his engine.

The truck was a paragon of utility. It had a number of nonstandard items welded to it: a vice stand, a small hoist, a homemade reel winder, and up front, a steel tool rack hung with axes, chains, a steel rod, a long-handled pruner, a coil of rope, and two old blackened railroad lanterns that obviously hadn't been lit in forty years. Everything was neat and well organized and it all seemed to blend, even the little wad of Coors empties lashed together with a rubber band in the back corner by the tailgate.

Clearly, the truck was old and worn, but it had the same well-groomed look as its master, rancher Grimes. Its homemade paint job was clean, bright, and unmarred. That was more than Andy could say at the moment about the rear quarter of his 1982 solid-blue Olds Cutlass, which had taken a good scratching from the fence.

"This your ranch?" asked Andy as the man dropped to his knees and started hooking a cable somewhere underneath the front bumper of the Olds. "Wait a minute, let me help with this," he said, squatting under the bumper with not the least idea of where to put his hands.

"No sweat. No use in you gettin' dirty—I can get this. Yeah, the ranch is mine, the family's, rather." He chuckled. "It's not clear, and never will be, but it's ours. We don't have much on it now anyway—couple o' thousand head." He finished the cable, picked up a long-handled steel cutter leaning against his boot, strode to the fence, and snapped the bottom wire to the outside of each back wheel.

After they pulled the Cutlass from its snare, Andy helped Dub Grimes repair his fence. It was by no chance that wire stretchers, staples, fence pliers, and a half roll of barbed wire were in their rightful places in the bed of Dub's truck. When they were finished, Andy was concerned because the fence, though fully repaired, did not look as good as it did before. Grimes assured him as to how a fence was a fence—first, last, and always—not a thing of beauty.

They shook hands, and Andy praised Dub's effort. "How much do I owe you?"

Dub Grimes was silent for a moment and started shaking his head mildly as he looked straight into Andy's eyes. Then he smiled timidly. "There's no owin', Andy. If you paid me anything, it'd mean I hadn't helped you."

"But, I just—I don't know what to say."

"There's nothin' to say; it's done."

"Well, I hope you know I'm grateful."

The rancher nodded and turned away. As he strolled to his truck, Andy called out to him.

Dub stopped and turned half around. "Yo," he said.

"I still say I owe you one."

"No way."

"Funny thing, though, uh … "

Grimes paused again, his hand already resting on the door of his truck, just waiting solemnly for Andy to finish.

"Well, you know," Andy continued, "you never did ask me what happened."

"Don't take much to tell what happened. How it happened might be interestin', but it's none of my business." He smiled and touched the bib of his little rinky-dink cap with two fingers—probably a rancher's salute. "Hang in there, son!"

Andy grimaced. "Right, sir."

The battered Olds crept along the shoulder of the highway for about twenty-five yards and stopped beside a mailbox mounted on a bent cedar post. The driver frowned and stomped the floorboard with his trembling foot. He stared at his shaky hands, and then doubled his fists and stretched his arms past his knees. He sucked in a full breath and puffed it out in one quick gust. He eyed the mailbox and poked a finger into his temple as he read the name: W. T. Grimes. Then he shoved the lever into drive and sped away.

Why a playground? thought Andy. Why had he been consumed by a simple schoolyard twelve miles back? One that, though he had caught barely a parting glance, had almost cost him his life. He was at a loss to explain to himself the curious fascination he must have unconsciously held for it. He could not fathom it at all, even now, as he tried to recreate the picture that had hung obsessively between him and the diffused red taillights closing on him through the drizzle.

Andy Boone rocked his head vigorously, suddenly aware that again he was starting to stare vaguely down the highway. Moments later, he hit the brakes and pulled to a screeching stop. Then he swung the car around and headed back toward Tillman where he'd noticed the little school while waiting for a traffic light to change. He had to put the matter to rest. He would assault the problem head-on. Such an approach was natural for him and was partly responsible for his spectacular rise, in just five years, to director of Employee Relations at Clay Cutter's large Southwest regional branch.

He would wade into battle, storm the little town of Tillman, park his car near the traffic light, and go stand at the fenced schoolyard and study it until he spied the thing that had soaked into his head without telling him it was there. There's something incredible about the human brain, thought Andy, that it records information whether or not the conscious senses are paying attention. Clearly he had seen something important that had registered without his conscious knowledge. It was just there in his head, like a faint breeze that leaks timidly through an open window and settles in, undetected, until it finds a lose paper to rustle.

Andy proceeded through the light and turned around at the next block so he would be headed out of Tillman when he was ready to go. He drove back through the light and pulled close to the edge, well off the highway.

It had started to drizzle again. Andy stood for a while looking over the top of his car at the schoolhouse. In that first moment, part of his mystery dissolved; he was at once taken with sadness, and now he remembered that it was sadness that struck him three hours ago when he passed through the little East Texas town. But that sense of sadness had lasted only a few moments. As he recalled, he was quickly through the town, and it was over with. The problem was that as sadness faded, it left something in its place, a strange obsession that still didn't make sense.

He walked over to the chain-link fence that sealed the triangular playground, holding up his shoulders against the drizzle. The light-brown brick school was only two classrooms wide and about three times as long. A wood frame addition stood at right angles close to the front of it facing the other way, apparently overlooking the next street. Andy shrugged at the absence of any special sensation about the school. He was still frowning and slowly shaking his head when he turned away and walked down the fence line to study the small playground.

The long side of the triangular schoolyard ran along the highway. Up near the school, there were two swing sets and one old, well-worn straight slide. Midway toward the point of the yard, two basketball hoops faced each other about nine yards apart across the patchy grass. Otherwise the yard was empty and silent, probably because it wasn't recess, or maybe because of the rain.

Whatever the reason, it was sad to look at an empty playground on a dark, dreary day. After all, it should never rain on a child's playground. Andy dropped his chin and closed his eyes. That wasn't it. He looked up again. The emptiness seemed to plead of pain, not fun, of childhood tears, not laughter, struggle that filled the lives of so many little kids throughout the world, even as Andy stood at that lonely fence. He looked back toward the school and stared again into the empty swings. He could very nearly see the children swinging back and forth, giggling and chattering like newborn chicks.

After a while, Andy pursed his lips and shook his head. He had not accomplished anything. Sad as it was, he knew positively that melancholy was not the enigmatic menace that had spooked him as he sailed down US Highway 175 oblivious to everything outside himself.

He walked a little farther down the fence line and gazed to the end of the playground. It was deserted—just wet, nothing else. Then something started to happen. A human figure was emerging through the mist. He saw a little dark-haired girl coming into focus as if through some special visual effects. He knew she was not really there, but the longer he gazed, the more real he was able to make her out. She was standing half turned aside as if she'd been hurt and was hiding it from her playmates. Now Andy was paralyzed. He stared numbly, his lips parted and drying, though rain was running down his neck. He was transfixed—Lorrie Dean!

His vision faded and came again. This time, the eleven-year-old girl was facing him, standing closer and looking right into his eyes. "Oh God, please! No!" he blurted through the fence. Lorrie Dean's face came closer, and in that instant Andy cringed at the thought of what had happened so many years ago. How foolish! How foolish to think of it now, to allow it such command. The little schoolyard had brought it all back, the longing and the guilt. There was no sane reason why such a thing should continue to haunt him; he had not even seen her since they were fifth-graders twenty years ago.

He laced his fingers into the fence wires like an eagle clutching its perch, gave it a vigorous shake, and stalked back to his car.

Andy sat slumped in his parked car, brooding about the rites of time, wishing they did not work such cruel magic. For him, time's strange ritual had quietly filtered events of his childhood and had buried most of them. But into a scattered few, it had cast immortal breath. She was one of those—Lorrie Dean.

2

Las Colinas rose out of the Texas prairie in majestic towers and a few classic low-rise buildings. They were the offices of giant corporations, rambling over the prairie floor amid spruced greens and flowering embankments and along the shores of meandering man-made canals. Many of them were only a couple of stories high. A few were one-story, winged colonials with columned porches and gabled roofs and fountains spewing in their courtyards. The place was a hive of human effort, a bristling colony rooted at the edge of a great metropolis.

Andy Boone and his battered Cutlass were in the heart of it. Over his left shoulder was metropolitan Dallas, Texas, and just ahead only a couple of miles was the Dallas-Fort Worth International Airport. He was going too slowly for the traffic behind him, straining to find the mid-level brick tower of Clay Cutter Industries and the Mandalay Hotel where he had been booked for a week. It should be easy enough to find his way, for Las Colinas straddled a main thoroughfare and there seemed to be no downtown district. As such, there was no noticeable retail commercial center.

The rain had ended an hour ago, and the sun, which had popped out for one last peek, was just setting over Fort Worth in the distance.

Andy spotted the Clay Cutter building just seconds before he reached the Mandalay Hotel. They were within reasonably easy walking distance of each other, a welcome development in a day otherwise filled with uncalculated trouble. He opted to park in the outer lot rather than stop at the lobby entrance. He lingered a moment after he parked, staring at the scratched, muddy rear of his car.

Inside the hotel, he hurried to the counter and pressed up close to it, hiding his muddy shoes, and dropped his attaché close to his soiled trouser cuffs.

"Good evening, sir." The young Spanish girl still held her dimpled smile as Andy looked up. She was pretty, and there was a gracious countenance about her. Her voice was warm and friendly, and she seemed genuinely pleased that someone had come to her counter for assistance.

"Hi, I'm Andrew W. Boone. I have reservations for the week."

"OK, one second." Her typing was easy and fast, and in a few seconds she pulled a sheet from the printer and read it as she stepped back to face Andy. "Yes, Mr. Boone, your company has already preregistered you. All I really need you to do is sign right here to acknowledge your registration."

He grinned as he signed the little form, thinking of the stereotypes that were rapidly vanishing. The attractive Spanish girl did not have a Spanish accent; rancher Dub Grimes did not dress or act like a cowboy. Something was surely awry in the great state of Texas. "Thank you," he said as he handed her the paper and pen.

"Thank you, and welcome to the Mandalay and Las Colinas. Have you stayed in Las Colinas before?"

"No, I haven't. I've just been transferred here."

"Oh, great! You'll love it. And if we can help you with anything at all, please let us know."

"Thanks. Ah, as a matter of fact, I'll probably call on you for directions at some point."

"Good deal, Mr. Boone, we'll be really glad to help. Here's your key card. Your room number is penciled here on this paper. May we help with baggage?"

"Oh, no thanks. I don't have anything to bring in right now."

"OK. Sleep tight, sir."

Andy nodded and headed for the elevators. He was only a few steps away when she called out to him.

"Oh, sir! Excuse me, Mr. Boone. I almost forgot—I have a message for you. I'm sorry."

"No problem," said Andy as he took the small folded square of paper from her. He nodded again and glanced briefly at the note before stuffing it in his trouser pocket. He was to call Wade Boliver, his new boss. Hot dog!

His room was actually two rooms: a small parlor with a love seat, two chairs, and a desk and a larger bedroom with one king-sized bed, another desk, a telephone table, and night stands. The walls of the bedroom were covered with silk, floral-patterned paper and held two large pictures, one a scene of Texas bluebonnets and the other a painting of a huge, well-endowed longhorn bull.

Andy was feeling good about his new quarters, nodding at every turn as he toured the plush suite. He was about to drop into an easy chair and start to unwind when he stopped dead in his tracks.

"Hoo boy!" He closed his eyes and dropped his head. Just as the day's pressure had started to ease, something clicked in his head. He was staring at his muddy shoes. He started to peel the sweater from his shoulders, and when it was off, he hooked two fingers in the neck of it, whirled it once around his head like a lasso, and slung it on the bed. Damn!

Still shaking his head, he drifted toward the draped balcony door to check the view. He stumbled over a lamp table, damned it, and staggered on. The view was mostly of flat land, mesquite trees, and a distant lake. He stood, frozen, gazing vaguely across the range into the distance, as if searching the horizon for spiritual help. Finally, he took a deep breath and, as he turned away, closed his eyes. Lorrie

Dean was still there. In his profession, he was always wholly in command. But not here. He could not shake the image of the little girl from years ago.

There was so much to do in the next two days. He needed the weekend to get his bearings, begin looking for an apartment, and prepare for his new assignment. He had planned to memorize the names of his staff and coworkers and a bit of information about each one to let them know they were important and that he didn't take them for granted. There hadn't been time for that during his wrap-up at the McLean headquarters, and now his concentration was divided between these tasks and Lorrie Dean.

He needed to call his parents to let them know he was safely in port. He sat down at the telephone and whopped the table once with his fist. He could not even get excited about his new career venture. In fact, what excitement he'd had was now dead. But he could tell this to no one, not even his mother. He had to shoulder it himself.

The death of excitement about his new job was small change compared to the staggering blow of Lorrie Dean's resurrection. Zeal was no match for hysteria, not for Andy Boone, not on this day when, without warning, he'd been very nearly shut down by a simple memory. It was a memory that, up to now, he'd managed to hold at bay through intense preoccupation with his work.

"Hi, Mom."

"Are you all right?" Even the voice of Anna Boone, world's premier mother, was powerless to change his mood.

"Yeah, I'm fine. Got in OK. Is your head any better?"

"Oh, sure, I'm all right. Didn't I tell you I'd be? Your trip go smooth?"

"Uh huh. Great, very uneventful. Daddy in yet?"

"No he's not. He's still working on one of the rip saws."

"Uh huh … ah, Mom, here's my room number—you already have the hotel phone number—room 7114."

"OK, Andy Woo. I'm glad you made it."

"Well, got a lot of things to do, Mom, so I'll let you go for now. I'll write you next week. Love you."

A warm shower and leisurely dinner would surely loosen the day's grip. Andy began to empty his pockets. "Oops!" He pressed out the phone note that had been wadded at the bottom of one of them. Call me, it said, signed Wade Boliver. What a hell of a note! Call me? That's it? Not, Welcome, Andy, give me a buzz when you get a chance?

"This is Andy Boone. May I speak to Wade Boliver?"

"This is he. Where are you?"

"Uh, at the hotel, here in Las Colinas."

"Good. Good. What you got?"

"Er, got your note to call you."

"Right. Glad you got in. I just wanted you to know that I can't be with you your first week. My brother-in-law and I and a couple of friends are going hunting in Colorado. But no big deal. Everybody there'll take care of you all right. We have a great staff. Check with Paige Ivy. She's your best bet. And I guess that's about ... oh, and, heh heh, better watch out for Kirk Daniels. Anyway, you'll find out for yourself later on I guess."

Andy waited. Apparently that was all of it. The regional director of Human Resources obviously had just finished his planned briefing. It was now time for him to pitch that ever popular last note, that instantaneous blurt that comes at the end of every veteran briefer's act: any questions? Not so this time. Andy waited a little longer.

"You there, Andy?"

"Oh, yessir. I didn't want to interrupt."

"Right."

"So, that's, ah, that's fine, then," said Andy. "I'm sure looking forward to the challenge, and I will give it—"

"Sure, no problem. See you in a week. Good luck!"

"Thanks. Have a good, er, hunt."

"Will do. Bye."

Andy was shaking his head, still clutching the cradled phone even after he hung it up. *Why, yes, Mr. Boliver, my room is just fine, and thank you for asking. Oh, and sure, I had a really good trip; thanks.*

He knew his limitations full well. The shower had indeed cleared his head. He could not use the weekend as he'd planned. He would be fit for nothing until he freed himself of his haunting obsession. He would have to go to Baytown, find Lorrie Dean, and clear his conscience. He would have dinner in one of the hotel dining rooms tonight and get started early the next morning, before sunup. The interstate to Houston would take him almost all the way. He could be there in five hours.

The next morning, Andy was strolling across the lobby, humming as he went, his new plans now in full swing, when abruptly he stopped. He started to walk on and then stopped again. "Hmm …" He turned slowly and moseyed over to the registration counter and asked the pretty Spanish girl for some information. He took note of her name, complimented her style, and then hurried out to his car.

Soon he was back on Highway 175, the road that would take him through Tillman and then on to Diboll where his parents lived and worked their small sawmill. Dawn was a good half hour away. Actually, it would not take that much longer to go the country route than the interstate to Baytown. After all, it was Saturday and the open highways wouldn't be too crowded—or would they? Anyway, it didn't mean a damn because Andy Boone had made a decision. He smiled as he thought of the case of Coors in the trunk and reflected back to the homemade roadside mailbox neatly lettered W. T. Grimes.

As he approached the site of the previous day's debacle, Andy looked at his watch—eight fifteen. Ranch people were early risers. They had probably finished their breakfast by the time he got in the shower. He slowed, crimped the corner of his mouth, shook his head when he spotted the patched barbed-wire fence, and then turned up the long, sloping dirt driveway.

The house sat on high ground to catch the sounds of the roving range, and it was ringed with double windows so it might see all that went on there. It stood over the land as though it was the supreme master. It was the epitome of simplicity and strength, in no way the image of a standard ranch house. It was two stories high, almost square, framed with old-style narrow siding, and painted—in the only way this house could be—entirely white. Its high-pitched roof was cut into lofty gables and most of them bore neat louvers.

A wide porch ran across the front and down the left side to cool the house on the western sides and yield a place of solace at the end of a day's toil. It was shaded with a flat roof and edged with a waist-high banister all around. Wooden swings, weathered slick and gray, dangled from its ceiling at the corner and front end; lawn chairs and old rockers were scattered along its course, and it was hung with ferns and trailing plants from one end to the other.

To the left of the house, Andy could see an orchard and beyond it in the distance, another orchard of a different kind. Toward the back on the opposite side, he saw a corner of freshly plowed ground, a garden plot close to the house. When he pressed the doorbell, he heard chimes faintly ringing inside.

The door opened, and there was a auburn-haired girl, probably fourteen years old, obviously tall for her age. Her face was the picture of youth—fresh, wholesome, clear as the country air—and it bore a faint spray of freckles across a trim little nose and a bright, sweet smile.

"Hi, I'm Andy Boone."

"Hi, Andy Boone, I'm Kelly." She snickered, and the youthful light in her face brightened.

Andy chuckled and twisted in place as he eyed the alert kid in her green fleece suit. She was tall and slender, but certainly not undernourished, and the contours that would someday shape her as a grown woman were faintly apparent. Andy felt his face soften in amusement, for she was a remarkable likeness of her dad—assuming, of course, that Dub was indeed her dad.

She must have caught his amusement. She tilted her head and

measured him too, her dark-brown eyes beaming as if from deep, knowing wonder. "Would you like to come in, Andy Boone? Grandpa's down at the tractor barn."

Andy stepped inside the screen door while Kelly held it open. "Well, maybe for just a second. Ah, is your daddy here?"

Kelly's smile faded and she dropped her eyes. She didn't answer; she just tossed her head slightly and looked up at him as if that was all the signal he needed in order to understand. Her eyes blinked a few times, and she waited, holding her faint smile.

Andy gulped and felt his face draw solemn. "Is Dub all right?"

"Oh, yessir. Dub's fine—everybody's fine." Now she was swinging her arms as she talked, her face alight again. "Grandpa's messing with a broken-down tractor, and everybody else is at the farm."

Andy sighed. "So you're minding store, huh, young lady?"

"Well, I'm in charge here all right. Do you need something?"

"Maybe you can just tell me how to get to the farm."

"It's out back."

"Out back?"

"Uh huh." There was a mischievous twinkle in her eye, and she stared innocently at her groping guest, coaxing more banter, teasing him, clearly believing it harmless.

Andy nodded and pursed his lips. His peers invariably enjoyed teasing him, perhaps because he approached even little things with great seriousness. He let them do it without challenge. After all, it was their thing. If he could contribute, great, he'd do it. Actually, his approach wasn't a matter of seeing the somber side of things at all; it was just a matter of being responsible. Now, here was this kid, trying to convert him in one quick meeting and just about to get it done. She was by far the most refreshing, most charming teaser he'd ever confronted.

"See," said Kelly, straightening her expression, "we have a two-hundred-acre front yard for a ranch and a hundred-acre backyard for a farm."

Andy grinned bashfully and Kelly waited, her rascally smile beginning to fill in again. She seemed to know that he was going to attempt the role her teasing game was trying to force on him. He cleared his throat and stroked his chin. "Any oil fields?" he asked, now grinning full tilt.

Kelly clapped her hands and danced a couple of hops. "Hey, good one, Andy Boone." Then she cleared her throat like a fancy woman at a swank party and held a hand to her chest. She pitched her voice into a mocking kind of soprano as she spoke. "No, we don't do oil, here. The price of oil is quite rather down, you know. Peanuts are better now. Do you understand me, Mr. Andy Boone?"

"Oh yes, quite so, my dear," said Andy, mocking her sophisticated play. "Thank you for reminding me—it was a foolish question." Kelly nodded and threw out her hands as if to say your score.

"Anyway, young lady, I was trying to find Dub Grimes. I have something for him. See, yesterday afternoon, I was cruising along the highway out there, and …"

"Oh, you're the guy who got hung up on the fence."

"You know about it?"

"He just mentioned it at supper last night. You OK?"

"Oh, sure."

"Actually, I was wrong when I said everybody is at the farm. Dub went into Athens right after breakfast. Probably be about noon before he gets back."

"Oh, well, that's … tell you what, uh, what I've got here is a case of Coors I wanted to give him, and …"

"Hey, great, we can have a party."

"Well, yes, of course. That would be fun. Wish I could stay around for it, but I have a ways to go yet and a long day ahead of me."

Kelly shrugged and raised her brow as if to say it was his loss. In a moment, Andy backed away, and she stayed in the doorway as he brought the beer up from his car.

"Is there someplace I can take this?" he asked.

"Ah, well," began Kelly, "let's just put it around here on the side porch on top of that barrel." Somehow she seemed to be losing her glee.

A few moments later, as he drove away, Andy looked back toward the house where Kelly was watching him leave. Now his bright, happy little farm girl looked solemn, maybe even a little sad. She waved good-bye and so did he. At the end of the driveway, he glanced in his mirror. She was still standing in the doorway.

Andy had already decided he wouldn't stop at the Tillman school yard—he didn't need any more of that. But as he drove through the little town, he glanced at the playground and in spite of his best effort faced again the image of young Lorrie Dean, standing hurt in the rain, half turned away, hiding something he now fought from his mind.

Soon he was free again, drinking in the soothing country scenery and singing to himself as he drove along. These were the best roads in the country, the only authentic overland routes, and most people who lived near them didn't mind slowing down and taking it easy. It could even be reassuring to fall behind a laboring log truck sometimes, to yield, to trail along in tune for a ways. He could think of the driver and wonder about his life and, after working a couple of hills, pass and wave, letting him know it was OK you had to wait. After all, he had a family and he was working.

Andy's route took him through Jacksonville and Lufkin and on toward Diboll. When he came into Diboll, he frowned as he stopped at a traffic light and looked in the direction of his parents' house. It was ten o'clock; his day was slipping away. He sped on out of town. He was no longer singing and no longer indulging in the country medicine. Minutes out of town, he slowed for a half mile and finally pulled off the highway. He looked at his watch again, then slowly pulled back onto the highway and headed on toward Baytown. His parents would understand his not stopping by—if they ever found out.

3

Baytown was a sprawling sea-level boomtown aged by polluted air and a rotting shoreline. It lay on a stretch of crippled land languishing beside Trinity Bay off the Gulf of Mexico. The air above it was stained with chemical waste, and it had lost its footing to industrial drain years ago. The coastal refineries had pumped out so much of its groundwater that the land had collapsed and the town was sinking inexorably before the waiting bay.

But it was a survivor, this town, and it was home, and nothing in creation can keep a hometown from being home. Most of the natives of Baytown had stayed, and they were among the most genuine and steadfast people in the world. Somehow they'd kept their sense of identity. Perhaps this was because the forces that had made the town and then crippled the land had rallied to save it and had assured its economic stability. And no doubt, the town was borne, in some measure, of the native character of those pioneers who migrated to the coastal boomtowns in the twenties and thirties.

Andy's nose twitched uncontrollably as he drove into town from the old Goose Creek side, just south of the huge Exxon refinery. Beautification efforts had turned the main street into a winding landscaped trail, but to no avail; it was still dead. Andy frowned as he passed his alma mater, Robert E. Lee High School just outside the old city center. It had burned and been restored years earlier but no longer looked as he'd remembered it. After he crossed the creek, he strained to find his old junior high school, but its once hallowed ground was now a field of oil tanks.

His breathing was quickening as he slowed into the little community of Wooster where he'd grown up—and where he now expected to find Lorrie Dean and her family. Nothing was the same as he remembered it, not even close. Where the bakery once stood was a modern office building. The corner grocery and the feed store had been taken by the widened highway, and the famed Yellow Jacket Inn was simply lost to destiny and the encroaching bay.

Andy could feel his body tensing, gearing up for what he was about to face, as he pulled onto the shoulder of the road and stopped. He leaned across the seat to stare at the little schoolhouse, and in that moment the inevitable paralysis grabbed him. David G. Burnet Elementary School stood alone on what high ground was left in that area. Andy looked away slowly and gazed toward the spot where he had last seen Lorrie Dean twenty years ago. It was awash with the tides of Scott Bay, but that did not temper the memory of what had happened there in that one moment of his childhood he could not escape.

He tugged at his tingling ears and heaved in a long, expanding breath, cursing the fear that had overtaken his bones and muscles. He was less than a half mile and only a few minutes away from solving his problem, and then it would be over. There was no reason to have to flail at the stupid rigor of his body. He swallowed the lump in his throat hard and sped back onto the highway and on toward the Heights.

Lorrie Dean's neighborhood was desolate, the houses all in ill repair, all surrounded by the waste of repeated hurricanes left to pile up where it had washed. One end of Crow Road had already been swallowed by the bay, but the LeMay house was near the turnoff and still safe for a few more years. In the driveway, Andy waited for his nerve and collected his thoughts. Then he set his chin, bounded upon the front porch, and knocked firmly.

"Hi, I'm Andy Boone. I used to live on Mapleton, around on the west shore."

The woman smiled and waited inside her screen door. Andy waited too. She was not Lorrie Dean by any stretch of perception, and she was too tall and too young to be her mother. But she was clearly somebody, so Andy cleared his throat and began again. "And, ah, so I happened to be in town, and … is this the LeMay residence?"

"Who?"

"LeMay—Lorrie Dean. This is their house, isn't it?"

"I never heard of them. Who did you say you were?"

"Boone, Andy Boone. We were schoolmates, Lorrie Dean and I."

"Uh huh. Well, it's nice to know you, Mr. Boone. I'm Louise Sadler. But I'm sorry, I just don't know those people. We bought this house just a little over three years ago."

Andy was stroking his chin as she finished. He looked again into the woman's face and tried to manage an intelligent response—he was having a lot of trouble coming up with one. The woman watched as he struggled. After a moment, she stepped outside to stand before him. Her smile mellowed and her eyes grew soft as she continued to explain. "I think most of the people on this street have been here for years, so I bet they can help you. We just haven't been here that long."

"Did you buy from the LeMays?"

"No, sir, we bought from a property company in Houston. I don't know who ever owned this house before we moved in."

"But, didn't … do you know where …"

"We don't really, Mr. Boone, not really. We had to do a lot of fixin' up, so the house must have been vacant a long time."

"Well, OK, I'm sorry … if I'd had sense enough to look in a phone book before I came out, I wouldn't have bothered you."

"Oh, it's really no bother."

Andy nodded. He looked down at the floor and waited, giving her a chance to take the hint. In a moment, she touched his arm and turned away. "Hold on a second," she said. "I'll bring our phone book out for you to look at."

As he reached the Ls in the book, he put a finger at that place, and when he did, he noticed that his hand was shaking. He let it drop by his side. "Could you possibly give me the name of the company you bought from ... the house, I mean?"

"Oh, sure. In fact, I think I have an old envelope from them. I'll be right back."

Andy glanced at the envelope in the seat beside him as he drove toward the next driveway. It showed the address and phone number of Channel Harris Properties in Houston, Texas. He had found no LeMays in the phone book.

The woman was right on one point; someone was home at most of the houses, an unusual situation for a Saturday afternoon. Most of the people remembered Andy and invited him in to share a few fond recollections. But nobody knew anything, not about Lorrie Dean—nothing! It was beyond all manner of reasoning that nobody, not one person knew at least a tiny fact or even a hint about Lorrie Dean's disappearance. Even his old high school buddy, Chester Rudman, whose family had lived on Scott Bay since the first road was paved, could not help.

"Do you know, Chester, if she was married?"

"No, she was not married. I do know that."

"Was she still living up there in the two-story with the family the last time you remember anything about her?"

"Yeah, far as I know she was."

"Do you have any idea at all where they might have gone, I mean just even a hunch?"

"You know, Andy, I don't. I just don't know, and what gets me now is that I can't even figure out why I don't know."

"When did you first miss them?"

"About ten years ago, I guess, about '82 or '83, somewhere along in there."

"Was there any talk about it around the neighborhood?"

"Noo-o-o." Chester's brow wrinkled as he stretched out the word and paused to look away. Then he frowned and continued. "I don't remember any talk." He paused again. "You know, now that you ask, it seems like they were here one day and the next they were gone. There wasn't any talk, there wasn't … there wasn't anything."

"Chester, I just don't get it."

"I know, Andy. You're right, entirely right. I don't get it either."

"I mean, it looks like somebody around here would know something about them. For that matter, you'd think everybody would know. We used to know everything about one another out here on the bay."

"Yeah … we did. I'm sorry."

"Oh, no, Chester, I didn't mean you. It's just that … it's so hard to understand."

The two men looked at each other for a while, each visibly deep in study about the strange situation. Finally Chester said, "Andy, why don't you check with some of them up there at the Mower Fix. They all have been around here all their lives. The saying goes that they have fixed every lawn mower and garden tractor in Wooster, Texas, at one time or another. They ought to know something about the LeMays since they had all that equipment back there."

"I don't remember that place."

"No, the place was put in after you left, but the people who hang around there were born and raised right here."

"Oh, OK, good idea. Where's it located?"

"Up on the highway about halfway between the turnoff and Slapout Gully, over on the left."

Moore's Mower Fix was a weathered, buff-colored shack about the size of a boathouse with a wide lean-to on the windward side. It sat just off the shoulder of the road, leaving barely enough room for a car to park headed in. Three men were outside the shack, and one little boy, about five years old, was romping dangerously close to the highway.

Andy watched the men for a moment before he got out. A young man was hunkered down trying to untwist the top of a wire clothes hanger, and a much older man was sitting on a stool under the lean-to humped over a grindstone working on a lawn mower blade, his bib cap turned around backward. It looked as though he probably could whip out up to two sharpened blades in a day if he got his second wind. Behind the wire-hanger guy was a fat popeyed grubby-looking kid with a face like a pumpkin and long, stringy yellow hair slouched over his ears. He was doing nothing.

As he got out of his car, Andy thought he would be extremely lucky if this motley crew knew anything at all. As he approached, the fat guy pointed toward the man with the wire hanger and Andy adjusted his course. "Hi, gang," he said—to anyone.

"Hey," said the wire man.

"Workin' hard?" asked Andy.

"Shit naw." The man chuckled. Then he stood up, groaning, and dropped the hanger by his side. "Hep ya?"

"Sure can," said Andy, reaching out to shake hands. "I'm Andy Boone—used to live down on Scott Bay. I'm looking for an old schoolmate, Lorrie Dean LeMay."

The man looked at his hand, wiped it once down the leg of his overalls, and took Andy's hand. It was a limp, dead-fish grip. No damn wonder he couldn't unwind a simple coat hanger. "I'm Buddy Moore," he said. "Who did you say you're lookin' for?"

"You know, the LeMays down on Crow Road."

"Oh, yeah. Shit yeah, I know them. They're reg'lar customers. I work on all their stuff."

Andy's heart jumped, and a little shiver ran up his neck. He had rarely felt such an instant sense of relief in his life. He felt like hugging every man there, even the little fat shit. He stammered as he talked. "D-do you have a phone number or an address for them?"

"Well, not exactly. You know, like you say, they're back yonder on Crow in that two-story about three houses down."

Andy froze. He looked toward the grinder man, who had been shaking his head while the other man talked. Buddy Moore caught it too and waved toward the grinder. "Ain't they there anymore, Stretch?"

"Course they ain't there. They been gone from here ten or fifteen years. Where you been?"

The fat kid was doubled over laughing. He slapped Buddy Moore on the back and said, "You been dead that long, ain't you, Buddy?" Then he turned to Andy. "What you lookin' for the girl for, like, what you say, Lorrie Dean?"

"I … we were … ah, we were just childhood sweethearts. Our two families were close—it's nothing. I just happened to be here and …" He could not finish; his throat was tightening, and his voice was trying to break up. Had he not been a man, he would have cried.

The boy had sobered some but continued to rattle on like a back-alley, stand-up comic. "What the hell," he said, grinning like an idiot. "I wouldn' worry about one girl. Find some more girls to look for. Girls is girls. Right, Buddy?" he cackled out again.

"No thanks," said Andy, and he started toward his car. He called behind him as he walked. "If anybody knows anything about where she might be, I sure would like to know about it."

"Actually, we don't, Andy," said Buddy Moore.

"Yeah, I don't know," said the fat kid, "but, well, I don't know, but I heard they died or something."

Andy spun around in his tracks and bounded back toward the boy. He stopped just short as the boy backed away with both hands in the air. "Hey, hey, hey," he said, "easy, settle down, Sport. I jus' said somethin' I heard. I don't know nothin'."

"You heard Lorrie Dean died!?"

"Yeah, I heard that. I don't know nothin' about it."

"When did she die? Where?"

"Like I say, man, I don't know none of that."

"Come on, fellow, help me, help me!" Andy was shouting.

Now the boy was shaking his head, dead serious. "It's probably not true."

"But you heard it. Where were you?"

"Wadaya mean?"

"Where were you when you heard it? Who was there with you? Who else heard it? Who said it? What exactly were the words said?"

"Hey—hey, aw right. I don't know, I'm tellin' you, I jus' heard Lorrie Dean had a problem, and they took 'em all away. I don't know who was around or where I heard it, or nothin'."

Andy looked toward the other two men, and again the grinder man was shaking his head as if to say the boy was lying. Andy wasn't sure. But the boy was an indifferent little son of a bitch, and that's what irritated Andy. How dare him treat Lorrie Dean with so little respect! But he was the kind of guy who could say anything he wanted to and get by with it because nobody would dare hit a fat, ugly little shithead who'd borrowed his brain from a zoo. Finally, Andy threw out his hands, as if conceding defeat, and said, "I'm sorry … I just …"

The fat boy chuckled again, the others shrugged, and Andy walked to his car, got in, and left.

It was near sundown. Andy drove back to the bay and on down to Mapleton Avenue where he had once lived. He could only get so for down the street: water now engulfed most of the area where his home once stood. He parked and got out to look around. The house had been hauled away, probably piece by piece, as had all their neighbors' houses. Not a particle was left. He couldn't even make out where the driveway once was.

He stood by the front fender of the Cutlass for a while, surveying, trying to fix where certain trees might once have stood, where the hill once took up, where the creek came in, trying to find something definite in the world he'd once savored as a child. He could smell the storms in the salt air, storms of years ago. It made him think of his dear mom and dad, and he marveled at the recollection of how quickly they would wade back in and begin to rebuild after a hurricane invaded. Now the water just seemed to lie across the land as though it were lost, as though it were alive and could think and somehow knew it didn't belong there.

He stared out across the bay from which Bird Island once rose. Today, it was just a dot in the wash. Suddenly he smiled as he remembered a monumental event of his childhood, when he was finally able to raft over to the tiny island—the unspeakable thrill at that conquest. Now he could feel his tension ebbing a little. He bowed his head and closed his eyes and began to sway while the bay breezes gathered in his hair. If in that moment he could have found Lorrie Dean at his side, he would have drawn her into his arms and dreamed them both into eternity.

* * *

Andy arose early on Sunday morning, ate breakfast at the Holiday Inn buffet, packed his car, checked out, and set out toward Saint Mark's Methodist Church. It was nearing the hour for Sunday School classes, so the church secretary was likely to be in the office. Saint Mark's had been the LeMays' church, and even Lorrie Dean's schoolmates had come to know of the family's extraordinary dedication to it.

The church secretary was pleasant and tried to be helpful, but the records she came up with failed to show any past members named LeMay. That, of course, was impossible, but Andy had pledged to keep his temperament in check while inside the church. She told him that Reverend Michael Lawson had been pastor there for only the last six years, but he might be able to remember at least some reference to the family.

"Do you think I could I speak to him today?" asked Andy.

"He's out of town this Sunday. Sorry, sir. But I'm sure he'd be glad to meet with you."

"Well, who's preaching today? I mean, do you have an assistant pastor or other church official I could speak to?"

"Possibly. Now, the assistant pastor, Reverend Dunning, has been here a little less than two years, but he has worked very closely with the stewards and the committees and lay people, so my guess is he has heard things related to past activities and members of those units. And the best part is he's in his office right now and I'd be glad to take you to him and introduce you. Would you like to do that? We want to help if there's any way we can."

Andy agreed, and in less than two minutes the secretary introduced him to Saint Mark's assistant pastor, Ashley Dunning, who shook his hand, smiling broadly, and invited Andy into his office.

"Thank you, Reverend, for taking your time. I really appreciate it. I just have something I think you can help me with, and …"

"I'll sure try."

"Uh, well, I am looking for an old native family of the Wooster addition where I grew up. Our families were very close, and it happens that I am indebted to the youngest member who was my … who I went to grade school with." Andy stiffened to hide a surge of guilt but quickly rationalized that the idea that he was indebted to Lorrie Dean was not entirely a lie.

"OK."

"They are the LeMays. The girl is Lorrie Dean."

"Hmm. Name doesn't ring a bell, son."

"No, sir, I'm sure you probably wouldn't … it's been at least twelve years, but I just thought if we could find some old records or some recollection of a steward or someone who may remember them—"

"Oh sure. I see. Problem is, we don't have any really old records as such. And I don't keep any documentation, personally, about the membership. But surely, someone in the congregation will remember that family."

"The church doesn't keep records on former members?"

"Oh yes, but they're not definitive in terms of what you're wanting, and we probably don't have anything that far back. Did you ask the secretary about it?"

"Yes. She doesn't have anything." Andy bowed his head for a few moments, trying to reckon with this shocking mystery—the literal disappearance of the LeMay family. His voice was weak as he started to speak again. "You know, if I could just find out something, just one little thing about them ... I wouldn't have to have their address."

"Wish I had it, my brother. I really do."

"I was out at Moore's Mower Fix yesterday, out on Market Highway, and a guy there told me that he heard they died."

Reverend Dunning laughed and said, "Oh, no, they didn't die! The guy's pulling your leg."

Andy's head bobbed up, and he stared at the holy man for a minute. Then he cleared his throat. "Excuse me, Reverend, but how would you know that?"

"Oh, surely I don't know it, but it just seems illogical the man told you this just because he might not know where they are." He seemed to be getting a little nervous. Andy held his gaze on the pastor, silently pushing for more. Then the reverend asked, "Do you have a church, Andy?"

"Not now."

"Well, I want to invite you to join with us in our worship services this morning. They'll be starting in a few minutes, and Andy, please know this—I'm truly sorry we haven't been able to help you. Let's pray at the chancel for a moment, just you and I, and I'll also keep you on my prayer list."

"I'm sure I could use it, I guess, but ..." Andy didn't finish.

"But what?"

"Well, uh, you wouldn't know what to pray for me about."

"Oh, I'll just pray for forgiveness for your sins."

"Well, you got something there, all right." Andy paused. "One thing, Reverend."

"Yes?"

"While you're at it, would you put in a word for Lorrie Dean LeMay?"

"Why, of course."

The sanctuary was aglow with candlelight, a peaceful shelter, accepting in every way, but it made Andy's heart ache all the more. Still, it was a solution, this holy shelter, and it was always there, each flickering candle glowing with deep rapture and all of them together a great procession of strength. Surely this sanctuary must have been Lorrie Dean's friend; surely it healed her from the likes of Andy Boone. He wondered how many times she had walked the aisle he descended toward the altar.

He accepted the invitation to stay for worship services, but it bothered him that it was for purely selfish reasons. He wanted to get the attention of some old-timers and talk to the ushers, who were mostly stewards, and any other potential sources of memory about the LeMay family. At once he began to feel the genuine warmth of a church family gathering around him, the sympathetic interaction of people, their warm smiles, the upbeat chatter; noticeably absent were complaints about coworkers and garbage collection. Andy felt good about all this, but the instant pride he felt for himself gave way quickly to overriding guilt for being out of the church for so many years.

Unfortunately, although a few did remember the LeMays, no one acknowledged any recollection of their departure. Andy stayed until the last handshake, then strolled back through the sanctuary and out the back door to the parking lot. As he stepped out of the church, he blinked in the dim light of a cloudy morning. He wandered toward his car as if under a magic spell. When he was in his car and backing out of his parking place, he glanced at his rearview mirror. Reverend Dunning stood in the doorway, holding a writing pad. As Andy drove away, he continued looking in the mirror. He could have sworn the preacher was writing down his license number.

Moments later, Andy Boone was crossing the San Jancinto river headed for Houston where he would pick up I-45 that would take him back to Dallas and Las Colinas. It was time to kiss Lorrie Dean and Baytown good-bye. He had tried and failed. So much for that! It now was time to condition his head with something else, to get psyched up for his first day at the Clay Cutter region. Time to replace all distractions with thoughts of his new duties and new colleagues and even his new boss, Wade Boliver, who wouldn't be there.

Boliver's curt tips hadn't given him much to go on: a Paige Ivy, he recalled, was supposed to be the good guy—er, girl—and Daniels somebody, Kirk Daniels was at this point the mystery man.

4

He had met the enemy. Or so it would seem from the rousing reception they did not have waiting for him on his first day at Clay Cutter Industries. Paige Ivy had left a note at the lobby information desk: come on up to 7E12. Someone will show you.

How sweet. And how very clever to sequester the band and streamers on the seventh floor to make the surprise welcome ever the more thrilling. 7E12 was probably a huge conference room, maybe even an auditorium.

Andy opened the door to 7E12 and stepped into a small reception room outfitted with one secretary desk and two work stations, each space properly loaded with a Clay Cutter (CC) computer, laser printer, and allied trappings.

"Good morning."

"Morning, sir."

"Are you Paige Ivy?"

"No, sir. Do you have an appointment?"

"Well, I hope so—I'm Andy Boone."

"Oh, yes, you're the new man. Nice to see you. Just a second." She smiled as she picked up the telephone and pressed one button. "New man's here," she said as she lifted her eyes toward the ceiling. After a moment she said "OK" to the phone and looked at her visitor. "You can go right on in, sir. Door on your left."

As he entered the office, a neat, conservatively dressed woman about forty years old rose from behind her desk and, coming to the side of it, extended her hand. "I'm Paige Ivy." Though her smile was a little weak, her countenance seemed warmer than any he'd met with so far at Clay Cutter. "I see you made it OK."

"Yes, thank you," he said as he clasped her hand gently. "The directions were very clear. It's good to be here."

Paige pulled out two chairs flanking a corner of the small conference table at one end of her huge office. "Have a seat," she said as she eased gracefully into one of them.

"Thanks. How's business?"

"Impossible." She laughed heartily as she leaned forward to slap the table. She continued to beam as Andy chuckled with her. He had said the magic word; business was obviously the operative one. That being the case, clearly this was a woman who relished hard work and tangible results—not a bad choice for the head of Recruitment and Staffing for a large, growing corporation.

"Anyway, Andy, I've been sort of appointed to show you around and give you an idea of what's going on out here. Because it's, ah, well, let's say—different." She snickered again as she stressed the word. "This is operations. It's hands-on. Know what I mean? Y'all probably didn't get into operations very much up there at headquarters in McLean."

"No, not a lot. It's, ah, you're right, mostly policy."

"Right. But—so, are you bedded down all right at the Mandalay?"

"Oh, yes, beautiful place. Wish I could stay there."

"Well, you know you're paid up through Friday, so you'll need to take some time over the next couple of days or so to look for an apartment."

Andy nodded. Before he could speak, the intercom sounded.

Paige apologized for neglecting to have her secretary hold her calls but took this one anyway.

It was a spacious office, carpeted and partly paneled, and it was well lighted by windows that filled the back wall. Besides the conference table, there was a small reading table in one corner. A wooden computer cabinet stood behind Paige's desk, and a credenza topped by a large hutch was set against the wall off to one side. There was a grouping of framed photographs, probably the Ivy family, and one trailing plant on the credenza. Everything was compulsively drawn. The room was brimming with files and books and racks of papers, but it was all orderly and neat and the papers were stacked precisely in little islands of work.

Paige stood up as she talked on the phone. She was a little above average in height, and she was slender almost to the point of being too frail. Her face was lean but courtly and somewhat attractive when she smiled. Her deep-brown hair was short and curly and styled away from her ears. And, like the office, it was completely in order, the evident product of rigorous daily care and a great deal of pride.

As he began to ponder what his own office might look like, Andy's eye caught the stack of recruitment literature lying in the center of the conference table. Most of it had probably been written at their headquarters in McLean, Virginia; that put him on familiar ground. Clay Cutter was a major, enterprising electronic data corporation that had enjoyed a spectacular rise to become a fully competitive marketer of everything about computers including the furniture.

The corporation was the masterpiece of Orbison C. Clay and Murlon Cutter, both of whom had jumped ship from other electronic data conglomerates and started their own company in 1979. The company had scrambled to a fully competitive status within about ten years. But its markets had settled a little in the last couple of years. It had only one major problem; its goods were a little more expensive than competing systems, the interminable menace of American-made products.

When Paige finished her phone conversation, she remained standing and asked Andy if he would like a short tour of the Personnel shops.

Andy started to rise from his chair and then hesitated. "Paige, who does ... I've been looking over some personnel rosters that were sent to me, and somewhere I came across, or maybe Wade Boliver mentioned, ah, the name of Kirk Daniels. Who does he work for?"

Paige leveled her gaze at him for a moment as though gauging the best way to answer. Maintaining eye contact, she said, "He's yours."

"Pardon?"

"Kirk Daniels works for you."

"Oh, OK, good deal. Yeah, I'm ready for the tour if you are."

Paige began with her own division, introducing most people near their route. She had eleven specialists, mostly women. They were all located in one big ward partitioned into small cubicles with freestanding screens. It was an unending source of fascination to Andy that the executives in any company were usually out of their grand, spacious offices while the people who did the real work were crowded together in little cutouts with barely enough room to lean back in their chairs.

After they visited the main areas, occupied by the divisions of Employee Benefits, Job Classification, and Management and Control, Paige introduced him to his secretary, Valorie Garreck, and the two of them showed him his own office—another elegant, spacious room, much like Paige's. Back at the secretary's desk, Paige invited Valorie to join them as she introduced Andy to each of his officers.

"Thanks," said Valorie as she glanced up at Andy. "Oh, maybe I ought to mention this first. Ah, Mr. Boone ..."

"Andy."

"Andy—OK, thanks, I have already received a phone call for you from a man who didn't identify himself. No problem—he said he'd call back later today—but I just thought maybe you ought to know."

"Sure, you bet. Was it someone from headquarters?"

"No. I mean I don't guess it was. They usually identify themselves."

"How did he ask for me?"

"He just said he'd like to speak to Mr. Andrew Boone."

"Hmm." Andy's brow furrowed, and he stared away for a moment.

He was still thinking about the call when Paige stopped at the first small office. "This is Willis Braley," she said. "Meet Andy Boone."

Willis was a tall, handsome black man with a quick and easy smile and a firm handshake. His expression seemed to brighten genuinely as Andy pumped his hand.

Next Andy met Morris Allgate and Calvin Berryman, and after an awkwardly brief exchange with them, they entered the office where a man was hovered over his work as if he was about to devour it. Inside, Paige cleared her throat and the man looked up. When they were introduced, Kirk Daniels raised only part way out of his chair and reached across his desk for the perfunctory handshake with his new boss.

They finished the review of troops with Miguel Berrero and Karsten Friedmann. Six seeming stalwarts, all men. Strange thing that in 1992 the prevailing corporate wisdom held that only men could deal with the tough, mean old labor unions, while the women scored applications and filled out employment forms. Only men could negotiate brilliant contracts, settle grave disputes, and stand up to hostile adversaries, while the women stoked company procedures and processed resources. Men still were the warriors, women still the nurses.

Andy sat in his office deep in thought. He was hardly conscious of its appointments for he'd gone straight to his desk after Paige left. He had his back to the windows and leaned slightly into his desk, propping his chin on one fist. Something clearly was amiss. With the exception of Willis Braley, all of the men, his men, were guarded—not cocky like Kirk Daniels, but noticeably cool, aloof. Paige Ivy had done what she was assigned to do, but even she seemed to be forcing politeness. She had been tasked to take him in tow for a morning. She did it responsibly, and although she had warmed some during the course of it, she never really quite became friendly.

He struggled on in his thoughts, but he could not figure it out. All the strangers he'd met in the last two days had been nicer to him than the people of his own company. Dub Grimes, hard, tough-minded rancher, had been gracious and accommodating, and the man's cute little daughter, Kelly, had opened the door to him and at the same time embraced him with genuine warmth and the kind of banter usually reserved for close friends. Maybe he was in the wrong place; maybe he should be on the farm with Dub and Kelly.

Whatever the situation, there obviously was an asterisk by his name, and he was painfully aware that he was a long way from finding the footnote. But he was a problem solver. At least he knew where he stood; as long as he had that, he could figure out how to deal with his situation. He dropped his fist to the desk and stretched tall in his chair. The solution was clear; the only weapon he had at the moment was to listen. That, he would do. If they had cast him in the role of enemy, he would be the most indulging enemy they had ever faced.

Andy had lunch with two of his men, Willis Braley and Calvin Berryman—the others had opted out. Lunch conversation was reserved and uninteresting. Afterward Andy took to his office again and laid his plans. He was about to take charge, issue his first orders. He would instruct his staff to brief him on their assignments—privately, one at a time—and he would listen. Somewhere in that process, one of the men would come forth as an informant without being prompted. In every organization, whether two or twenty in size, each person assumes a self-assigned personal role, and for whatever selfish or noble reason, one of them always emerges as the boss's confidant. There was absolutely no exception.

At one o'clock, his staff sauntered in one by one with about as much animation as day workers at a night safety meeting. When they were seated, Andy spoke of how pleased he was to be there and how privileged he knew he was to have this assignment. He pledged his support to them and then invited questions and discussion. Consistent with his plan, he told not a word about himself. He jumped straight into his instructions. Each man was to come in the next day and brief him on his work.

"Be ready to tell me what your job is," he said, "what you're doing. I'd like to know of the projects you're working on and what their status is, and any specialty areas you may have and so forth."

When he finished, Andy let the silence settle. After a few seconds, Kirk Daniels twisted forward in his chair, lifted his chin, and stared just past Andy for a moment, his lips puckered like a fish about to suck in a seed. "Ah, Chief?"

"Yes, Kirk."

"That's a little short notice, isn't it? I mean, just overnight is all we have to get this together."

As Andy answered, he pretended to study a piece of paper on his desk and spoke in an unassuming, calm tone of voice, "You mean you don't already know what you're doing?"

"Well, yeah, but that's not the point. We want to do a good job of it, you know, to respect your time and have it organized."

"That's OK. It'll be completely informal, relaxed—nothing to worry about."

Kirk sat back and frowned straight at Andy's nose. Andy looked, in turn, at each of the other men. During the meeting, Miguel had been staring down at his lap rolling his thumbs together while Willis was laid-back, a slight grin breaking across his lips. The other three were pulled uncomfortably forward in their chairs, their mouths slightly agape.

Finally, Kirk spoke again. "OK, Chief, whatever you say—it's your show. But tell me this. Are you going to tell us what your job is?"

Andy didn't flinch. His instinct quickly disposed him not to take the bait. This man had come to fight, and he would try to draw Andy into battle if he could. If Andy accepted the invitation, he would not be able to find out all that he wanted to know. He could not both listen and play games. "Touché, Kirk," he said, grinning broadly.

"Oh no you don't," said Kirk. "You're dodging the question. Answer the question!"

"I'm just going to listen. That's my job for the next couple of days." As he was talking, Andy began to tug on his shirt collar with one hand and point toward Kirk with the other. He finished by saying, "Incidentally, Kirk, your collar is turned up on one side." It really wasn't, but it made the man think of himself, and as Kirk slapped at his collar Andy dismissed the meeting.

Andy doubled his fist and jabbed the air when the last man was gone. Then he smiled and began rocking and nodding at the piece of work he'd just completed. In a moment, he held out his hands and saw they were steady as steel. His job was his element. He could take any challenge, speak in public, deal with company presidents, wrestle with rank and file, and be a rock of confidence and stability. Yet a seemingly innocuous little task like looking for the name of Lorrie Dean in a phone book in Baytown had made him tremble. Instantly, his mood faded.

Just then, Valorie came in with some papers, apparently the mail. She seemed preoccupied. She was looking straight at Andy and almost missed his desk with the papers as she laid them teetering on the edge of it. "Mr. Boo ... uh Andy, that man called again."

"What man?"

"The one who called before you got to your office this morning. He asked for your home number this time, but I refused to tell him where you're staying. Is that OK?"

"Why, of course, Valorie. Way to go! You handled it just right. But, I wonder what is with this man?"

"I don't know, but he gives me the creeps. He has a hard voice and he talks very stern and businesslike."

"Oh well, don't worry about it. We'll find out."

That night at the Mandalay, Andy wrote a letter to his mom and dad, confessing that he had been to Baytown to check over the old home place and apologizing for not having the time to stop by when he went through Diboll. Then he wrote to Channel Harris Properties in Houston, asking for any information they were free to give him about the sale of the LeMay house in Baytown. He thought they could at least give him some dates and names and indicate where he might find any relevant public records. He had already resolved to drop the Lorrie Dean search because he was fully occupied with other priorities. Even so, it would not hurt to make this one inquiry, academic as it might be.

After dinner at the Mandalay, he looked at a few apartment ads and fell asleep with the paper in his hand. The next day, he met with Valorie Garreck for a few minutes as soon as he got to work. Then he asked her to hold any calls for the duration of his interviews with his staff.

Most of the men were well prepared, confident in what they were doing, and articulate in explaining it. Their handling of labor issues seemed to be strictly institutional, by the book. But they also conveyed a genuine interest in hard work and effective results. Two men were assigned to each plant, Burleson and Durant. Two others serviced the great bulk of the white-collar work force, which was not covered by any union contract. Another was a rover, and the sixth man mostly handled employee counseling, morale questionnaires, and related matters.

His interview with Kirk Daniels was much shorter and testier than he had even predicted. Nevertheless, the man did an excellent job of the technical briefing and it left no doubt that he was competent and on top of his job. It was also evident that he was frustrated with something.

"Well, Chief," said Kirk, "better enjoy this while you can."

Andy nodded. If he quipped back, the man might start a word game with him, and Andy wouldn't find out what was really bothering him. It was clear that he wanted to needle his boss, that something was seething in his gut. Andy waited. He could wait all day if necessary.

Finally, Kirk leaned his head against the high-backed chair and swiveled back and forth as he continued. "You know what I mean?" he smirked. "You never know what's just around the corner."

"True."

"But what the hell, don't let that worry you." Andy still didn't answer, so Kirk stopped swiveling and leaned forward to squint directly at his boss. "Don't get too comfortable, though. You're lucky to have this job."

"I agree." Andy snickered and took his own turn at leaning back in his plush chair. "I'll take all the luck I can get. Glad you think so too."

"No, Chief. You don't get it. But you will. I mean I'm sure if anything happens, they'll take care of you in some kind of way, since you've invested in this big move."

"If something happens?"

"Well, maybe I should say *when* it happens."

"Oh?"

The two men stared at each other for a while, each sweating the other, testing his grit. In a few moments, Andy said, "Anything else?" As Kirk shook his head, Andy stood up. "OK, that's all. Thanks. You did a good job."

Finally, the confidant emerged, Morris Allgate. He was about fifty years old, and he probably felt more self-assured than the younger officers. His briefing was average—not as good, actually, as Kirk Daniels's had been. But he did offer some observations after he finished the technical patter when Andy asked if there was anything else he thought it would help him to know.

"Well, I think, Andy, you're probably just going to have to give this thing a little time."

"What thing?"

Morris looked surprised but apparently felt he had opened a door he couldn't abandon. "Well, you can probably tell, people around here weren't overjoyed to see you coming."

"Sure 'nough?"

"Yeah. See, you were touted as the bushy-tailed young tiger, the place favorite at headquarters who was going to sail in here and start changing everything. That shakes people up. Status quo is our motto. Know what I mean? I guess everybody resented you before you got here."

"Morris, do you think it's really more because they thought I was the palace favorite than the idea that I'm going to upset everything?"

"Yeah, probably."

"Hmm."

"I don't really feel that way, myself."

"I could tell you didn't, Morris. I appreciate your support." He paused a moment. "You know, I'll just have to work on the others. I'm sure I can allay their fears and maybe even their resentments. It'll probably take more effort with some than others. Kirk, for example, is pretty frustrated. That's very obvious."

"Well, Kirk is something else. His is a totally different case."

"How so?"

Morris pondered for a moment. "Are you sure you want to know?"

"Absolutely."

"Well, Kirk's problems go a long way back. But the main one that concerns you is that, well, he thought he should have gotten your job."

"Hoo boy! That does muddy the water."

"Well, that's not all of it, but I've probably talked enough."

Andy did not press. Morris Allgate would remain a tipster only for as long as Andy didn't try to push him into that role. He'd had about all he wanted to know at that juncture anyway. "Morris, I appreciate your time and the effort you're obviously putting into your work. Hang in there!"

As Morris left the room, Valorie came in. "Your mystery man

is right on schedule, Andy." She smiled this time, seemingly no longer anxious about the mysterious caller, probably because he was becoming an accepted phenomenon.

"You know, I don't have any sympathy for that man. If he had any gumption at all, he'd leave a number where I can reach him."

"He did this time."

"Hey, Valorie, our first breakthrough."

"Right, boss, here's the number. He wants you to call him after seven tonight."

Andy frowned as he took the note. "After seven? This guy must be some kind of spook."

When he got to his room at the Mandalay that evening, Andy dropped his briefcase into a chair and fell across the bed. He was too frustrated to look for an apartment and too tired to call some dolt who couldn't figure out how to get him during office hours. As much as he longed for an hour relaxing on a barstool, this was no time for it. The mystery man was trivia, and Andy was not about to let petty harassment drive him back to drink. He'd dealt with the drinking issue before he left McLean.

5

Only a simpleminded fool could stalk a man for three days in broad daylight and still not catch him. By the end of his third day at the Clay Cutter region, Andy had sorely tired of the mystery caller. For some inexplicable reason, the man would never leave word as to who he was or what he wanted. He was a pest. He was an intruder, a threat to a man's freedom. Kirk Daniels was sheer trivia compared to this relentless slink. Kirk, with his patent hostility, was but a curious, almost delightful challenge and he was right up front with it. But the mystery man was hiding out.

Andy was fuming when he snatched up the phone at the Mandalay after work on Wednesday and dialed the unknown number.

"Hello." The voice was dead, a fat frog's croak.

"Ah, I have your number. This is Andy Boone."

"Oh, yeah. Glad you called." The voice had perked slightly. "You're a hard man to get in touch with, Mr. Boone."

Andy lowered the phone and grimaced at it. Then he shoved it back to his jaw and grumbled into it. "Not really—most people don't have any trouble finding me at all."

"Heh heh. Sorry 'bout that, Mr. Boone. But I think you'll

understand when I tell you what we need. I'm Chadwick Jarrigan. I'm with the Federal Bureau of Investigation."

"Sorry, but so far, I'm not impressed. You could have left that word three days ago."

"OK, I hear you. I understand what you're saying, but just take it easy. I only have ..."

"I'm damn close to taking it easy, right now, by hanging up this phone and giving my time to something a lot less irritating."

"Now, hold on, Mr. Boone!"

"Hold on, yourself. I'm on for about another thirty seconds. So if you can prove to me ..."

"OK, the thing is, I need to talk to you, and we need to do that in a meeting, you know, face to face."

"Mr. Jarnigen ..."

"Jarrigan!"

"Whatever. I don't appreciate your approach at all. So what's your question?"

"Like I say, Mr. Boone, we have reason to believe you have some important information." His voice was a frog again.

"So, go ahead, ask me your information."

"No, sir! I told you, already. We have to do this in a face to face—"

Kaplunk!

* * *

He was in his office, one hand resting on the phone, the other holding open the directory listings at the FBI, when Valorie came in and interrupted. It was Thursday morning, and he was in a desperate hurry. He had a scheduled meeting with union officials across town in Grand Prairie, and he had only a half hour to get over there.

"Excuse me, Andy, but your taxi is waiting down at the front," said Valorie.

"What do you mean, taxi?"

"Yeah, we have to use them sometimes, when the company cars are all checked out."

"No, no, Valorie, I already have a car reserved."

"I don't know, sir, but that's what they just said."

"Who said?"

"The transportation officer, Vanster—you know."

"Excuse me, Valorie. Why don't you just tell me what's going on."

"Well, Vanster just called and said the cars were all being used for the board. I guess it just came up unexpectedly."

When he reached the front entrance, only one taxi was waiting. Andy walked up to the car and leaned down to catch the driver's eye. The driver turned his head slightly, obviously waiting for Andy to get in. Finally Andy said, "You waiting for Boone?"

The driver nodded. Andy got in the back seat. Still the driver said nothing. Andy sat forward in his seat, frowning, as the taxi pulled away from the curb. As they were leaving, he looked back toward the spot reserved for company cars in the Clay Cutter parking lot. He saw three company cars. He turned back to stare at the back of the driver's head and was aware suddenly that his hands were pushing against his seat.

When the driver glanced into his rearview mirror, Andy looked at it too and drilled his eyes straight into the face he saw there. The driver twisted around in his seat. Then, without turning, he held his hand just above his right shoulder and let the black leather folder flop open, revealing a badge. Instantly, Andy slid forward and gaped at the FBI badge and picture of Chadwick Jarrigan.

"OK, score one for you," said Andy. "What do I have to do to get you out of my space?"

"Just a few answers. We might can do it right now if you cooperate."

"Why should I? Am I supposed to cooperate just because you're the almighty government? Why don't you cooperate?"

"I'm going to. We just think you may have some information we need."

"Write me a letter!"

"Don't be difficult! Please!"

Andy held the silence for a moment. Then, with his best effort to sound conciliatory, he said, "This is kidnapping, you know."

The man snickered and glanced at Andy in his mirror. "Really," he said.

At that, Andy pulled up to the front seat-back and shouted into the man's neck. "Listen, Jarrigan, nothing incites me more than taking away my freedom. I can cool just about anything else that ever comes along, you name it. My life's work is patience and calmness. But I can't stand … I absolutely can't take a violation of my freedom."

"Nobody's violating your freedom," said the FBI man. "We were trying to keep this low-key to give you the benefit of the doubt, but you …"

"What damn doubt?"

As the taxi came to a stop at a traffic light, Chad Jarrigan turned toward his passenger who, with his last outburst, had slid over against the right door. The man tried to sound calm and unaffected, the cool, fat frog back in his voice. "Like I say, I've been trying to do this the easy way, and it's obviously not going to work. So, it's only right for you to know that we have ways …"

He was cut off by the clamor of the back door swinging open. Andy Boone was on the sidewalk when it slammed shut.

* * *

It was after four o'clock when Andy got back to his office. Surprisingly, the meeting with union officials had gone well despite his tardiness, and he was encouraged by the early rapport it seemed they had come to share. At his desk, he picked up the telephone and dialed the only FBI number he could find in the Dallas directory.

"FBI."

"Ah, yes, I'm calling for the director, please." Andy tried to sound matter-of-fact.

"Who?" asked the man who had answered.

"The, ah, I'm sorry, I just got out of a meeting and my head's stuffed. Anyway, last Friday, I was contacted by your, ah, by Mr.—"

"Wadkins?"

"Right. Thanks. I need to touch base with him for a second."

"Who is this, again?"

"This is Woodson." Andy had scrambled quickly for his middle name. Just then, Valorie came in and shoved a note under his nose: Wade Boliver is holding on line 2. "I'm sorry," said Andy, "I'll have to call you right back—I have a red phone call holding. Thanks. Bye."

"Hey, Andy, how's it going?"

"Fine, sir, fine. How's the hunting?"

"Super."

"Glad to hear it. I just got back from a union meeting, and ..."

"Good. Paige taking care of you all right?"

"Oh, absolutely. She's a pro. Lucky for me, she's on the team." Andy chuckled awkwardly.

"We're all lucky to have her. You get an apartment yet?"

"No, I haven't. I've been so consumed in the new job that ..."

"Better give it some priority, you know."

"Right."

"OK. Listen, Andy, I've got a note here that Kirk Daniels is trying to get in touch with me. Before I return his call, do you have any idea what he wants?"

"Not at all. Want me to get him on for a conference call?"

"No, no. I just thought you might know what he's up to."

"Can't imagine. I've been working with him every day since I got here Monday, and he hasn't mentioned any special interests. I'll be glad to get on the line with the two of you in case it's, you know, something I will need to follow up on."

"No, Boone! Don't belabor the point—I already spoke to that the first time you asked me. See you next Monday!"

After he hung up, Andy swiveled around to admire the horizon through the window. Then he closed his eyes and let his head drop toward his chest, propping it, finally, on one thumb. Maybe Kirk was not the up-front guy Andy thought he was. He was the man's boss now. Nothing should emanate from him that didn't go through Andy first. Slowly, he swiveled back around and folded his arms on his desk near the phone. After a few moments, he reached for the phone to resume his call with the FBI, then stopped and let his hand flop back down on the desk. "To hell with it!"

It was Friday—finally—a seeming lifetime since Andy had thrashed his car through the rain on a country road heading for his new job and a bright, exciting new future. He was sitting quietly at his desk, his mind drifting back to the little Tillman school yard. Suddenly he flinched and caught his breath as the intercom buzzer shattered his dream.

"Andy," said Valorie, whispering diffidently, "there's a Mr. Jarrigan here to see you … said you were expecting him."

Andy fought instinctively at his first reaction. "But I'm not expecting anybody, Valorie—you know that."

"Yeah, but he, ah, he wants to see you anyhow and—hold on, er, just a minute." Andy waited. "So, ah, Mr. Boone, he's holding a police badge for me to see."

"Tell him to go to hell!" Now he could hear mumbling in the background, and when Valorie came back on he apologized to her. He was being unfair, unnecessarily putting her in a very difficult position.

"Oh, that's OK, but anyway, Mr. Jarrigan says he can do this discretely if you cooperate, and nobody will get embarrassed."

Andy stayed at his desk. Chad Jarrigan sat in front of it. The two gazed at each other for a while. Then Jarrigan cleared his throat and, in a nonchalant, somewhat sarcastic style, said, "Mr. Boone, let me just tell you where we stand." When Andy only nodded, he continued. "I must ask you to come to our office downtown. Another agent and I have some questions, which shouldn't take long, and then you are free to go."

Andy shook his head but spoke calmly. "I'll never understand it. Why can't you just ask me, here, right now, in my office."

"Oh, be assured, we could have done it that way, and as you recall, I've tried to meet with you. But now I'm afraid your own behavior—your resistance, so to speak—has made you somewhat more suspect than at first."

"It's your own damned fault. I haven't done anything wrong, and I'm trying to get started in a new job and you are working like hell to deny me that chance."

"Well, sir, sorry you feel that way. I really wish you'd come on down. If you haven't done anything, you have nothing to worry about."

"I have my time to worry about, and right now, time is very crucial to me. Besides, I expect to be given my basic citizen rights."

"I have no problem with that."

Neither man said anything more for a long time. Finally, Jarrigan said, "So, shall we go, Mr. Boone?"

Andy rubbed his head and looked past the FBI agent.

"Well then, I must tell you that I have with me an affidavit, an arrest warrant."

"Then arrest me!"

"It doesn't have to be this way, Mr. Boone."

"You're damn right it doesn't!"

Jarrigan got up and moved beside Andy's desk. "Stand up, please."

Andy didn't move. He stared straight into the man's eyes and waited. They had dug in their heels, each man sweating it out, waiting for the other to break, utterly uncompromising. It was a game of chicken, like two daredevils racing toward a head-on collision, still vowed to crash rather than budge.

Finally, Andy scooted back in his chair and Jarrigan stepped back and relaxed his shoulders. They stood face to face, and Andy shook his head, still holding the FBI man's gaze. "I'm sorry. I'm not going with you."

The man breathed deeply and drew out a set of handcuffs. "Have it your way. You can choose to accompany me without these, you know."

"Unh uh. If you have an arrest warrant, you're going to have to arrest me. I'm flat-ass not conceding. You're the one who's causing this. It's your stubborn, inexplicable unwillingness to read me in, to let me know what's going on, why you want me, why I'm a suspect …"

"I didn't say you were a suspect. I said that your resistance had made your actions suspect."

"You know something, Jack, you're full of gibberish."

"Chad!"

"Well, OK, Chad. Shit! Are all you guys like this? Is this your great, clever game, to squeeze blood out of people by treating them like children, acting like they don't have sense enough to know of your skullduggery, to understand the awesome mystery of FBI work? I'm not impressed with your authority, and least of all your underhanded methods."

"No comment, Mr. Boone. Hold your hands together in front."

"Aren't you going to read me my rights?"

"That doesn't apply here. We're just going to question you. We're not going to hold you or file any charges."

Jarrigan snapped the cuffs in place. Then the two men lifted their chins and strutted resolutely out of Andy's office, like two little boys who'd fought to a draw, each claiming victory. Valorie was not at her desk. Andy hesitated, and they stopped in the middle of the room.

"Hold on a moment," said Andy. He breathed deeply, letting his anger drain and then raised his bound hands up toward the agent like a child pleading for redemption. "I'll go with you. I can't afford the way this would look to my company, what it would do to their image if I go out of here in handcuffs. Of course, you know that—you're counting on it. But I don't understand it. I don't understand the way you operate … but some day I will, my friend, because I'm damn well going to figure it out."

Just as Jarrigan was releasing the cuffs, Valorie's door opened and Kirk Daniels stopped abruptly.

"Check with me later this afternoon, Kirk," said Andy. He nodded toward Jarrigan. "We have to go to a meeting that came up suddenly. I'll read you in later." Andy slapped Jarrigan on the shoulder and chuckled as they passed Kirk, who stood absolutely still, looking puzzled. Whether or not he'd seen the handcuffs was anybody's guess.

At the FBI office, Andy and Chad Jarrigan were met by a second agent. The two of them led him into a small room and invited him to have a seat at a table. Chad sat down across from Andy, and the other agent remained standing, leaning nonchalantly against a wall. The room was boredom. The gray, painted walls were bare. There were four wooden, low-back chairs and a small table about the size of a card table. That was it. There were no other props of any kind, not even any books or papers or files: nothing—desolation.

It was suddenly and emphatically clear to Andy why they wanted him out of his own environment. He was now in their court. They had full advantage here. He was in a room apparently designed to average people out, to melt down their personalities. There were no comfortable, familiar surroundings to help shape one's answers, to coax one's thinking, nothing to stimulate the senses or get an impulse from. The hard reality of it was that all you had was you.

"OK," said Jarrigan, "state your full name."

"Excuse me," said Andy, matter-of-factly, "but at this time, I am demanding a writ of habeas corpus."

"Don't worry about it—we're not charging you. Please try to understand we have to question you, that's all. If anything changes that situation, you'll get all those rights you're worrying about."

"Well, I want my one phone call. I want to call my lawyer."

Jarrigan tossed his pencil down on the table so hard it bounced, and then he let his chin drop down to his chest. Finally, he looked up, clearly struggling to stay calm. "OK, Mr. Boone, go ahead and call your lawyer."

Andy frowned. "I don't have one."

For one fleeting instant, Andy thought he detected a slight, knowing smile softening the face of his adversary. "OK, my full name is Andrew Woodson Boone."

"And your address?"

"Well, I don't have a permanent address yet. Right now, I am staying temporarily at the, ah, Mandalay in Las Colinas. Otherwise, my address is my employer, Clay Cutter Industries."

Chad Jarrigan stopped scribbling and waited a few seconds after Andy's last answer. Then he laid his pencil across the pad and shuffled around in his chair. "All right, now, to begin with, Mr. Boone, how about telling us what you were doing in Baytown last weekend."

"That's none of your business!"

At that, the other agent stepped up to the table. "Take it easy, Mr. Boone. You're going to get nowhere with that attitude. All you have to do is answer the question. What interest did you have in Baytown?"

Andy sprang out of his chair and stood to face the agent. "Baytown is my home, OK? I grew up there, went to school for twelve years there, played there, worked there, paid taxes there, supported my church, rooted for the football team, took the local paper, scurried in to build back after the storms there, sweated out the sinking, forsaken land there. My dad gave twenty-five years of his life to the Exxon refinery there. That's my interest in Baytown."

"We appreciate that," said the agent, "but from what we have, it doesn't look like it was old home week when you dropped in last weekend."

"You don't have to have a family reunion to go home," said Andy as he sat down again and pulled up to the little table. "Besides, what do you mean by what we have?"

"Just questions, that's all," said Chad Jarrigan.

"Bullshit! That is sheer unadulterated bullshit! I'm fed up with all this secrecy, this sneaky stalking and shinnying around the point. Do you guys think I'm stupid?"

"Of course not," said the other agent. "Another question, here, ah, what …"

"Forget it! You're not getting another thing out of me until you tell me what's going on. I can sit here all day if that's what you want."

"Come now, Boone," said the agent, "Surely you don't want to embarrass your company by prolonging this into something noticeable. Surely you don't need any more visibility."

Andy stretched tall in his chair and waved a finger at the agent as he talked. " Let me tell you, my company is a big company, a great economic factor here, and I hold a responsible position in it, one I didn't just stumble into. I'm sure my company can withstand this little absurdity better than you can afford the publicity. So let's don't talk about my company."

"OK, OK, hold it, guys," said Chad. "Let's just, ah—maybe we can fill in a little here. I understand your situation, Boone. Here's the thing—well, let's put it this way, what would you think? Here's a guy, a stranger in town asking strange questions, showing his temper and driving a car with Virginia license plates with fresh scratches in a strange pattern over the rear end of it?"

"I was home, and most of the people I talked to know full well who I am and why I was there."

"OK, next question," said the standing agent. "What do you know about the Michael LeMay family?"

Andy flinched. He stared alternately between the two of them, his heart suddenly pounding, anger changing to passion. He pushed up to the edge of his chair and leaned toward Chad. "Do you know where they are?"

"Come, now," said Chad, "you first."

"I don't know anything about Michael LeMay. I know his daughter, Lorrie Dean. I'm …" He rapped a fist on the table and swallowed hard. Why was he suddenly having trouble talking? He had no problem dickering with the agents. His fury had been instinctive because, by damn, he was right. But in the heat of such effort, he'd suddenly drained when they brought up Lorrie Dean. That one crowning blow was more than he could take under the circumstances. He stammered on, hating himself for succumbing to the situation, for going from assertive, insistent, confident citizen to struggling, impassioned prisoner. "I'm trying to find her."

The FBI men let him wait to say more. They looked at each other, that knowing uh-huh look. When it was clear Andy would go no further, Chad said, calmly, "Why?"

"I just am."

"Yeah, but why are you looking so hard for her, Mr. Boone? Are you related to her?"

Andy decided that they'd harassed him enough to justify a little white lie. Actually he was related to her in terms of their childhood association; that is a relationship; they hadn't said blood relative. "Yes, I am. I am related to her."

The other agent snickered and leaned toward Andy. "Well, why don't you explain for us just what that relationship is?"

"Why don't you go shit in your hat?"

The two agents stared at him for a long time, obviously waiting for him to crack. Finally Chad sighed and looked up at the other agent. Then he wrinkled his brow quizzically, pursed his lips, and rubbed his chin. "OK, we already know you're not related to her, so what else can you tell us?"

"Oh no you don't. It's your turn again. Like I say, I don't appreciate this cat-and-mouse game y'all are trying to play, but if that is the game, then I'm in too. So, now, I'll tell you more if you'll explain why you want to know."

The other agent leaned over the table, pointed a finger at Andy's face, and was about to respond when Chad interceded, brushing the man's arm aside and then holding both hands up in a peace signal. "It's OK, not a bad bargain, I guess. Mr. Boone, we are seeking surveillance of a man who is trying to make contact with Michael LeMay, or most particularly, his wife, Charlotte. This man has …"

"You don't have to tell him all that," said the other agent.

"It's OK. Hold on. Mr. Boone knows the trouble he'll be in if he divulges any of this. Anyway, this man has violated federal laws—I'm sorry, that's all I can tell you about that. We know you're not that man, but surely you can understand how we had cause to think you might be involved with him."

Andy was shaking his head as Chad finished. Lorrie Dean had come to rest in his mind as though she somehow still suffered from his own conflict. He longed for her, just to kneel down and take her small hands and say, "I'm sorry." His head jerked abruptly as he suddenly realized that he wouldn't have to kneel. If she was alive, she was no longer a child.

As he began to tell the only truth he knew, Andy was pining, his anger completely subdued. "I never did know Lorrie Dean's parents, except what they looked like. I just … we were close childhood sweethearts. Something terrible happened between us one day. I won't tell you what it was, just as you can't tell me what laws your man broke. It doesn't matter anyway. The point is, I am trying to find Lorrie Dean. Mostly, I just want to find out if she's all right."

"You say she was simply a schoolmate?" asked Chad.

"Right."

"What school?"

"High school."

"What high school?"

"Sterling."

"You didn't go to that high school."

"She did. Anyway, our friendship was in elementary school, David G. Burnet in Wooster."

"You're looking for a friend from your elementary school?"

"Yes."

The agents smiled at each other; the one standing shrugged and turned away. "OK, that's all," he said to the wall, and Chad nodded agreement.

Andy could feel the heat in his ears again. He gripped the arms of his chair until his knuckles strained white at the damnable indifference of these two men who'd searched him without mercy. The intrusion of Lorrie Dean was burden enough without the merciless torture of two dogged G-men. Why did people assume lasting friendships aren't made in grade school? For Andy, grade school was where life began. It was where character was made or broken. But now he began to wonder what Lorrie Dean truly meant to him. Maybe he was just crazy.

6

Rank fury raced toward Baytown. The '82 Cutlass with its scratched-up butt burned asphalt as it charged down Interstate Highway 45, its driver ready to kick ass. Someone in that dear town had fingered Andy Boone, and the FBI had trodden on his freedom and questioned his intentions, his word.

Andy had checked out of the Mandalay and packed everything in his car within two hours after Chad Jarrigan let him go. He had not found an apartment—had hardly even looked for one—and his time was up at the hotel. It was a hell of a way for a young man to spend Friday night, but Andy's goal was to wake up in Baytown on Saturday morning so he would have the full weekend to do what he had to do.

The two G-men had put fighting words in his head. He'd started out to find Lorrie Dean to clear his conscience, free his mind, and make sure she was all right. Now he had a whole new challenge. The FBI had come to his place of business, handcuffed him in front of his people, hauled him to town, stuffed him in a little hell chamber, drilled him for two hours, and then warned him to watch his step. Finding Lorrie Dean was no longer a mere urging of the heart; now it was a maddening of the brain.

Andy was two hundred miles down the highway, near the town of Conroe, before he quit thinking about the FBI caper. As his anger faded, his thoughts mellowed and he became largely unaware of his surroundings. Two taillights glowed in his memory and then faded as his vision dropped back to rancher Dub Grimes rescuing his Cutlass, and on back to the little schoolyard in Tillman where Lorrie Dean had been resurrected after twenty years. Where had she come from, anyway? Why had she picked that time and place to show up again? Had she been hiding, waiting, or had he been hiding her from himself? Maybe he had locked her away in some far corner of his heart that he never planned to go back to, and then somehow she'd roused and, in stirring, had wakened a long-lost, deep sense within him.

Now the search had returned to the heart. Andy longed to find Lorrie Dean—right there, in that instant. As he cruised down the mesmerizing highway, he seemed to be floating and everything became dead still and quiet. He was filled with a strange sensation, as though he had been lifted outside himself and was looking down at his own body. He saw himself as a little boy again, and the little boy seemed to be rambling around inside the grown-up man's heart, casting about for a little girl.

The little boy is alone, a small wanderer in a strange land. He is afraid but pushes on. He calls out for the little girl and somehow knows she will not answer. Please hear me calling; hear me calling, Lorrie Dean. Do you hear me, sweet Lorrie Dean? Suddenly the little boy stops in his tracks and cocks his head to one side. What if there is no little girl? What if there never was a Lorrie Dean? No matter—he has to find her anyway. He crouches now, for the hollow is ever so much darker than before. He is lost. He drops to his knees and lets his head fall to his chest. The little boy begins to cry—and the man kills the dream.

The grown man rattled his head, shaking away the vision. He laced his fingers and stretched them backward until his knuckles popped. Then he clutched the steering wheel and pushed hard against his seat. It was time to settle down. Reverie would not find Lorrie Dean!

＊ ＊ ＊

Andy's mind still raced as he lay in his Holiday Inn bed thinking through his plans for the next day. He had just turned off the ten o'clock news, and the room was dark and quiet. Clearly, he was calculating about more than he could likely accomplish in two days, but he had to try, and he had to get it all down in his mind in some kind of order. He had to visit the church, the library, two high schools, the newspaper, the police station, and all the people he'd previously talked to in Wooster where Lorrie Dean once lived. The odds were that his opportunity to make some of these contacts would be limited; many places normally close by noon on Saturdays.

He was up and finished with breakfast by eight o'clock the next morning. A half hour later, he pulled into the parking lot of Saint Mark's Methodist Church. By now his fury over what happened at the FBI had subsided. Perhaps that's what church was supposed to do—defuse. At this point, what did it matter if the reverend had copied down his license number. After all, in a sense Andy had trespassed on their territory.

Unfortunately, neither Reverend Lawson nor Reverend Dunning were at the church. Andy accepted the invitation to return at two o'clock that afternoon when one or the other was expected to be there. Meanwhile, he headed for the library and got there just as the doors opened. There were two things he wanted to do: look through the phone books for surrounding cities within a hundred-mile radius of Baytown, and leaf through references on the subject of locating missing persons.

As expected, there were very few LeMays listed anywhere. He found only seven: three in Houston, one in Freeport, two in Beaumont, and one in Lamarq. He copied their phone numbers and addresses so he could call them on Sunday when he had more time. As to his research into the matter of locating missing persons, he found that the few books they had on that subject offered little guidance beyond what his own initiative would lead him to do. He had already determined that the emerging Internet didn't yet have a sufficient database to offer much in this particular area.

By ten thirty AM Andy was at the Ross Sterling High School, hoping that even though it was Saturday there would be someone in the office. Since the school year was ending in about six weeks, he predicted there would be some weekend activity involving at least part of the faculty and staff: putting records in order, giving final touches to the yearbook, making plans for graduation, and bringing transcripts up-to-date, particularly for the seniors.

He figured right; the office was open. That was the good news.

There were two people in the main office: a man seated against the back wall posting some oversized graph sheets from a huge, rickety stack of file folders, and a woman standing near the counter working with a calculator.

As Andy stepped to the counter, the woman looked up and smiled. "May I help you?"

It was the warmest greeting he'd received during his two visits to Baytown. The woman was neat, pretty, and poised. She looked to be about fifty-five years old. Her blonde hair was simply styled. She appeared to be wearing very little makeup, yet her face reflected a soft glow. She was the picture of a calm, gracious, confident human being.

"Yes," said Andy. "I'm Andy Boone, a 1978 graduate of Robert E. Lee."

The woman's smile broadened, and she nodded.

"A close friend of mine graduated from this school the same year, and I'm having trouble locating her. Do you think … I was wondering if perhaps you have some records that would show a forwarding address or where … or something like that."

"We don't post forwarding addresses, but let's take a look at what we have. What's your friend's name?"

"Lorrie Dean."

The nice woman started writing on a small, blue square of paper. "Dean," she said as she finished.

"No, excuse me. I mean, Dean is not her last name. It's LeMay."

"And you think she was here when?"

"Probably 1978, somewhere in there."

"All right, sir, excuse me for a moment. Our hard-copy files are in another room. We didn't get anything into computers until 1987. But it should only take a couple of minutes. Have a seat over there."

Andy sat down at the front of the office near the glass door next to a leggy artificial green plant. He kept his gaze aimed straight at the counter, where he expected the great deliverer to appear in no time with all-consuming good news that would lead to a quick and pleasant end to his search. But then he frowned. He was at once aware of heaving in his chest and tightness in his shoulders. He twisted in his seat, tried to make his shoulders droop to relax, and even jabbed himself in the sides a few times, as if signaling his lungs that everything was all right and they didn't need to labor so much.

After a few moments, he looked away from the counter and stared through the glass door. Now and then, a student passed by, sometimes a couple of them walking and chatting quietly together. He could also hear conversation and occasional laughter coming from a few doors away. He looked at his watch several times but could never remember what it read from one glance to the next. Time was dragging on. The woman had said a couple of minutes, but it seemed that a good half hour had passed.

Andy rose from his chair and stepped quickly to the counter as the woman came into the office through a side door. He watched her face as she approached to see if there were any immediate signs of the news she had. She looked serious but not discouraging.

"Mr. Boone, I don't have much on Lorrie Dean LeMay, but I can verify that she graduated in 1978. We have an address, but I checked the phone book and there's no LeMay in there anymore. I'm afraid that address wouldn't help you."

He felt a weight nudging his throat and chest and started to brush at the hot tingle that shot across his forehead. He lay both hands on the counter and tried to sound relaxed. "Do you show where her transcript might have been sent or where she asked that it be sent?"

"No, sir. There's no notation about any college plans at all. It really is an unusually brief record."

"Are there any notes at all about her family, any relatives, or next of kin, or anybody?"

"None."

Andy stood still and silent, trying to reckon with the moment.

The woman looked down at the tiny note in her hand and then raised her head to look at her visitor. The smile was gone, her lips had tightened, and her eyes seemed to cast genuine sympathy. "I'm sorry, Mr. Boone. I really am sorry that I wasn't able to help you."

"Thanks. I know you tried. Ah, would you have the yearbook for 1978 that I could look at?"

She smiled broadly and her eyes twinkled; she was apparently relieved that she could fill at least one request of this solemn young man. "Yes, yearbooks are in the library, which is, of course, not open today. But I can get in there and get the annual you want and bring it to the conference room just down the hall from here. Why don't you come with me, and I'll take you to a table there. Then I'll bring it to you."

A small group of young people were at the large conference table, both boys and girls, probably all seniors. They were all clean-cut and casual but neat. They seemed carefree and happy. A little stream of friendly banter chased around the table, sometimes meeting a burst of abrupt laughter. It was a fascinating little symphony, light melodies darting here and there, themes building, fading, returning, a volley of pomp at unexpected times, and all of it driving, always proceeding.

In a few minutes, the kind lady returned and set a 1978 yearbook on the small table where Andy was seated. "Take your time," she said. "You can just leave it here when you're finished."

As she turned to leave, Andy stood up and said, "I can't thank you enough." Then he immediately turned his undivided attention to the yearbook.

He remained standing and thumbed straight to the Ls in the senior pictures. He made a quick pass through them and failed to find LeMay. He was at Lomax when he realized Lorrie Dean was not there. He started to sag over the chair. He could feel blood pulsing in his throat, a faint feeling in his head. He braced against the chair and stared down at the merciless yearbook.

After a while, Andy took a deep breath and flipped the pages back to the beginning of the Ls and started through them again, this time tracing each picture with his finger, saying the names under his breath. When he touched LeMay, he whispered the name and went on by it to the next picture. Suddenly, he gasped.

No word, no thought, no sense of any kind could capture in the tiniest degree the impact of seeing the little round solemn face that rose stoically out of the page. He held on to the chair and stared at the innocent little girl—the pretty, loving, precious, beloved child of heaven. He was choking. He wanted to talk to her, and it took every ounce of presence he could muster to keep from crying.

There was nothing printed underneath Lorrie Dean LeMay's name. Not a word. Her classmates, pictured all around her, had notations under their names reflecting honors and achievements: Band, Science Club, Baseball, Track, History, Student Council, DE, DO, Choir, and so on. Some had as many as five such listings beneath their pictures. There was nothing there for Lorrie Dean. The simple picture was the complete story of Lorrie Dean.

Andy was still standing. The yearbook rested on the table at arm's length. He started to sway and then reached out and touched her picture. He held his finger there a while and let the moment take him all the way back to the fifth grade at David G. Burnet Elementary School in Wooster, Texas.

Lorrie Dean was one of those rare little girls who was pretty—just plain pretty—even without smiling. The only difference was that her eyes shined a little brighter when she did smile. But she smiled very little. Instead, she was almost always solemn—warm and sweet, but solemn. Andy hadn't thought about this as an eleven-year-old, but now, as he recalled those childhood school days, it struck him odd that one so young should bear such a serious countenance. Maybe that was just part of her style.

The yearbook picture was black and white, yet Andy could see the rose in her cheeks, the dark black hair that fell just above her shoulders, the pink in her little turned-down pouting lips, the deep brown of her serious eyes. No wonder the face of Lorrie Dean haunted him so, if only on its own merits. As he could remember, it was a face of perfection, softly rounded and favored by a dainty, almost pug nose and small feminine ears. Her chin was curved perfectly, fading to her slim, smooth neck. She was all class.

Andy slowly lowered himself into the chair. He didn't break eye contact with the picture of Lorrie Dean as he sat. He tried to figure out what he was feeling, but couldn't. At once, he was aware that the chatter in the room had stopped—it was stone quiet. He looked around to see if the little group of kids was still at the table and found that they were all looking at him. One of the boys asked, "Are you all right, Sport?"

Andy nodded and turned back to his book.

One of the students, a girl, came over, stood beside him, and followed his gaze. Andy glanced briefly at her and slowly pointed to the picture. "Lorrie Dean," he said, and closed the book.

Back in the school office, Andy was greeted again by the nice lady and asked if he had found his friend in the yearbook.

"Yes," said Andy, "I found her. Thank you! But here's something I forgot to ask you when I was in here."

"Oh, all right, what else may I help you with?"

"Well, you remember you said there was an address given for her, but they weren't in the phone book any more?"

"Yes, that's right."

"Was that address on Crow Road in Wooster?"

"Oh, no. No, it wasn't a Wooster address. You know, if she was living out there, she would have attended R. E. Lee."

"Can you tell me what it was?"

"Ah, it was a north Baytown address. Ah, hold on, let me take another look."

"Oh, ma'am," said Andy, "I also forgot to ask if there were any notations as to her mother's maiden name."

The lady returned in a couple of minutes and gave Andy a piece of paper with the address written on it: 99301 Jones Road. She also told him there was no maiden name listed for the girl's mother. Andy thanked her for all her trouble and left the school.

It was high noon. Andy decided to catch a fast-food lunch before heading for his old high school. He found a Wendy's en route and was on his way again in less than twenty minutes.

As he drew near the Robert E. Lee High School, Andy suddenly slapped his forehead. "Oh, no!" he said. He continued to chastise himself aloud as he banged on the steering wheel in rhythm to each word. "I could have looked through pictures of Lorrie Dean's class! Damn!" If he had done that, he might have spotted some people he knew from David G. Burnet who might remember something about her. He vowed, however, that he would not go back and bother the office lady anymore. She had been absolutely super.

The atmosphere and activity at Lee were about the same as that at Sterling. Andy had a simpler mission there, so did not have to press anyone with questions about Lorrie Dean. He was there simply to search his own yearbook for names of classmates he'd been with from the first grade all the way through the twelfth. These were the people from Lorrie Dean's neighborhood, people most likely to remember something about her and her family. The office people were responsive, and he finished his job and was out of there in a little over an hour, leaving him just about enough time to get to his two o'clock appointment at Saint Mark's.

As he approached the church, Andy reflected on the ending of his previous visit when he imagined the assistant preacher was recording his license number as he left the parking lot. But he couldn't be sure of it, and it would be entirely unproductive to attempt any investigation of that possibility. It was not likely that Reverend Dunning was the person responsible for the FBI's intervention in his life. In fact, he also recalled that during the FBI interrogation, Chad Jarrigan had made a speech likening him to a stranger driving a scratched-up car with an out-of-state license, asking strange questions, and showing his temper. The only time he'd actually displayed any temper was to the little insolent blimp at Moore's Mower Fix in Wooster.

Reverend Lawson was still out, but Reverend Dunning came forth pledging his interest and whatever assistance he could provide, just as before.

"You know, Reverend," began Andy, "you prayed for me before, and I just thought I'd bring you up-to-date on what's happened to me since you did."

Andy spilled out the whole story, including his struggles with the new job, the apparent lack of enthusiasm for him among the Clay Cutter people, his arrest and interrogation by the FBI, and the complete absence of any success at finding a clue to Lorrie Dean's whereabouts.

Reverend Dunning seemed genuinely surprised when he mentioned his experience with the FBI. He expressed his sympathy for the other problems and offered to pray with him again. Andy accepted, then told the reverend he mainly wanted him to know that he was still interested. He added that he would appreciate it if he would keep it on his mind in case anything at all should arise that might help figure out how to look for Lorrie Dean.

By the time Andy got to Mower Fix, having intended to beat the shit out of the little fat fart, he had lost all his ire. He had begun to question his own emotions and confront head-on his uncharacteristic anger. Now he was beginning to accept the possibility that he was letting the prospect of revenge take over his real mission, which was first and foremost to find Lorrie Dean. He would get nowhere with the distraction revenge entails.

The place was deserted. Andy stared dumfounded at the little Mower Fix shack, his Cutlass motor still running. The building was all closed up, and there was no sign of anyone anywhere in the yard. He thought back to his previous visit and recalled that the man who seemed to be in charge was referred to as Buddy Moore. He could call him from Chester Rudman's house, assuming his friend would be home when he retraced his interviews with the Crow Road people of Lorrie Dean's old neighborhood.

As he started to back out, he thought he heard noise from somewhere around the shack. He hesitated and listened, leaning his head half out of the window. Nothing! As he resumed backing out, he thought he heard another sound coming from the back of the shack. He pulled back in, cut the motor, got out, and stood at the front of his car. Now he could hear a definite racket coming from the back. He walked slowly toward the rear of the shack, and just as he turned the back corner saw the tall, lank man who'd been sitting at the grindstone under the lean-to on his previous visit. They called him Stretch. He was the one who kept shaking his head at the silly kid's attempt to guess at what might have happened to Lorrie Dean.

"Good afternoon," said Andy. "You're Stretch, aren't you?"

"Well, that's what they call me." He studied Andy for a moment. "Ain't you the guy lookin' for the LeMay people?"

"Right you are. I'm glad you remembered. And, sad to say, I'm still looking."

Stretch just nodded and looked Andy over.

"Y'all not open this Saturday?" asked Andy.

"We close early most ev'ry Saturday 'less there's some business. See, I'm s'pose to be the senile one 'round here, so they have me come in on Saturdays to pick up 'round the place."

Andy looked straight into the old man's face, and they held easy eye contact for a few moments. The man's face softened, and Andy felt confident that this man had credibility because of his willingness to look him straight in the eye. "Stretch, as I said, I'm still looking." He shivered at the melancholy sound of his own voice. "And I just stopped by to let y'all know that. I guess what I'm saying is I don't want anybody to forget, and … ah, that way, if something accidentally should surface about them, you'd be reminded at once about me. I really don't mean to bother anybody, but I can't stop trying. I owe it to the little girl."

"Well, I don't reckon she's so little any more," said Stretch, as he smiled for the first time.

"Hey, you're right." Andy grinned too. "I still think of her that way because she was so little the last time I saw her."

"Well, le's see, ah … Andy, ain't it?"

"Oh, yeah, Andy Boone."

"Andy, I'm gonna be honest with you." He paused, and Andy waited patiently. "The way they all left outa here is sort of a mystery." He looked down at his scrubby shoes and twisted one of them in the sand. His mouth was slightly agape all the while, and he started scratching behind one ear. Then he looked up squarely at Andy and continued. "Yeah, I remember the little girl, awright. Mostly, I jus' remember that she was cute as a bug and always come with her daddy when he brung somethin' to get fixed. And they had a lot. A lot that they was always havin' fixed, that is."

"So, I guess you knew them about as well as anyone around here."

Stretch cocked his head and flexed one corner of his mouth as he squinted up at Andy. "Yeah, I think you could say that."

"What was the mystery you mentioned?"

"Oh, it was jus' that they was here one day and gone the next and nobody knew what to say about it. They had got to where they didn' much have anything to do with anybody. And the next thing you know, psssstt!"

"Do you have any ideas?"

"Not really. I figure somethin' must o' happened that maybe they didn' know was comin'. But don't ask me what. I have no notion outside of jus' thinkin' somethin' was wrong."

"Were they in some kind of trouble?" The old man just shrugged. Andy tried again. "Do you know who any of their friends might have been?" Stretch shook his head. "What about the mother, Charlotte LeMay? Do you happen to know her maiden name?"

"Oh, naw." He chuckled. "I don't know nobody's maiden name."

"Who did the daddy work for?"

"He worked for Miller's dairy, but that ain't been here in years."

"What about before that?" asked Andy.

"Well, le's see, his name was Michael. You know, he come down here from Orange or Beaumont—one of them—with that dredgin' company, Coastal Dredgin', somethin' like that. And, ah, they was dredgin' around the Exxon docks in Baytown. But that played out, and Michael took on at the dairy."

"Do you know anybody else who was with that dredging crew?"

"Not really."

"Did they move to North Baytown at some point that you know about?"

"No. They didn'. I was still deliverin' stuff to their place on Crow Road that Michael had brung in here right up to the time they left."

"Do you know if Lorrie Dean lived with someone else over in Baytown for a while?"

Stretch shook his head. He kept shaking his head, his lips pouting, as Andy continued to ask questions: where did they shop, who was the family doctor, who was Charlotte's hairdresser, where did the family come from, was Lorrie Dean born here, who else might know these things?

The shank of the day! That's all he had—not nearly enough time to finish the ambitious schedule he'd planned for Saturday: the police station, the newspaper, a round of interviews with his previous contacts in Lorrie Dean's old neighborhood, a shakedown of the address found in her high school file, dinner, and at least twenty phone calls. Now, he had no choice but to take them in some kind of order of priority.

Officers at the police station did not categorically deny that Michael LeMay, or any other LeMay, had ever been arrested but they professed that they had no record of any such event. When asked what his interest was, Andy indicated that he was a security investigator for Clay Cutter Industries to whom Michael LeMay apparently had applied for employment. At first, they questioned his right to have access to such material but relented when he pressed his citizen's right to public information. Nothing worked, however, and he left the police station as ignorant as ever.

His luck ran no better at the newspaper. When asked if they kept a home delivery subscription list, they said they did but that the only way they updated it was to rub out a subscriber's name when, for whatever reason, they no longer received the paper. Nobody he talked to admitted ever hearing of LeMay, nor could they verify that they ever delivered papers to the Crow Road address. When he tried to take out a missing persons ad, they balked, claiming concern over possible invasion of privacy and pressing him for justification. In the end, he could not persuade them that Lorrie Dean LeMay was either a missing relative or a missing heir of a deceased person.

As he left the newspaper, Andy trudged toward his car and grumbled as he struggled to open the door. He let his body slam into the seat and immediately slumped there to gain strength. It had become a weary battle just to get in and out of his Cutlass and drive it from one stop to the next. The rest of his work would have to wait until Sunday.

Thoughts and feelings competed for his attention as he continued to sit quietly in his car—thoughts about the academics of his search, feelings born of his emotions about Lorrie Dean. During those times when he was pumping people for information, he was not conscious that he actually felt for Lorrie Dean. He was driven by the heat of the effort, the sheer challenge of problem solving. These were actually the easier times because he wasn't thinking of his feelings. At such times, the grief abated, at least temporarily. Now, with the day's work done, it was back.

7

An unprecedented class reunion would surely shake Lorrie Dean out of the air. Reunions have status. And the alumni committees who put them together enjoy two of the most compelling elements of leverage in the world: power and innocence. Community support is implicit and unconditional. Alumni councils seem to have carte blanche privilege to track down classmates by any means possible, including newspaper ads. It is axiomatic that the people of a given graduating class constitute a family, that they are somehow relatives. At least, these were the convictions of Andrew Woodson Boone.

Andy was up early as usual. He sat in the hotel dining room, fidgeting and frowning, indifferent to the boiling coffee steaming in his face. He was anxious to get on with his work, but it was Sunday morning. He felt obliged to hold any contacts until the afternoon in deference to those who did not share his early-bird nature and others who would resent being bothered while they were getting ready for church. At the same time, if he waited, he wouldn't be able to finish half of what he needed to do and still have time to drive back to Dallas. With that thought, Clay Cutter suddenly loomed in front of him like a dark cloud.

He decided to go ahead and call the neighborhood people—some of them old friends—in Wooster and remind them of his continuing interest and ask the same questions he'd put to Stretch at Mower Fix. His conversations would be very short. It was now clear that if anyone knew anything, Andy would be able to detect it in a couple of questions or in less than two minutes, whichever occurred first.

He was able to reach most of the Wooster contacts. The story was the same. Nobody knew anything, not even a remote clue. So, he set about to call the seven LeMays he found listed in the phone books during his Saturday visit to the library. No hit! Not a single hit! They all reported pell-mell that they never heard of a LeMay who once lived in Baytown and that they had no relatives who might have migrated to that area. It was as if they had gotten together and voted to give the same answer if ever questioned on the subject. Lorrie Dean was a nonentity.

Andy shoved the phone back so hard it banged against the lamp on the small hotel desk. He started shaking his head, incessantly. Then he set his chin against his neck, grasped the sides of his chair, and stretched as stiff as he could. He continued to push stiff-armed against the bottom of the chair until his elbows ached.

Searching head-on was not working. Lorrie Dean would have to be lured into the open. Andy released the chair and relaxed. A class reunion just might do it. The trick would be to find the right person to put in charge of the effort. Andy could finance the undertaking himself and even do some of the legwork on request, but he knew full well that he did not have the raw talent, the finesse, the personality needed for the job. Further, he didn't have the Baytown contacts. Last, but by no mean least, he didn't have the time. Clay Cutter was already after his butt.

The project clearly needed a woman's touch. A man might well miscalculate the role of a reunion organizer and see it as a matter of big deals, quick action, and volume results at the expense of small but important details. This approach would be no match for the unrelenting effort of a local female graduate, preferably a little extroverted, socially adept, and blessed with personality, an eye for detail, the finesse to attract the interest and cooperation of others, and the perseverance to see it all through with the maximum possible response.

Mildred Finway! Andy smiled as he checked her name on his short list of people originally from Wooster who had attended Ross Sterling High School. She had all the qualities; she would be perfect. He would support her in every way possible. He would be eternally grateful to her and find ways to show it. But with his luck of the past two weeks, he probably would be unable to locate her, and if he did, she would likely tell him to go fly a kite.

He pulled the phone back within reach and started to lift the receiver. He hesitated. He closed his eyes and propped his chin on praying hands: "Please, God, let me have this one!"

Mildred Finway's mother happily gave Andy her daughter's phone number and her married name, Panacek—Mildred Panacek. He immediately called her and made a date for two o'clock at her apartment. Piece of cake!

The tide was turning; no time to let up now. He had three hours before it would be time to meet with Mildred. He decided to check out the address given for Lorrie Dean in her Sterling High School file: 99301 Jones Road.

It was a white frame bungalow in a modest neighborhood. It looked clean and in good repair, and it sat on a medium-sized, well groomed, neatly landscaped yard. Two vehicles were parked in the driveway, a late model Mercury sedan and a Chevrolet pickup of mid-80s vintage.

A young man answered Andy's knock at the door. He said nothing, just looked at Andy, apparently waiting for whatever speech he had prepared.

"Hello, sir, I'm Andy Boone, a former ..."

"We don't need any!" The man started to close the door.

"No. Sir? Please! I'm not selling!" Andy raised up on his toes and waved his arms high in the air, as if beseeching the gods.

The man hesitated. "OK, then what do you have?"

"I'm trying desperately to find a friend. I used to live in Baytown, was raised up here and graduated from Lee. After I left the state to work for a computer company, I lost track of someone who had been very dear to me." He was spitting the words out as fast as he could for fear he would lose the man again.

The man held up one hand as if stopping traffic at a school crossing. "OK, who is it?"

"Well, her name is Lorrie Dean LeMay."

"Sorry, you've got the wrong house, Buddy."

"But … could you just help me with one more thing—then I'll go. The reason I'm here is because her high school record shows that she was living at this address in '78 when she graduated from Sterling. Can you tell me anything?"

"Never heard of her. My wife and I have been in this house since '81. Never heard of her. Too bad. I'm sorry." Again, he started to close the door.

"But please! Forgive my intrusion … I'll go, but if you could just tell me who had this house before you."

"My friend, I have absolutely no idea."

"Could you tell me who you bought it from?"

"That's none of your business. Who do you think you are, barging in here asking a lot of personal questions? Butt out!"

Andy pleaded with everything he had. He offered to buy dinner for the man and his wife, that very night, and give them a chance to know him and maybe understand why he was searching so hard.

Ultimately, the man relented and invited Andy in. "When I said I didn't know who had this house before us, that was the truth, Andy. You might ask some of these neighbors around here. They might remember more about who was here."

"That's a good idea. I'll do that this very day. Meanwhile, can you think of anything at all about the previous ownership of this house that you believe might help me?"

"Not really. We bought it on auction."

Andy flinched. "On auction?"

"Right."

"I don't under ... what does that mean?"

"It was being auctioned off, and I just mailed in a bid, and it was awarded to me."

"Can you give me any names?"

"Don't have any. It was a strange and very quick process, but I got a warranty deed to the place and that's all I care about."

"Who was behind the auction?"

"The government."

"What government? The city, state ...?"

"Just the government—that's all I know." He thought for a moment and continued, "Now, I did ask a few questions, but they would always say it was confidential as to how the house came on the market in the way it did. They said confidential a lot. I finally quit asking. 'Cause, like I say, I got the house."

"You've been very kind. Thank you for your patience and for trying to help me. Again, I'm sorry to barge in like this."

There was no answer at the house immediately next door, so Andy started knocking on doors elsewhere around the neighborhood. Some of the people were in and, unlike his first contact, seemed jovial and quite willing to talk to him. Most of them recalled that the house became vacant very suddenly and the woman who was living in it moved out lock, stock, and barrel without saying good-bye, kiss my foot, or anything. When he asked if they remembered a little girl, they admitted that they did and that she was there most of the time but not always.

He decided to try the house next door again before leaving the neighborhood, and this time he was in luck. He was invited in by a very polite middle-aged couple who seemed confident in their own security and appeared to trust Andy up front. They unhesitatingly acknowledged that there had been a young high school girl living next door and they said her name was Lorrie Dean.

Andy closed his eyes and drew a deep breath. To hear someone else say her name, to openly admit that she was persona grata—that was a stirring experience.

The nice couple also told Andy that the woman living next door was Lorrie Dean's aunt and that her name was Sophia Easlie. They didn't know if she was a sister to Lorrie Dean's mother or her father. They did report, however, that Easlie was her married name, which offered no clue as to the maiden name of Charlotte LeMay. Otherwise, they knew nothing of the LeMays. They confirmed that they woke up one morning and Sophia Easlie and the young girl were gone. They never came back.

* * *

Mildred Panacek lived in a fashionable apartment complex in North Baytown. When she answered the door, she giggled happily, held wide her arms, and whooped, "Andy Boone!" Andy walked chuckling into the warm embrace of a very dear hometown friend. They held the hug for a long time, much to Andy's pleasure. This was something special, he thought, reserved only for those who are very close.

As she led him into the living room, she started chattering, "I'm glad you thought to call Mother and get my married name, although, as you can see, I'm no longer married." Before Andy could comment, she continued uninterrupted. "Irreconcilable differences—know what I mean? Mostly about raising the kid. I have an eight-year-old, Jenny—brilliant, pretty, perfect in every way. She's at a little party this afternoon." She paused just long enough to smile and toss her head as if to say "just kidding" and then plowed ahead. "But, that's OK, that's OK, I'm doing fine." She pointed to a couch and said, "Pull up a cushion, Andy." Then she hurled her body into the adjacent recliner and settled into it as gracefully as one can when planning to sit on one's foot. She sighed and rocked her head, smiling at Andy as if to ask whether he was going to say anything.

"I'm impressed," began Andy.

"Hey, Andy, you're looking good, my man. How did you manage to stay so slim and trim?"

Andy smiled and shrugged modestly.

"Still favor blue Dockers and knit T-shirts, I see." She laughed and slapped her leg. "But, then again, why not? After all, you can handle it."

"Thank you … I think," said Andy, still grinning. "Actually, you're looking darn good yourself, Mildred. But that's the way I remember you. I don't know if you ever knew it or not, but I admired you when we were little kids. All us guys did—your charm and good looks, and your special way with people."

Mildred tightened her smile, and her expression settled a little. Uncharacteristically, she didn't try to talk for a moment. Now two old friends sat, momentarily quiet, each gazing slightly past the other and thinking warmly of the past.

It was not customary for Andy Boone to pay much attention to the details of what women looked like. They were either overall pretty or not pretty. But in this moment he was fascinated by the way this special woman had put herself and her environment together.

Mildred Finway, now Panacek, was bright and vivacious, and though she obviously had suffered some bad times she seemed genuinely proud of herself and showed no bitterness or self-pity. She was medium height, borderline plump—which Andy tended to favor—and blessed with a delightfully expressive and handsome face. Her light-brown hair was short and fluffed and styled away from her face, with a scatter of bangs across her brow. She looked comfortable and neat, though maybe a little mischievous, in her light-green argyle pullover, tan acid-washed skirt, and bone flats. *It all seems to fit,* thought Andy.

Mildred's apartment was equally cultivated. Its walls were of paneling, painted ivory, with contrasting darker trim around doors, windows, and baseboards. There were two easy chairs, the emerald green now holding Mildred and a deep purple armless chair across from the jewel-toned striped couch where Andy was seated. The walls were conservatively decorated with only two large paintings, both landscapes, and two little clusters of family pictures on either side of the hallway entrance. Against one wall was a large TV. A stereo cabinet and speakers were spread along another. The place was neat and orderly, not compulsive but definitely clean and picked-up.

"What are you grinning about?" asked Mildred, leaning forward in her chair to stare straight at her visitor.

"You," he said.

"What?"

"It's you, Mildred. All of this. This apartment, the way you look. It makes me think of our childhood days, of us, the good times, of years ago—and before I go any further, thank you for seeing me."

"Listen, man, I'm flattered! I couldn't be happier to see anyone. You're right, we all knew who we were back then, didn't we? Nobody seemed to be trying to figure out what their thing was or where they were supposed to be going. Know what I mean? I'm just glad we didn't have to go through what the earlier generations did—and for that matter, what the later generations have to compete with."

She was in constant motion as she talked, bouncing on her leg, leaning forward and back, rocking her shoulders, and sometimes waving a hand in the air. And she said you know what I mean a lot. But she was candid and easy to understand, and Andy now realized that with all her animation, the welcome embrace with which she greeted him was not a loving hug; it was a figure of speech. No matter. She was precious. The world was full of pain, and this was her way of dealing with hers. This is where personality comes from, the need to cope.

"But Andy, tell me what's going on? Your phone call got my curiosity up. What's this about Lorrie Dean LeMay?"

"Mildred, I'm going to tell you everything, absolutely everything. First of all, I am mainly just trying to find her. I must find her. I can't live with not finding her."

"Did she mean that much to you? Was she your sweetheart or what?"

"We were sweethearts, in a way, as much as grade school kids can be. You know, it was just a mutual crush. But that part of it—well, that didn't last any time. Something happened one day, something terrible. I did something that hurt her, and she didn't deserve that."

"Hurt her physically or emotionally?"

"I'll get to that in a minute, but let me start at the beginning."

Andy proceeded to tell everything he could think of about his search for Lorrie Dean LeMay, all the background that was involved and the strange circumstances that seemed to set loose within him a demon madly determined to find the long-lost schoolmate. He told of everything he'd done, of every person he'd talked to, and of the total absence of any clue of any kind, all the sources he'd checked out, and even his confrontation with the FBI.

"Well, Tiger," said Mildred. "I never knew you to be that aggressive with anyone. You were always the dreamer, the inventor, the quiet, silent type. Why did you take on the FBI like that? That was never like you."

"Because they caught me at a bad time and because they acted secretive and stupid about it. So, anyway, coming on up to this—I need your help."

"Andy, my boy, I'm yours. What can I do?"

"I can't just keep scrapping like this, trying to chase her down with just sheer energy and logic like some kind of special agent. In the first place, I'm not qualified."

"Well, I don't know. I guess you're doing pretty good from all you've told me."

"Yeah, well, but that's—I'm not getting anywhere. What I want to do, what I'd like you to help me do—is organize a class reunion for Lorrie Dean's graduating class."

"Wait a minute, Andy. They had their tenth reunion in '88."

"I figured that, but maybe we could have a makeup reunion on behalf of those who didn't get to attend that one and, of course, invite everybody else too."

Mildred's head dropped into her hands and she began to rock back and forth, holding her head and laughing until her plump frame was shaking all over. "Andy, I'm sorry." She wiped tears from both eyes, all the while trying to suppress her laughing. "I'm sorry," she said again. "It's not you. It's just that you're so serious, so like I remember you." She reached out and patted his knee as she continued talking, "And believe me, I love that little boy in you. Know what I mean?"

"So, will you help me?"

"A makeup reunion. It's so … unprecedented. Andy, I just don't think it would work."

"Let's don't call it that. Let's just have another reunion."

"A fourteenth reunion. That's just as …" She stopped, caught suddenly in Andy's poker-faced, unrelenting stare. They looked at each other for a long time, and in those moments an unspoken bond seemed to arise between them. As it was emerging, they were both nodding agreeably.

"Thanks," said Andy, when Mildred started to smile sweetly.

"You got it," she said. "I'll start right away."

"When you get a response from Lorrie Dean, I'd sort of like to know it at that point."

"Well, all I can say is, we'll try."

She slipped a writing pad and pencil out of the table drawer next to her recliner. "OK, let's go! Let me get some of this down. Wait a minute, Andy, would you like a beer?"

"Sure."

She leaped out of her chair and scurried away. She was back in less than a minute, carrying two beers in one hand. She popped the tabs on both, handed Andy his, and dropped back into her chair, tucking one foot underneath as before. Then she edged forward with the writing pad over her knee and started poking the pencil's eraser at her forehead. She started to write as she talked. "Andy, you say her aunt's married name is Easlie?"

"Yes. So we can't tell if she is a sister of Lorrie Dean's mother or her father. You know, it would be a real break if she turned out to be the mother's sister. If we could get her maiden name, we could trace through that lineage as well as the LeMay side."

"Right. Tell you what. I'll call this Sophia Easlie's ex, assuming I can locate him. So, what about this work you did at Sterling yesterday?"

"They don't have much of a record. They didn't have a forwarding address for the LeMays and they didn't have the mother's maiden name. All they had was this Easlie address."

"Did you ask them where Lorrie Dean was born?"

"Ah, no, how would that—"

"We could dig up Lorrie Dean's birth certificate in the county records where she was born. That should give us her mother's maiden name. Also, if we could find out where her parents were married, we might get something off the marriage license."

"Hmm. I should have had you in on this long ago."

Mildred's chatter had subsided. She was obviously getting involved, getting her teeth into it. From the change in her behavior it seemed to Andy that she was beginning to take it on as a personal challenge, as something important for its own sake. She was writing and thinking, paying no attention to her beer, and from time to time, looking at him. Abruptly, she raised her pencil in the air and half pointed it at Andy as she spoke. "Andy, you ought to … have you talked to your own mother about this? You know, she and Charlotte were in the PTA together. She may have a wealth of knowledge on this."

"Well, I thought of that, but I haven't … ah, no, I haven't."

"Why?"

"The problem is figuring out how to pick Mother's brain without ... well, I'm afraid she'd ask more questions than she answered."

"Andy Boone! You rascal! She's your mother! You talk to her. You hear me?"

"Right."

"By right, do you mean you'll talk to her?"

"Yes, Mildred. You're right. She has a right to know as much as I've told you. But ... it's just going to be hard telling your own mother about some very deep feelings and some that you don't understand yourself and that you don't want anybody trying to explain to you."

Mildred just stared at him.

"Right," said Andy—finally.

"OK, I'll try to trace down Sophia Easlie through her husband, and since you won't have a chance to go back to the Sterling office, I'll find out where Lorrie Dean was born. And if it's not too far away, I'll even check on her birth certificate. Plus—plus, Andy, I'll talk to some of Lorrie Dean's old teachers. Know what I mean? Teachers know things. Meanwhile, I'll get me a working committee—they're going to laugh at me at first—and start the ball rolling. What we have to do is figure out a way to generate some unprecedented excitement over this very unusual homecoming. Maybe that's it—we could call it an urgent homecoming."

"The only reservation I have, Mildred, is that it's putting so much on you. You're a very precious, adorable human being, and I don't want to take advantage of you."

"Your gratitude is all the reward I need, Andy, and I know I already have that." She had become suddenly a little sentimental but was trying to maintain her effervescent self. She was having some trouble doing it. Andy did not push her or interrupt. It was proper that she be allowed to go at her own pace. She was taking on a lot, and she deserved all the consideration he or anyone else could give.

For the first time, Mildred didn't look at Andy directly as she talked. "I wish somebody wanted to find me." She swatted a tear from one eye as she guided her habitually waving hand to her cheek. She struggled to look carefree and unaffected, as if her last remark was intended to be a joke, and her voice had the slightest crack in it as she continued. "Maybe after you find Lorrie Dean, I could disappear and you could hunt me down." She forced a halfhearted giggle.

"Believe me, Mildred, you'd surely be a worthy object to hunt. But please don't disappear on me just yet. I couldn't take two of you at the same time." He laughed and walked over to take her in his arms. He held her, and she held on. They lingered, their embrace steadily tightening, for quite a while.

After they slowly pushed apart, Mildred asked, "Why are you trying so hard, Andy?"

Andy sighed and held her hands for a moment as he talked. "I think that it's because of the way it came to me. It almost cost me my life. After I passed that school yard in Tillman, I was the saddest person in the whole world. And after I went back there, to the school yard, I sat in my car for a long time, trying to figure it out. It's one of those things I can't explain to myself, but that I no longer question. Now, with all the mystery that's been added, their strange disappearance and everything, it's as if Lorrie Dean was calling for help when I passed that school yard."

"OK, all I got to say, Andy, is—keep your head!"

"I know."

"One other thing, Andy, ah, well, what would you do if you found her?"

Andy's reflexes piqued as though the question was a shock, an unexpected jolt. He didn't try to answer at first. Finally he said, "I really don't know what I'll do." He paused, still considering the matter. "I think I would try to figure out what the truth is and tell her that. I just don't know, I don't know. I want to find out that she's all right, and I hope to find out that she's happy. I want to find out if there's anything at all in the world I can do for her. Even if she has a husband, I could tell her that. He'd understand."

"Do you love her?"

8

Andy Boone's sensational rise to eminence crumbled to a pathetic crawl at the feet of Wade Boliver, his wayfaring boss. He met Boliver's wrath Monday morning, just seven minutes after he reported to work bleary-eyed and road-worn, after only three hours sleep after his late drive back from Baytown.

When he walked into the Human Resources director's huge office, the man was slung way back in his oversized, judicial chair, smirking straight ahead over the bare top of a solid oak desk. He extended his hand as Andy approached but did not offer to get up. He invited Andy to have a seat facing him across his desk.

Wade Boliver was a tall, surly man with a flat, wide face that looked as though it had been stamped on his skull as an afterthought. He was wearing a light-brown, baggy, ugly suit that needed pressing. It seemed that his office stretched halfway across one side of the Clay Cutter building and it was draped and carpeted and lavishly decorated as if it were a royal throne.

Andy lowered himself into the overstuffed chair Boliver offered and continued to sink into it after he landed on what he thought was its bottom. When he was fully docked, he was at once aware that this was a tactical chair, designed specifically to disadvantage its occupant. His rear was so near the floor that his knees stuck up in the air like goalposts. And his head was so low, he strained to look up at the man on the other side of the desk. Worst of all, while it only took a couple of seconds to submerge into the chair, it would seem to take at least ten minutes to struggle out of it.

Wade continued to lean back in his chair as he talked. "Just a couple of things, here, Boone, ah, before you get too far along with things."

Andy wrinkled his brow, trying to look attentive while waiting for what he was afraid was going to be another unilateral conversation with his boss.

"It's been brought to my attention," continued Boliver, "that you have done some things that perhaps may have rankled some of the troops here."

That cinched it! It had been Andy's experience that whenever anyone started out a meeting with "it's been brought to my attention," you were, indeed, about to get a one-sided lecture with no opportunity to ask questions or explain anything. Andy decided he needed to level the playing field, that his awkward physical position was a bit untenable, so he began to squirm out of the mammoth, bottomless chair.

"Excuse me, Wade," he said, as he continued to rise. "I have a serious back problem, and my doctor wants me to sit in support chairs as much as possible. He probably doesn't know what he's talking about, but if you don't mind, I'll just grab this straight-back chair from the conference table over here."

While Andy retrieved a better seat, Wade Boliver leaned forward in his chair as if mounting some kind of major offensive. When his underling was settled, he leaned back again and continued with his speech. "As I say, it's been brought to my attention that you might have ruffled some feathers around here, and I just wanted you to be aware of it so you can … so you can be, you know, careful about things."

"What have I done?"

"Just hold on! I'm getting to that."

"Sure, boss, go ahead."

"First of all, Boone, I'm not trying to criticize you at this point. It's just that I want to make these ... ah, these impressions—available to you, so you'll be sensitive to everyone around here and be careful."

"You have my undivided attention."

"OK, so the word is out that you gave your men a ridiculous deadline to prepare detailed briefings for you."

Andy sat tall in his chair and looked the enemy straight in the eye. "Not so, boss," he said. "First of all, there was nothing to prepare. Secondly, they should be prepared all the time to discuss what they're doing. And finally, all I asked for was an informal account of what they do."

Boliver lunged forward in his chair and leaned toward Andy, squinting and raising a finger in his direction. "Don't get defensive, dammit! I'm trying to give you some counsel, some advice."

Andy shrugged.

Boliver snorted and continued. "Sorry, I didn't mean to get so hot. Anyway, they said you talked down to them, that you were demeaning and cocky, and that you pointed your finger at them and made fun of their clothes, and that ... why are you shaking your head?"

"It's not they, Wade, it's Kirk Daniels."

"There you go again. See what you're doing. It doesn't matter who all said what. The point is these impressions were left."

Andy was still shaking his head as Boliver talked. "Boss, I can be an incredible help to you—to your mission. I'm not trying to be insubordinate. I just want to be fair with all of my staff, and I know they didn't all come running to you with grievances about me."

"Well, you should be sensitive to Kirk Daniels and to all of them."

"I am, and I will continue to be, but it won't work for me to be afraid of him or let him anger me into making mistakes. That's why it's perfectly all right with me if you concede that the lone complainer is one Kirk Daniels. I can deal with that. I'm not going to leave here and punch the guy out."

"Quit trying to put words in my mouth. I never said it was Kirk Daniels, and you're getting defensive again."

"Please bear with me, boss. I plead with you for that. Now, I remember you warning me about Kirk Daniels during our first contact, on the phone the day I arrived at the hotel. And I recall Daniels called you last Thursday, because you asked me if I had any idea what about."

"Well, the fact remains, Boone, that these complaints have been made about your early behavior."

"They're ridiculous. No way did I talk down to anyone, and I didn't comment on anybody's clothes. All I did was tell Kirk his collar was turned up. Check me out, Wade—let's talk to the others."

"I know what the others will say."

"So, let them say it. That will give you a fair picture."

"You know, Boone, I'm getting tired of this conversation. Do you get my message or not?"

"Loud and clear. And I pledge to follow your counsel. It's just that I've only been here a week and I already have the distinct impression that Kirk Daniels is not an easy man for Clay Cutter, and not an easy man for you as the personnel director."

"Human Resources director," corrected Wade.

"Right. But … so, Wade, if you could just tell me a little bit about the man, if I know what the problem is, I believe I can relieve you of a lot of responsibility for him, save you some trouble and grief. Is he somebody's sanctified brother or something?"

"Don't get silly," smirked Wade.

"Well, what?"

"Boone, why do I get the feeling you've forgotten who you're talking to?"

"OK, I respect you. Please know that. But I know you don't want your employee relations chief to fall down and play dead."

"This meeting is over. That's all. Do you understand?"

Andy rose from his chair and set about to leave. Near the office door, he turned back and said, "One thing I'm positive of, Mr. Boliver—Kirk Daniels wants a fight. His ego sorely needs a victory, but I will not knowingly make a bad decision just so it can have one."

He hurried to his office to keep from thinking about his fiasco with Wade Boliver. Discipline was his main ally at this point, the one thing he could rely on to keep him on course and off the path of anger and remorse that might otherwise lead him astray. He needed to be creative in deciding how to deal with his increasingly tenuous situation at Clay Cutter, and brooding about the way he was being treated would clearly kill any hope for something constructive on that level.

At his desk, he immediately turned to two phone messages and a tiny stack of incoming mail and sank himself into the immediacy of these tangibles. He returned the two phone calls and read through the mail, mostly routine memos and forms about upcoming meetings and other events related to the Employee Relations program.

There was one person in Human Resources he could talk to who he was convinced would be candid and would not have some kind of self-serving hidden agenda—Paige Ivy. She was, in Andy's estimation, the singularly best asset Clay Cutter had, patently competent, thoroughly committed to hard work and quality results. He could talk to her and not lose his present discipline until the effects of the Wade Boliver meeting wore off.

Paige welcomed him into her neat, well-organized office with the same grace and slightly reserved warmth she'd shown his first day at Clay Cutter. As she pointed to a chair for Andy to take, she said, "You look like a guy who just missed his bus."

Andy smiled, a little chagrined that his deliberate discipline had failed to completely hide his somewhat tangled frame of mind. "Oh,

I'm still getting settled," he said, "still trying to figure out my role around here."

"Know what you mean. Can I help?"

"Well, knowing I can lean on you at times will be a great help in itself. I have a lot to learn, much more than I realized when I first got here." Paige smiled and nodded and waited for Andy to continue. "I just had an ever-so-brief meeting with Wade."

"How did it go?"

"Wish I knew."

"Hmm."

"There's one thing I do know," said Andy. "That's one awesome chair he's got in there."

Paige laughed outright and gestured her agreement. She tried to stop a couple of times and couldn't, and Andy began to laugh with her. While they snickered together, Andy saw in her what he'd sensed from the beginning: a quality human being, keenly responsible, all business most of the time but genuine and true and capable of relating in a warm and human way.

After their laugh, they looked at each other, neither obviously tempted to say anything for a moment, and in that time it became clear to both of them that neither was about to badmouth Wade Boliver. Momentarily, Andy felt himself waxing solemn again and looked straight into her eyes as he spoke: "Paige, have you heard any complaints about me around here?"

"No, not at all. Why do you ask?"

"Because it's plainly clear to me that one of my men, namely Kirk Daniels, sees me as an adversary. And I can't figure out what the problem is."

"Uh huh," began Paige. "I really don't know what the deal is with Kirk or what his plan is for himself or you or anybody else. I try not to find out—the more I know, the more I'll be expected to gossip about it, and I don't have time for gossip."

"Oh, by all means. I'm not trying to draw anything out that

would make you uncomfortable. I guess I just had to express that to someone."

"I understand," said Paige.

Andy squirmed in his chair for a moment, thinking Paige might say more. When she didn't, he decided to change the subject to business, a topic that he knew was dear to her heart. "Paige, you know ... our divisions are the only two in Human Resources that are really concerned with what people are like and how they behave. The others, Classification, Management, Benefits, they're all pretty much procedural and it doesn't really make any difference to them what the people do, or want to do, or can do, or what they're up to."

"Oh ... well ... perhaps," said Paige hesitantly.

"Just a thought," said Andy. "Anyway, I think that you and I probably should—er, could—meet together from time to time on matters where our areas of interest overlap. What do you think?"

"Well, Andy, I don't know. See, we've never had much coordination among the divisions here. I don't know if it's really necessary. I know my job and what's to be done, and all, and I never really thought of it as overlapping anywhere."

It was Andy's turn to nod while Paige shrugged and crimped one corner of her mouth as if inviting him to answer her last point. Then Andy looked at his watch and leaned forward in readiness to get up. "Well, I guess it's time I got out of your hair and back to my own bailiwick," he said, smiling at Paige.

Paige held his gaze, her expression changing several times, at once quizzical, then pondering, and at times, calculating—never hostile, but serious. Finally, she nodded, smiled, and started to rise from her chair. She escorted her visitor to the door and opened it for him. As he started out, she touched his shoulder, smiled, and said, "Hang in there!"

9

Paige Ivy told Andy The Lamp was his best bet among nearby apartment units, and she was probably right. The only hitch was that its popularity, particularly among working singles, sometimes made it hard to get into. In fact, on Andy's first visit, he had to settle for a place on the waiting list, with six applicants ahead of him. But in a remarkable and uncharacteristic turn of luck, he received a call in three days, announcing an unclaimed vacancy for a one-bedroom efficiency apartment, which would be repainted in one day.

The Lamp was a quiet, cultivated compound of two-story balcony apartments on the outskirts of Las Colinas in Irving. It was surrounded by a waist-high brick wall that followed along a trail of trimmed hedge-holly, climbing roses, and little islands of early spring flowers, mostly blue and yellow petunias and deep-purple and white pansies. The apartment village was served by a narrow one-lane road that emptied into small parking sections at intervals and featured old-fashioned street lamps along the way. On the inside, The Lamp was by no means lavish but fully accommodating. It should amply serve the young man for as long as he needed, which according to the way things were shaping up at Clay Cutter—especially with the frolics of Kirk Daniels and Wade Boliver—might not be very long.

Shortly after noon on Wednesday, Andy was in his room resting up from the arduous task of packing his sock drawer, making his bed with new linens, and ticking off completed items on his to-do list, which included registering his car in Texas, transferring his bank account, and applying for a Texas driver's license. It occurred to him that he had unread mail from Channel Harris Properties. He was frowning as he stirred the little pile of papers on his dining table, and that irritated him because there was no particular reason to be frowning in advance. He found the small envelope and held it in the air for a moment, still perturbed at himself because of the foreboding mood he seemed to have slipped into. He eased open the envelope and shook out its contents, which consisted of one page with letterhead that took more space than the terse message typed across the middle of the paper:

Dear Mr. Boone,
Re: your inquiry about the residence at 317 Crow Road in Baytown, Texas. Our records show that we purchased this house and resold it, but the name of the seller and date of record are not shown. We have no other relevant information. If deeds were filed on this property, you may find some details in Harris County tax records. Please let us know if we can be of further assistance. Signed, Rayford Mott, President.

Andy sat stone still, musing aimlessly, with one fist covering the small note on the table. He sat that way for several minutes, motionless except for his heavy breathing. In a while he labored up out of his chair and strolled aimlessly to the balcony. Still he waited, trying to gain some sense of what was taking place in his head—and perhaps in his heart. He picked out a spot on the horizon, a water tower, and mumbled to it: "Why does it have to be so hard? Why couldn't I just wake up some morning and ... bang—Lorrie Dean! He fell silent again and then turned to go back into his room. He heaved a series of agitated breaths and started mumbling again as he fell into bed.

When he awoke the next morning there was no "bang—Lorrie Dean." Instead there was just the usual bang—Clay Cutter. It was time for another smashing day of fun and games at the big corporate playground. Andy was in his office but five minutes when Wade Boliver's secretary called him to come to Wade's office. Andy thrust an arm in the air as he sprang away and sang out, "It's Boliver time!"

Boliver was leaning back in his chair, scowling, as Andy entered the office. Before his visitor could sit down, he straightened up, still sneering, and said, "Wanna tell me about the FBI, Boone?"

"Not much to it," said Andy as he pulled up a chair from the conference table. "They thought I had some knowledge about a man they're looking for."

"I don't really buy that story. Couldn't you just call them and give them your, er, knowledge ... or go see them and make your important—knowledge—available to them?"

"As a matter of fact, I tried calling them, but they wouldn't have it that way. I refused to take time from my job and meet them in their office downtown, so they came out here and insisted. That's when I went with them. I figured they were going to be a habitual distraction until I met with them on their terms. As it turned out, I didn't know anything anyway."

"Well if all that's true, why did it have to be such a big damn secret? Isn't this the kind of thing you keep your boss informed about?"

"Right, sir, but it just wasn't a big deal."

Wade Boliver glared at his visitor for a while and then bobbled his head and said, "You know, Boone, you haven't gotten off to a very good start around here."

"Can you tell that in just two weeks?"

"First of all, that's a sassy comment, and second, in case it slipped your mind, I'm Human Resources—I can tell it in two hours."

"Well, I'm truly sorry, Wade. I promise to keep you better informed, and I'll try harder at my job. I never meant to cause you any trouble or discomfort. I pledge to be more sensitive to, ah, to your concerns."

Wade Boliver's head had started to dance, and Andy could see the pulse pounding in his neck. Then the man leaned forward over his desk, listing slightly over his right elbow with his finger pointed straight at Andy's nose. He narrowed his eyes and said, "Let me tell you something, young man, you're not the palace favorite around here; you're not headquarters any more, and they can't help you."

Andy held eye contact with Boliver, which seemed to anger the boss all the more as he continued to scold. "Don't get it in your head you can call headquarters to bail you out." He paused and then huffed and rattled on. "In fact, I welcome you to call your cohorts in McLean and complain about how we're treating you. Go ahead, young tiger, do it!" He flopped back in his oversized, utterly impractical executive chair, swiveled around sideways, and sneered, "They can't help you, Boone. They don't give a damn what happens to you now."

"Do you, Wade? Can I count on your help?"

"You've got such a sarcastic tongue, Boone. No wonder the troops are riled at you."

"Who's riled?"

"See what I mean?" Wade rolled his lips as though exercising them for word battle and started to speak while his mouth was still distorted from the harsh exercise. "I'm just telling you, Boone ... that your record before coming here doesn't mean a damn thing. It is of no use to you anymore. Your career starts and stops here. Try to get it in your head that when you left headquarters, your reputation stayed there. You don't have a reputation here. You're starting from scratch."

Andy continued to look directly at his adversary without offering a word. He just listened, content to let the man shoot up all his bullets before Andy spoke. Then, without changing his countenance, he said,

"I couldn't agree with you more, Wade. All that you say is clear and reasonable. But what isn't clear is why you felt tempted to make those comments. What prompts this onslaught, boss? Tell me what's really bugging you about me. Give me something to work with."

"Don't you get it, Boone? You just said you agree with me."

"Yeah, I accept the logic of what you said, and … I mean, a man doesn't just up and make a speech like that—about all that headquarters stuff—without some precipitating reason."

"I'm just warning you. Watch your step!"

"That's another thing I can't decipher. Why am I getting all these warnings? You warn me, Kirk Daniels warns me, others caution me to be on the lookout for trouble … what's going on? Have I been marked for some inevitable disaster? Am I the designated whipping boy here? Is there some kind of conspiracy—"

"Shut up!"

"—to run me off?"

"If you ever again disgrace this company by the likes of bringing the FBI to our door, there will be disaster."

"If that's what you're hung up on, you should know that this unblemished company was duped by the FBI before one of its agents ever showed up at my door. Let the company, including our obviously fallible transportation officer, explain why they were conned by an FBI agent posing as a taxi driver and lured into carting off one of their officers—actually kidnapping an employee right under the company's nose. Check that one out, and you'll know something about where the disgrace really is."

Wade Boliver's face was drawn tight and his eyes were squinted nearly shut and drilled straight at Andy. "That's all, Boone. Get out!"

Andy left the room without another word. He paused outside the door and then wandered toward his office, passing it briefly until a squealing phone stopped him in his tracks and made him check his bearings. Finally he fell into his plush chair and sat quietly.

"Are you OK, Mr. Boone?"

He'd been barely conscious of a faint shuffling at his office door and the sound of Valorie politely clearing her throat. "What? Oh, yeah, I'm fine—thanks for asking."

"Sure."

"As a matter of fact, why did you ask?"

"Oh, it's just … I, ah, well you looked to be in a daze—or, I mean, in deep concentration."

"Just a little tired, but yeah, you're very perceptive. By the way, have you heard any rumblings around the organization about me lately?"

"Rumblings? You?"

Clearly, he hadn't gotten her with that one. She was too diplomatic, too much a professional to jump on a baited question like that. So he decided to cast about in more abstract terms to see if she was mindful of any scuttlebutt or imminent trouble around the organization. He avoided bluntly asking her if she'd heard of any impending trouble for him or anyone on his staff. That would have been unfair to her in her particular situation. In any event, Valorie appeared perfectly relaxed and natural throughout the conversation. There was nothing about her demeanor that made it appear she felt awkward in dealing with him. So maybe he shouldn't worry. Still, something was going on: his boss was deliberately after his butt.

When they finished, Valorie handed him some papers. "I don't see anything urgent or extraordinary in today's mail, Mr. Boone."

"Thanks, Valorie."

"Sure." She walked to the door.

"Valorie?"

"Yes, sir."

"Thanks for all you do."

Her instant smile was radiant. "Thank you, Mr. Boone, for saying that."

At that moment, Andy ached to see Paige Ivy, just to be in her presence and let her countenance and calming demeanor heal him. In his mind, Paige stood out in the Clay Cutter organization as the most genuine, most trustworthy, and capable officer on the roster. He'd never detected any signs of pretext in whatever she said. She was top shelf.

"Hi, Andy, pull up a cushion."

They sauntered toward the conference table where they'd sat during their first meeting. After they were comfortably situated, Paige looked quizzically at her visitor and said, "Are you OK, Andy?"

"Oh sure—I think. Thanks for letting me barge in like this ... you know, unscheduled."

"No problem. I don't have a schedule anyway," she said, grinning mischievously. "Obviously, I should have, with all this work I've let pile up."

Andy looked around the room at stacks of files, applications, and computer printouts. "Can't you farm some of this out, Paige?"

"Not really. I have two new technicians, but I have to thoroughly audit their work for a while, and I'm still catching up on backlog left by the two they replaced. There's no one to give that work to. The really disconcerting thing is that 75 percent of it is purely clerical."

Andy pushed his chair back from the table and twisted around so he could rest an ankle over one knee. When he was all set, he looked up at his friend and caught her smiling pleasantly, knowingly. "I guess you heard about the FBI caper."

"Seems like I heard you talked to an FBI agent, but that's about it."

"I did indeed, but at their demand and in their office. They thought I might be able to help in their investigation involving a suspect from my hometown. Turns out, I knew nothing." Paige didn't respond or even raise an eyebrow. She showed no surprise at all, which probably meant that she had heard talk. "I think, Paige, I probably should work on keeping a low profile around here. Maybe I should just treat Kirk

Daniels like the fair-haired young prince he is purported to be. What do you think?"

"Andy, I think you needn't do anything but be you. We have to presume that's what they hired you for."

"Guess you're right. I trust your judgment in things—that's why I sort of sought your counsel in this thing."

"You're OK, Andy. Just keep that in your puddin' head. Just keep saying, I'm OK."

"Thanks for your confidence. I'll keep trying, but I'm not naive. I know positively that I am not off to a good start."

∗ ∗ ∗

The Lamp was a welcome port in the storm, a refuge from the day's squabbles and scuffles. Andy gulped down a take-out hamburger and a can of Coke, then dropped free-fall into his recliner. "What a day," he grumbled aloud. "One more like this and they can take Clay Cutter and shove it, or whatever." He picked up the only piece of mail from the night stand, ripped open the envelope, shook out the single piece of ruled notebook paper and began to read:

Dear Andy Boone,
Hope you don't mind me gittin your address from your mother. Grandpa says thanks for the beer. I don't drink it myself, but he does. I kept thinkin of how you was worrin about trouble you caused us when you crashed the fence. It didn seem like you worried about some damage to your car. You didn even look it over much, but only what it done to our fence. Anyway, your thankfulness sort of stood out, and we'd like you to come for dinner—I guess I mean lunch—this comin Sunday. About 1 o'clock. We'll play like it's May Day even if it is a coupla days late. You probly need a break, so come on out here where it's peaceful. See ya. Dub

He started reading the newspaper, yawning and instinctively letting his eyelids droop. After a while, he awoke with the newspaper still loosely held in one hand. Now the embattled company new-guy waited for strength to get up and go to bed. As his thoughts took on energy again, he was struck with a sudden feeling of guilt. He pitched his head back over his shoulders and looked straight up toward the ceiling and said, "Forgive me, Lord." Then he pushed up out of his chair and strolled toward the foot of his bed, and there, his hands prayerfully touching his chin, he prayed, "Oh, Lord, I have neglected so much in the last days, most of all you and my mother and dad, the most precious gift from your hands in my whole life. Even looks like I don't know how to pray anymore. Please know, Lord, that I am grateful for my life, just the way it is tonight, just the way it went today, and just the way it's been all my other days. And I'm back, Lord. Thanks for not giving up on me. I praise you for your love and mercy. Amen."

Now in pajamas, Andy Boone flipped off the nightstand lamp and sat down on the edge of his bed, at once overcome with uneasiness about his own behavior, lastly whispering into the night, "I'm sorry, Lorrie Dean."

10

The young warrior marched resolutely back to battle. This time he pledged to make it a conciliatory offensive and score without casualties on either side. On his way in to work, Andy mailed a note to Dub Grimes, accepting his invitation, and saying how gracious and kind it was of them to have him over for Sunday lunch.

At the office, his first act was to begin rounding up all the information he could find about Clay Cutter operations in the Las Colinas jurisdiction, mumbling to himself as he set away. "It's study time! Time to learn something about this place besides the wrath and emotional insecurity of Kirk Daniels and Wade Boliver."

He decided to give himself an unguided tour throughout the organization, reaching most of the units. He talked to specialists and officers and retrieved books, pamphlets, fact sheets, and other publications about local procedures, precedents, policies, and company protocol. He would have to glean the scuttlebutt and unwritten rules from conversations with the rank and file. He very likely could pick up most of that from his own division, assuming his six humorless stalwarts would open up to him. He felt no compunction about crossing division lines in this search. After all, this was an honorable

undertaking, and he was, in fact, a key company officer. *If I'm not,*
thought the young tiger, *now's the time to find out.*

"Valorie, could you find the contracts for the last two terms for
both Burleson and Durant for me?"

"Sure—they're over in the library. I'll be right back."

"Hmm ... OK." That's dumb, why don't we have them here?

At the door, Valorie asked, "Anything else I can get for you while
I'm there?"

"Oh, glad you asked. How about files on rejected union
proposals?"

"Rejected ..."

"Well, ah, proposals proffered by the unions that never made it to
the contracts, you know, that were negotiated out."

"Oh, yes. We don't have them separated out like that, you know,
as rejected. We just have a folder labeled Proposals, and they're all
in there."

"OK, that makes sense."

All in all, the day went pretty well, no run-ins with his usual
hecklers, and the company information was really piling up. At The
Lamp he flopped across the bed, dead tired, and was fully prepared
to doze off until he remembered his upcoming trip to the farm. He
struggled up and lumbered over to the phone and called his mom.
She was thrilled at the news he'd be spending Saturday with them
and immediately began to rattle off all the preparations she would
make to get ready for his—as she put it, rare—visit. There was no
way he would tell her not to go to any trouble. That would be a slap
in the face. This is what moms do, and this particular mom was, to
Andy, the dearest and most precious mom in the world—*even if I
have neglected her,* he thought. His dad was equally a gem, but dads
and sons are buddies, and their caring is just different. Isn't it? Andy
mused.

Suddenly, the near forgotten menace hit him again. Out of the
blue. Something he'd managed to hold at bay for the last several

weeks. He'd gone on the wagon before leaving the headquarters assignment because he believed it was beginning to detract from his creativity. His career was the one priority in his life, so it was easy, then, to make concessions that might foster his advancement. It was just a vow he had made to himself. But now, inexplicably and without any forewarning, he yearned for alcohol, maybe just one little drinky poo to help settle the fatigue, maybe two. He was too tired to change clothes, so he just peeled off his coat and tie, flung them on the bed, and headed out.

Cylie Moe's Bar was not far from the Mandalay, where Andy had stayed his first week at Clay Cutter. As he reached for the door, he stopped abruptly and looked around as if he were being watched. He turned partly away, trembling slightly, and his mind was consumed with something that was always at the edge, nagging, even when he wasn't conscious of it. He cleared his throat and breathed deeply as he turned back toward the door and whispered under his breath, "Would you approve of this, Lorrie Dean?"

* * *

Andy ambled toward the bar, instinctively glancing at the ceiling and surveying the lounge as he made his way. On a quick take, it all looked a little expensive but very inviting and comfortable. Like old times, he thought, as he wiggled up onto the tall barstool.

"Good evening, sir, what may I serve you?" charmed the barmaid.

How pedantic, thought Andy. "Hi. Yeah, I'll have a Manhattan, ah, straight up."

"Excuse me, sir?"

"Manhattan."

"Manhattan. Right. Coming right up."

While Andy waited, he continued his scrutiny of the swank tavern. It was Thursday evening and not many people were there. It all looked so upholstered, he thought. The bar was in the shape of a horseshoe, and its counter was covered with a layer of emerald leather. The bar itself glistened with bright fixtures and rows of stemmed glasses dangling upside down from shiny holders. Swinging around on his barstool, Andy studied the lounge, which was filled with round tables on chrome pedestal footings. The tabletops looked to be of faux marble, possibly some kind of hard plastic. The floor was of narrow hardwood planks, and the ceiling was hung with small lanterns that gave the room a dusky, peaceful atmosphere. As he gazed at his surroundings, Andy pondered whether the absence of bright colors induced people to drink more or less and whether this issue was even considered when saloons are designed.

"Here we go. Sorry it took so long. We had to chase down some rye whiskey. Seems we don't get orders for cocktails very much except for martinis." She chuckled and squeezed her lips as if to say that was their shortcoming. "Anyway, that's a good order, and I apologize for not being completely ready for it."

"Oh, no sweat." said Andy, "It's worth waiting for."

"Thanks. Enjoy."

As she twirled away, a side view revealed that her neat smock stood out noticeably in the front. Andy felt a broad grin tug at his face as he reflected on this polite little lady. She was attractive and smiled easily. She didn't try to flirt, which seemed admirable considering that she was clearly pregnant and didn't need to encourage any folderol. Andy's grin broadened as he thought, *I don't think I've ever seen a pregnant barmaid.* But—why not? He enjoyed his drink, and he was beginning to loosen a bit. That felt good, and he smiled to himself. As he was near the last swallow, the barmaid returned.

"How are we doing over here?"

"Great. I'll have another."

When his mom-to-be showed up with number two, Andy said, "So you don't get many orders for Manhattans."

"Yeah," she said, very slowly, apologetically. "I don't know why. It's really good to serve one for a change."

"So, what do the men drink mostly?"

She laughed and spread her arms in front as if anointing a throng of patrons. "This crowd drinks mostly bourbon highballs, scotch and water, that sort of thing—oh, and beer. Lots of beer."

"Well, maybe I'll have Wild Turkey and Coke the next time."

"So you're not just passing through?"

"No. I just moved here and started a new assignment with Clay Cutter Industries."

"Wow!"

"Yeah, woo hoo!"

After the second drink, Andy decided, since he was out of drinking shape, he'd better cut himself off and head back to The Lamp. He paid up and headed out.

* * *

The next day went reasonably well at the Clay Cutter camp. Andy attended exclusively to the material he'd collected about the company's operations. He would need several days to go through it all, but he was already making remarkable headway. He was interrupted only once, when Willis Braley came in to ask for leave.

"You got a minute, boss?"

"Sure, Willis, my time is yours. Come on in."

"Well it looks like my daughter is to be in a play next Tuesday and she insists that all parents are supposed to come. Mind you, Andy, she didn't tell us this until the last minute. Anyway, I could really use the whole day off to help around the house and support her that night."

"Absolutely, Willis. You take the day, try to relax, and enjoy it."

"Thanks so much."

"Willis, thank you for giving your child some priority. I think that's very important, and I admire you for supporting things that are big in her life. Way to go!"

"Oh, why thank you, boss. By the way, are things beginning to quiet down for you around here?" he asked with an uninhibited wink.

"Willis, I think so." Andy laughed as he decided to embellish a little. "I'm still tiptoeing around here like I'm walking on eggshells and trying not to belch."

Willis shook with laughter. Then he looked more serious, gazed straight at Andy, and softened his expression. "You know—well, this is just something that I've thought of before, in my own case. It's kind of like this: See, when a visiting football team comes to town, they know they can quiet a hostile and disruptive crowd if they can score a quick touchdown. I guess, well, maybe that's what you could use. I don't know, ah, I just, well, you need a quick touchdown!"

"Willis, my fine compatriot, you're 100 percent right. I thank you for that."

"Hang in there, boss. I'll get on out of your hair now. Thanks for the leave."

Andy nodded, smiling broadly, and Willis left.

That night, Andy fell asleep easily, drifting away as he thought of his early departure the next morning and, just before he passed out, vaguely pondering the idea of a quick touchdown.

11

It was barely sunup when Andy rolled out of his parking space at The Lamp and headed for Diboll, Texas, home of the world's finest parents, who in three months would celebrate their fiftieth wedding anniversary. Nothing much was stirring in Las Colinas or Dallas as he pulled away.

In about an hour and a half, he passed the turn-off to the Grimes farm driveway. As he glanced toward it, he pitched a thumbs-up signal in the direction of the farmhouse. At once, he thought of the cool, collected Dub Grimes and the irresistible little girl. "Why am I grinning?" he mumbled as he cruised on.

When he pulled into the driveway of his parents' place, Mom was standing on the porch, waving, smiling. And, as country people always do when company stops by, she called out, "Y'all get out and come in."

Andy flashed a big smile and waved back. He was thinking as he opened the car door, *I never have understood why you have to remind people to get out first before they come in. But it doesn't matter, because it is a genuinely warm and friendly greeting.* By now his wonderful old dad was also standing in the door, holding it open. On the porch, they all hugged and headed for the den, where they dropped onto cushioned seats and started chattering about all that had been going on in their individual lives. It was genuine fun, and they laughed often and heartily.

After lunch, Dad went out to piddle around in the garden while Anna Boone and her son continued to sit at the table and leisurely visit and talk about the good times, which most of them were. Mom was an indulging kind of woman who liked everybody and related well socially. She liked a good yarn and a playful tease with anybody who'd interact that way. It was a thrill to her if somebody played a little prank on her. She knew that meant two things: she was important, and they loved her. She was very creative in her own right, both in artful matters and in the business of life itself. After their table-side visit, she took her son around the house, showing some of the craft projects she'd been working on: needlework, ceramic creations, and even some drawings and paintings. She was really very good and all without any formal training.

Later, Andy went out to visit with his dad and mosey around the place, looking at and talking about things Dad said he "had to get to pretty soon." Dennis Boone was a thoroughly reliable, responsible-minded man of his word. He didn't mind labor; in fact, he enjoyed it. He'd pretty much done heavy labor work all his life, going all the way back to his boyhood days on the family farm just outside Lufkin, Texas. He liked people, but he didn't relate socially as well as Anna, the love of his life. But like her, he was also creative, particularly in the matter of problem solving and inventing devices to help him in his work. He, too, was an expert at making life work. After a while, Dad and son were poking along back toward the house, hands behind their backs, heads bowed, looking at the ground as they reminisced.

At dinner, their family reunion continued and they savored their time together. The chatter was still warm and cast with feelings of love, and although the volume of it was less, it was no less rewarding. Clearly, they were beginning to catch up and didn't have as many new things to say. It was precious and very dear to Andy, yet it made him revisit his feelings of guilt about not indulging more in his parents. Nevertheless, this clearly was a grand day for all three of them.

After dinner and the dishes, Dad dozed off, sitting upright on the couch, and Andy and Anna continued to murmur softly. The time had come, thought Andy, for him to broach a subject with his mother that was high on his list. He had great hopes of a breakthrough in his search, because mothers were inquisitive people and they just simply found out things about others in their environment.

"Hey, Mom, remember when I was in grade school?"

"How could I forget?"

"Right. Anyway, do you remember Lorrie Dean, one of my classmates?"

"I think so. Why do you ask, Andy Woo?"

"It's just that I've been thinking about my childhood for a profile the people at Clay Cutter are drawing up on me, as they do all employees."

"So, why do they have to go back so far?"

"See what you mean. Something just made me think of Lorrie Dean and our little puppy-love crush. Remember that?"

"No way."

After a few silent moments, Andy looked up at his mother, squinted, and said, "You probably don't remember Lorrie Dean's mother's maiden name, either, do you?"

"Never knew it. Don't care. I'd forget my own if I didn't use it as a password on these—"

"Mom," shouted Andy, "never use any family name as a password!"

"Well, they say use something you can remember."

"I know, Mom, but you don't have to … you can choose anything you want."

"Well, anyway, what's the deal with Charlotte's maiden name?"

"Actually, nothing. Just forget it!"

"Don't get huffy, Andy Woo!"

Andy sighed and smiled diffidently. "I'm sorry, Mom, I didn't mean to be critical."

"Why don't you go down to Baytown and ask around?"

"Right." He closed his eyes and bowed his head in his hands.

"What's wrong, Andy Woo?"

"Oh, Mom, please forgive me. I think I am more tired than I realized. We had an extraordinarily busy week at work. No problem, though. I'll rest it off."

* * *

When they broke their tearful embraces on the front porch a little before noon the next day, all vowed it had been a reunion blessed by God, and Andy pledged to better stay in touch. As he walked to his car, his mom shouted, "Oh, by the way, I gave your address to a Dub Grimes out at Tillman several days ago. Gosh, I hope that's all right."

Andy beamed at his mother and said, "It is indeed all right, and thanks for doing it."

As he pulled away, still waving good-bye, Andy started grumbling to himself as a new surge of guilt flooded his brain—and his heart: "Damn me anyway. I should have told them that I am visiting the Grimes farm this afternoon. Again, I'm not giving priority to my parents. How would I like it if they ever failed to give me priority as their child? But they would just never understand that I opted to spend part of this weekend with another family. They wouldn't understand. They wouldn't. That's no excuse. Damn!" He sped on toward Tillman, shaking his head and chastising himself in his thoughts.

As Andy drew near the Grimes farm, a picture of the little girl flashed in his mind, "Kelly," he muttered, smiling—amused, fascinated. As his trusty Cutlass drifted on up the winding driveway, he felt his shoulders quiver a little, more noticeably at first sight of the stately farmhouse.

At the door, deep into the rambling old front porch, he was met once again by an engaging young girl, standing straight and confident in her light-blue slacks and rose-colored shirt. "Kelly?"

"Mr. Andy Boone, how wonderful to see you again. Please do come in." As they both stepped into the huge front room, Kelly hesitated and turned gracefully to face her visitor. She smiled, tilted her head slightly, and said, "Have you been getting along OK?"

"Yes, thank you. I guess you can say as well as I deserve."

"Oh, I'm so very sorry, Andy Boone. Maybe things will get better. Just don't give up, you heah?" Kelly laughed outright at her own jesting. Andy laughed too, for he was fully satisfied that his little auburn-haired charmer had already discerned from his countenance that it was OK to tease him. And as a matter of fact, he felt honored that she already had such confidence after only one brief pervious encounter.

Kelly glanced back over her shoulder at her trailing guest as she led him toward a volley of babble and laughter coming from a back room. "We're about to enter the main room in the house, the den of our social lives, our playground, so to speak. In fact, that's what we call it, the den. Everything goes on there—laughing, weeping, playing, partying, praying, planning—you name it."

"I feel privileged to be a part of it today," said Andy in his most humble and earnest voice.

As they entered the den, a hush fell over the little covey of four people. Then they turned toward Andy and began to applaud.

"Why are they applauding?" Andy asked his escort.

"Love at first sight, Mr. Boone," chided Kelly, as she winked at her obviously baffled visitor. "Seriously, Mr. Boone, they all know of your grace in coming here that time just to say thanks for the help Uncle Dub gave you when your car, ah, crashed. Everybody just felt that you were a class guy."

Soon the revelry wound down, and the six of them gathered at the big round table in the center of the room. There was a pleasant echo in the den as they all shuffled into their cane-back chairs, which were already arranged in a preplanned order around the table. The room was essentially rectangular, moderate in size, with a high ceiling, wallpapered walls, and hardwood floors. There were two other doors besides the door through which Andy and Kelly had entered from the front room, one opening into a hallway, apparently leading to bedrooms, and the other leading to the outside.

Lunch was a delightful flurry of interaction, with everybody trying to talk to Andy at once. He hadn't gotten this much attention since he was a young child. Afterward, they all took turns meeting him personally, and to the person, promising to visit with him in depth as the afternoon unfolded. Andy just nodded to each one, grinning and remarking that lunch was really delicious. He didn't let on, but he thought the meal was a little surprising in one respect. Since he had a certain stereotype of ranch dining, he fully expected to have barbecue and baked beans, but what he got was pork chops and sweet potatoes—and a lot of other really wonderful food. *Let's hear it for the peach cobbler,* he thought, smiling.

After lunch, Dub was the first to buttonhole Andy, edging in front of Kelly, who jerked back and rolled her eyes as if to say he had failed properly to get permission to interrupt. Dub bowed to her as if to apologize and turned back to face Andy. "Wadaya think of this crowd, Andy? Are we a hoppin' bunch or what?"

"Hopping? Yeah, I guess so, Dub. But I gotta tell you, this is no ordinary bunch. I think this is an absolutely admirable family of good-natured, bright, fun people. I'm impressed!"

From somewhere close by, a sort of husky half-whispering voice, said, "Good one, Andy Boone."

Uncle Dub quipped back, "Are you still here, Kelly dear?"

"I'm always here. Maybe Mr. Boone would like a short tour of the grounds."

"How 'bout it, Andy?" asked Dub.

"Sure. Sounds great. Lead on."

As they strolled along a tractor-wide trail through the woods, Dub and Kelly pretty well let the surroundings speak for themselves. They did tarry briefly when they came upon a little cove cut into the woods. It felt good to be near it. Dub remarked that each of them would come to it from time to time for quiet meditation. It just seemed to be waiting there for any who needed a peaceful sanctuary for a moment. Soon they came to the edge of a huge field of plowed ground, and Dub said probably they should turn back at that point. "I'm sure the others wanna visit with you before you have to cut out for the big city."

When they approached the farmhouse, Andy sighed and said, "That was very relaxing. It was a good tease—makes me want to see more of it."

"Yeh," shouted Kelly, "does that mean you'll come back sometime?"

Andy chuckled. Then he reached out to lay a hand gently on Kelly's shoulder. "Only if I can have one very pretty, very sharp, very gracious, very special little girl meet me at the door."

Kelly's reaction seemed out of character. She nodded wordlessly and peered at her visitor and eventually had to touch a finger under each eye. After they got inside the house, she disappeared without a word.

Andy headed straight for Grandpa, who was still seated at the table, seemingly about to nod off. Although this courtly man had been fairly quiet during lunch, he had been friendly and responsive to any conversation that came his way. Andy took an instant liking to him and felt that, although he seemed maybe a little eccentric, he probably was the sage of the family. They talked easily and unpretentiously, and Andy was taken by the twinkle in his eye and the mischievous glow in his countenance.

While they were talking, the lady of the house, the one they all called Mom, sidled up to the table and winked at Andy as she turned to Grandpa. "Are you trying to monopolize our guest?"

"Absolutely," said the old man of the world. "He's my friend … but I'll share him with you."

"You're so understanding—and kind, yes, kind." She laughed

vigorously. Mom was somewhat heavy—well, OK, fat—and very outgoing. She allowed as how she wasn't anybody's mom in their little troop, but everybody called her Mom because she acted like one and because she took charge around the household, and they were all glad to concede that role. She and Andy talked amiably for a good half hour.

Later, Andy met the fifth member of the tight-knit little club, one they called Aunt Leah. She was shy, quiet, and skinny, and they talked only briefly. Yet their meeting was still warm and unpretentious.

Finally, it was time for Andy to leave. He and Dub were alone at the door linking the den with the front room. "You know what, Dub," said Andy, "I feel like I now have five new friends in my life, and I feel very blessed."

"You bet we're your friends, Andy, and we feel blessed too. There's a very unique and interestin' story about each of us around here. We are just sort of a collection of strays from other family units. But that's for another time."

Andy shuffled in place as Dub talked, craning to peer down toward the hallway that supposedly led to the bedrooms, scratching the back of his neck and instinctively frowning. He stopped fidgeting and smiled instantly as Dub turned to face him directly. "I guess Kelly's all right," said Andy. "We probably wore her out with the long walk and all, and—"

"Mom said she's in her bedroom, that she doesn't feel well."

"OK, ah, well, say good-bye for me and tell her I missed her."

Andy was on the road to Dallas, yawning and peering into the night, deliberately alert for any taillights that might try to back into him. Clearly he was tired but very happy about his visits. Still, he felt a little dispirited somehow. *That's silly*, he thought. Then he shook his head and sped on homeward to resume the masquerade with his Clay Cutter partners. Yeah right—partners.

12

It was Monday morning, and Andy Boone was ready to take the field. He had but one thought as he cruised along toward the Clay Cutter camp: score quick! He kept stirring those words around and around in his head, convinced he could pull it off. He would have to score at least one early touchdown and then go on to soundly defeat that rag-tag pair of juvenile, crybaby scalawags whom he'd secretly labeled, in his own mind, the Clay Cutter Clowns, proprietors of the petty bowl. As he rode on, he could picture his mom and dad and Dub and Kelly and his other new friends standing on the sidelines cheering for him, and he could just hear the excited play-by announcer in the booth:

They're in the shotgun. Costello and Boone, the setbacks. Here's the snap. Oh my God, look at that! Boone leaps across and intercepts the ball before it reaches the quarterback and shoots through the line knocking linebackers left and right. Oh my, oh my! He's already in the secondary, hurtling straight for the safeties. This is your Andy Boone, folks; he's running like a shot-at young tiger, this highly sought-after acquisition from McLean. Oh no! He stiff-arms one safety so hard his head jerks backward and he falls to the turf. Oh, that's gonna hurt in the morning—here comes the other one and, oh my God, he goes down the same way. Uh oh, here come two angry defenders closing in on Boone from a really good angle. Hang on to your seats, folks. Boone spots the two speedsters and spits at the turf—did y'all see that? Oh my! Now they're really closing in, and it looks like—touchdown!

Folks, this hometown crowd is stunned into utter silence. Now, you gotta know the play wasn't designed to work that way. Yeah! Hey, look at the quarterback still frozen in place where he would have caught the snap, just standing there with both hands slapped on each side of his head. As you see, the visiting team bench has emptied onto the field, smothering their hero, and that little handful of visiting fans over there keeps chanting, Boone-Boone-Boone-Boone."

At the office, Andy was in his element: inventing, creating, exploring, venturing, and working like a drone. And somewhat surprisingly, his ordinarily sedate staff was working with unprecedented vigor and interest, including Kirk Daniels, who had to join the movement or look like a fool. Over the next three days Andy had completely revamped the Employee Relations program and was finishing plans for new interfacing with the other divisions. Even the union officials were excited about prospects for their future roles, and officers from other divisions were coming to Andy for ideas,

By week's end he was thoroughly exhausted, so he decided to check himself into Cylie Moe's Bar for therapy.

"Wild Turkey and Coke, please."

"Right on," said the polite barmaid who'd served him on his first visit. When she returned with his drink in about thirty seconds, she said, "Try this—it'll cure a hard day's work in no time."

"That's encouraging. I'm afraid in my case, it's got a whole week to work on. But I'm patient. I'll give it plenty of time."

She chuckled. "And you might have to get some more support for it, you know."

"Right you are."

"How's business at Clay Cutter?"

"Oh, you remembered. Well, it's going OK … so far."

"By the way, I'm Polly and happy to be your, er, server."

"Thanks, Polly. I can't visualize having anyone else do that. You have a very calming manner."

"I'm flattered. I'll look forward to you coming in for as long as I'm here. As you can see, I'll be having to take a little break in a few weeks." She smiled, her face aglow, and winked.

"Well, I'll be pulling for you," said Andy as Polly whirled away to help a new customer. He watched as she sailed over to greet the newcomer. *People are right*, he thought. *Pregnant women do seem to have an uncommon glow. Wonder what explains that. Maybe it's just the expectation itself … or maybe it's physiological. Whatever.*

When he was about midway through his third highball, Andy flinched reflexively. Then he shuddered, trying to shake some slack into his tired muscles. What's going on? Happy as he was about the week's work, there was something nagging his conscience, a kind of foreboding he didn't understand. It was threatening to take the edge off his euphoria from a week of extraordinary achievements. Then he tossed his head back and sighed, as a faint image started creeping into his mind—Lorrie Dean. Unfortunately, everything had its price, and his all-consuming effort to score a quick touchdown at work had precluded any momentum in his search for the little girl—or rather, woman—he so yearned to see.

✶ ✶ ✶

The next two weeks at work stayed pretty much on a high note. Kirk was really into it because he saw a way to make fame for himself. Strangely, Wade Boliver was not a factor. Andy hadn't heard anything from him one way or the other, and nobody mentioned his name. He smiled as he thought about that little mystery: good riddance.

During that very satisfying period, Andy brought unheard-of innovations to union relations. He arranged for negotiations to take place on their turf, where they seemed to feel less threatened, and which possibly motivated them to withhold some of the more outlandish proposals that had been so prevalent in the past. He also developed new ways to utilize the individual strengths of each member of his staff, appealing to Kirk's sense of pride by making it profitable for him to do his personal best.

One day Kirk came to him and, grinning mischievously, made a proposal that was loaded with risk. When he had finished, Andy said, "Let's do it. You get it started, Kirk."

"Well, hey. OK, boss. Course it's a good deal risky, but if it doesn't work, I'll have to say 'my boss ordered me to do it.'"

"Oh, Kirk, you'll make it work. It'll prove your claim to fame, so to speak, and highlight your outstanding skills. I have complete confidence in you."

Kirk squeezed his lips, lifted his eyebrows, and turned to leave, "Uh huh. Stand by," he uttered, and walked out.

Then came the fourth week since he had made the touchdown resolution, and things continued to roll—still no little challengers falling out of the woodwork to rival his siege of the playing field. Kirk stayed low, Wade was invisible, and his own staff kept on burning and churning. Paige Ivy was supportive and welcomed his suggestion that the two might trade personnel from time to time for brief periods so that, with such depth of training, they could help each other out when workload piled up. He also enjoyed several very pleasant conversations with her and remained steadfastly impressed with her acumen and bearing.

These events marked the culmination of six weeks of employment at Clay Cutter in Las Colinas. On that Saturday, Andy received a call from Mildred Panacek, his old high school chum who'd pledged to help chase down information about the family of Lorrie Dean LeMay.

"Hi, Andy, this is Mildred, what's going on, old boy?"

"Oh, hi, Mildred ... the usual nickel and dime, you know. It's great to hear your voice."

She giggled and said, "Well, I don't have a lot of information, but I have clarified two or three things, and I thought I'd pass that along to you."

"Mildred, you're a jewel."

"Thanks. Anyway, I've learned that Sophia Easlie is the sister of Lorrie Dean's mother. Unfortunately, she doesn't know one iota about what happened to Charlotte LeMay or where she went or anything. Shoot! Dead end there! However, she did say that Lorrie Dean was born in Beaumont ... she thinks. Again, no help, 'cause I drove over there, and a friend of mine who lives there and I looked at the county records for 1960, and there is no record of birth for any LeMay. We also looked at 1959 and 1961 with the same results. I'm so sorry, Andy."

"Mildred, don't be sorry. You've done way more than is right to expect of you. I'm just amazed and very, very grateful for your effort."

"I don't mind, Andy. I haven't heard anything from the reunion stuff I sent out. Actually, it's really too early to expect much response on that. But I'll keep you posted."

"You're very dear, Mildred, I don't know how to thank you. I just don't. But I thank God for friends like you."

"It's a pleasure, and it's been refreshing to me to feel that I might be of some value to somebody in this world. Thanks for the chance."

"You're sure welcome. You know, Mildred, the more I think about it, the more I think I should make a trip down there next weekend and look around some more. Would it be OK if I paid you a visit?"

"Come on down," she said as she laughed warmly.

"Maybe I could pick you up early that Saturday morning and we could go out for breakfast and explore some things together. I could call you when I check in Friday night if it's not too late."

"Great. I hardly ever sack out before eleven."

"Then it's a deal. By the way, how's your little Jenny doing?"

Mildred clearly liked the question. Andy could hear the jingle in her voice. "Jenny's just doing fine. You know what, Andy? She is damn smart—everybody says that."

"I would have bet my bottom dollar on it."

"Well, she really is, all right, for a third-grader. She's got to where she likes to dress up in little frilly girl things and wear classy shoes. If she had her way, she'd do that every day of the week, the little punkin. Actually, she's been a little like that since she was old enough to wear real clothes. Anyway, guess I'll give you a break before your ear gets sore and look forward to your visit. Take care, young tiger—bye."

"See you."

*   *   *

And then there was Monday, more push toward the goal line. So much to think of: touchdown, Lorrie Dean, and what about little Kelly—what happened there?

Things at work seemed to wind down some toward week's end, not a heavy fizzle but some fading of effort, at least enough to wrinkle Andy's brow slightly. *Just a normal cycling of dynamics, nothing to really worry about,* he thought. *Crap, then why is that little nagging furrow still teasing my brow. I didn't call for it. Go away, dammit!*

On Friday, Andy skipped his customary happy hour at Cylie Moe's and headed straight for Baytown right after work.

13

Nighttime in Baytown didn't seem to hold its usual charm. It was more than just dark; it was noticeably uninspiring, virtually repelling. Andy was in the motel by nine thirty. He called Mildred, who sounded warm and upbeat when she agreed to an early start the next morning. When he asked if Jenny would feel comfortable knocking around car lots and office buildings with them, she said Jenny was already looking forward to it and planning what to wear. "What a priceless little jewel," Andy remarked before they hung up.

The next morning the three of them headed out, laughing and cutting up like bosom buddies bound for a happy day. Mildred and Jenny both looked pretty in their tasteful outfits. "We'll start with the first new-car lot," Andy sang out.

"Super," said Mildred, "and remind me, Andy, what are we going to do there?"

"Just want to see if they have any records or any personal memory of the LeMay's buying a car from them sometime in the seventies. I know it's highly doubtful that there'd be any records, and there may not be anyone still there who has even a remote chance of remembering the family, but I've got to try. If they have a record, maybe I can get the vehicle ID number and check other states to see if it might have been registered there."

"You know, though, not all states require registration."

"Mildred, please!"

"I'm sorry—I didn't mean to be negative. I just thought maybe it was something to think of. I'm sorry."

"Oh, Mildred, forgive me. I'm the one who should be apologizing. I've just gotten so temperamental about everything, but there's no excuse for me to put that on my dear friend."

They looked at each other, each a little peeved, and neither said any more on the subject. Soon, they pulled in front of the Ford showroom. All got out, including Jenny, who reached for her mommy's hand. *What an absolute living doll*, thought Andy.

No luck. Still, they held hope as they headed for the Chevrolet dealer, mostly because Mildred knew one of their salesmen. Sure enough, when she asked about Trent Cooper, the greeter pointed to a salesman strolling around cars in the outside lot.

"Hi, Trent."

"Well, if it isn't Mildred, the charmer, with her cute, adorable little daughter. What can I sell you today?"

"Thank you for the kind thoughts. Hope you won't be upset when I tell you we're not exactly shopping." She giggled in her inimitably disarming way and continued, "Anyway, this is my high school friend, Andy Boone."

"Hey, Andy, nice to meet you," said Trent as he thrust out his hand.

"Same here," said Andy with the broadest smile he could muster. "It's good of you to give us a minute of your time. Actually, we—both of us—are missing very dear friends from our past, and we thought y'all might have a record or a memory of a purchase they might have made. That might help us in our efforts to track them down. It's the LeMay family. We're thinking about some time in the late 70s or early 80s, somewhere in there."

"Hmm." Trent was rubbing his chin and looking toward the horizon as he talked. "We don't keep records like that, at least not that long. Now hold on, let me think, let's see … . no, I just can't picture them, although there's something about that name that rings a bell."

At that moment an older man came around the front of the car. "Did I hear somebody mention the LeMay bunch?"

Andy practically jumped out of his skin at the idea that somebody may have just popped up who actually knew something. "Yes, sir, the LeMays are our friends from way back, but when we tried to visit with them, we found they were no longer around here."

"Well, I tell you—wait a minute now, ah, oh yeah, did they live out on the bay?"

"Yes, yes!" Andy cried out, shuffling in place. When he tried to say more, his voice cracked, and he smiled his best smile and kept nodding. Mildred put her arm around him and snuggled into his side.

"By the way, I'm Sid," said the older man, and he and Andy shook hands vigorously as Andy, still nodding, said, "Andy Boone."

"OK," said Sid. "I remember them. Yeah, they were here. See, their kid, the girl …"

"Lorrie Dean!" shouted Andy, now fisting both hands together and rocking them in the air as if pleading for the heavens to open up.

"Right, Lorrie Dean. Anyway, her and my kid were both christened on the same Sunday at Saint Mark's. Like me, the LeMay couple only had one kid. So I guess I sort of kept up with them for that reason, you know, mostly at the church."

"Do you know where I can see them?" pleaded Andy, still dancing around.

"Not really."

"Were you aware of it when they moved away from Baytown, er, the bay area?"

"I'm still trying to reckon what I do remember. Like I say, we were in church together. I think it was in the summer about ten years ago. Seems like I remember Mrs. LeMay—Charlotte, yeah, Charlotte—seems like she was testifying in a drug trial or something like that. I think it was held in Houston. Really, that's about it."

"Sid, you're a gem. If you happen to remember more as you think about it, will you call Mildred, or ask Trent to?"

"Sure, you bet, I'll try to help if I can. I know what it feels like to lose a friend."

Although that comment invited sympathy, at least some acknowledgment, Andy just couldn't shake his near hysteria enough to keep up a sensible conversation. He just nodded knowingly and patted the man's shoulder.

Jenny was still holding her mommy's hand as they left. Andy reached to the child and said gently, "Jenny, do you think I could have the honor of walking along holding your hand. It would make me happy?"

Jenny looked up at Andy and smiled that radiant, accepting smile that was so natural with her mother. "Sure, Mr. ah … what am I supposed to call you?" she asked politely as she reached her hand for his.

"I'll tell you what, sweetheart, some people in my family call me uncle. Why don't you just call me Uncle Andy."

"I like it. Let's go, Uncle Andy." They tootled off together toward the car, swinging their arms in stride and glancing cheerfully at each other after every few steps.

"Can I come too?" asked Mildred as she shuffled along behind.

Their visits to the other new-car dealers were not as productive, if indeed the other one had been. At least it held some hope, Andy thought, thin as it was.

"Well, that wraps that up," said Andy. "I thought maybe next week, if you don't mind, you could make a quick check at the tax office. I'm sure it's not open today. Anyway, if you could just find out if there are any property tax records still on file there for the LeMays. They may scream invasion of privacy, but you don't have to actually see the record—all you want to do is determine whether they exist, and if so, when the last tax notice was served to the LeMays. That information should be public, I think … I don't really know. Just thought we could try. Trying is all we can do."

"Andy, I'll be glad to. In fact, I think I know somebody who works over there. Sure, I'll take care of it."

"For now, what say we have lunch and rest a bit. I know you two are bound to be getting tired."

* * *

After lunch, Andy briefed Mildred on his plan regarding the daily newspaper, *The Baytown Sun.* As he drove toward it, Mildred was frowning a little, not disapprovingly, but as though she were trying to puzzle something out. Finally, she turned to Andy. "Now, what are we looking for?"

"Huh?"

"In the paper. What are we supposed to watch for when we look through the old issues from that period?"

"Darn if I know. Anything that might just jump out, any unordinary event, like maybe something on a drug trial, even if Charlotte LeMay's name isn't mentioned. You know? Keep in mind that Lorrie Dean's picture is in the Sterling yearbook for 1978, so we know they were here then. Unfortunately, that was fourteen years ago. Oh well, whatever."

"OK, I'm in. Let's see, the paper was already a daily by then, so that's a lot of newspapers we need to go through. But we can peruse fast because, as you say, we're looking for something to just jump out at us."

"You know, Mildred, dear precious Mildred, let's face it. I'm just grasping at straws."

"No, no, I just wanted to know how to help, like—"

"I know. And I don't really know what to tell you. Really, I don't. I think I'm just being stubborn and stupid. There's nothing that can happen with a search like that. Let's face reality, Andy Woodson Boone!"

"It's OK. You're giving it your all, and I admire you for that," said Mildred softly. She turned to face Andy, brushing a tear from her eye, and tried to manage a smile.

"I'm not putting you through any more of this," Andy said. Then no one said anything for a while. Finally, Andy cleared his throat and glanced at the back seat. "You know what I'd like to do for the rest of the day, Mildred?"

"What, dear?"

"I'd like us to dedicate the rest of the day to Jenny. Let's do things that will please her, make her happy."

It worked. Jenny was bubbling with excitement when they emerged from the Disney movie. And when they stopped briefly to pick up a jigsaw puzzle and two coloring books, she hugged her mom and Andy and then hopped into the car, singing merrily.

That night at the motel, Andy reflected back on Mildred's mood of the day, particularly when the two of them really sobered from time to time, realistically trying to face the music. She seemed sympathetic and clearly disappointed for him. What a beautiful human being. Then, as he climbed into bed, he recalled his promise to stop taking advantage of this fine friend.

Mildred hugged him at the door early the next morning and swept him into her home with her usual animated flare. She seemed completely recovered from the solemn mood that had caught her from time to time the day before. She smiled the entire time she was stirring around getting breakfast on the table and talking to Andy at the same time.

Clearly, Mildred hadn't opted for just an ordinary, humdrum breakfast. She spread the table with ham and cheese omelets and sauce, fruit, hash browns, and all the trimmings. *What an honor it is to be in her presence*, thought Andy. He was aware that he didn't exactly feel a romantic attraction for her, yet he could not have loved her any more deeply. She was just quality, and she was deserving of the very best life the world could offer her. Andy thought it was probably too early to tell, but somehow he was convinced that Jenny would grow up to be just like her. Thank you, God, for sweet people.

All three lingered at the table for a while after they finished eating—laughing, teasing each other, and making big fun. Somehow the exuberance soon started to dwindle, and ultimately, Andy and Mildred looked at each other solemnly and mused quietly together for a bit. The frivolity was gone. They continued to stare knowingly at one other, looking down from time to time, fiddling with their napkins, as Jenny scampered off to play with her new puzzle.

Andy garnered what he hoped was a soft, caring smile, the best he could manage under the circumstances, and held it as he gazed into Mildred's sympathetic eyes. Finally he swallowed, cleared his throat, and began, ever so slowly: "Mildred, never mind the property records. I'm being ridiculous. They won't show a darn thing! Why would they when nothing else we've checked even gives the tiniest clue about that family?"

Mildred nodded, looking serious and concerned. "I know."

"In fact, there's no use checking anything. It's done. But what baffles me is ... well, I can accept how nobody anywhere knows what happened to them, but how can the records fail to show they were at least here?"

"Andy, you know, this is some endless mystery. It's like they just left the face of the earth. And you know what else? Let's face reality— it's really naive of us to think a reunion is going to surface Lorrie Dean."

"You're entirely right. For my part, you needn't even pursue that any further. And dear Mildred, I thank you from the bottom of my heart for all you've done and thought to do. I love you big time."

"My pleasure," said Mildred, smiling sweetly. "But you're right."

"Yeah. Still, something is clearly wrong here. This can't happen."

"You think there may have been some kind of foul play somewhere, sometime?"

"I sure don't discount that possibility." The next instant, Andy jumped straight up, almost knocking over his chair. It was like lightning had hit him, like a flash of memory about something forgotten, or something neglected in the heat of the hunt. "Mildred," he stammered, "your comment just made me recall something the FBI man told me, which I didn't pay much attention to at the time because I was preoccupied with despising the guy. Now it all comes back! Mr. Chad Jarrigan is going to be my first order of business when I get back."

Mildred laughed heartily. "So, young tiger, it ain't over after all."

Andy smiled, nodded, and winked. "Now to more important things, Mildred. I have to tell you that you and your adorable Jenny sure looked pretty yesterday, and you never missed a step."

"Thank you," she said, giggling, "we try to act our best around special company."

Andy was staring at the little pair of shiny red shoes left under a chair in the adjoining den. "Yeah, Jenny looked very tasteful in her blue dress and red shoes."

"She really did. Her favorite dress color is what the little dickens calls soft-yellow, but we haven't found the just-right thing yet."

"What would you say of her? Is she short, tall, about average size, or what?"

"Andy, for her age, that kid is average in everything."

"She's a doll. Well, Mildred, it's time. I want to say good-bye to Jenny and if I can, get a little hug."

Mildred's smile faded as she waved toward Jenny's bedroom.

* * *

As he reached cruising speed on the interstate, Andy tried to put the visit behind him. *It's done,* he thought. It was hard for him to allay his disappointment, but that, too, had to be put to rest. He bemoaned the fact that neither this visit nor the other two visits to his hometown had clarified even one simple question about the LeMays. However, one thing was now crystal clear. Something bad had happened, something incapable of being discovered by ordinary thinking or conventional inquiry.

The disappointment only refueled Andy Boone's resolve to find his little girl of so many years ago. He would find Lorrie Dean— somehow. At this point, he had no conscious plan. He would just have to pray about it and follow his instincts. Logic wasn't working. Now, he was certain that he had to make friends with FBI agent Chad Jarrigan.

14

Touchdown or Lorrie Dean—Lorrie Dean or touchdown? How do you hit two targets with only one dart? These were Andy Boone's worrisome thoughts as he sat pouting at his desk. *How can I do this? All I have is me—one dart!* Then he slapped his head, managed a slight grin, and chided aloud, "Poor baby."

The day had begun with the usual Monday morning buzz at Clay Cutter, sidestepping busybodies chasing around with uncoordinated action papers left over from the preceding week and frantically dashing off to staff meetings. Andy had elected not to hold a meeting with his Employee Relations staff on the conviction that these affairs often produce nothing new or valuable and essentially hinder momentum rather than inspire effort. Even so, his staff was immersed in their assignments and no less animated than the other rank and file as they posed technical questions for their boss and set about their business. They seemed to be moving with the same determination and resolve that had awakened them in the last few weeks, but their facial expressions didn't reflect the same level of confidence and optimism as before.

Andy, ordained juggler, was still studying how to keep both balls in the air when he slapped the top of his desk and slid the phone closer.

He dialed the FBI number and, after someone answered, waited on hold for Chad Jarrigan to come on.

"Hey, Andy, what's up?"

"Hi, Chad. Thanks for letting me have a minute of your time."

"No problem. Good to hear from you."

"Well, I have something and … well, this is probably going to shock you out of your jock, but I'm a hankerin' to buy lunch."

"You got my attention," said Chad as he offered one of his rare chuckles.

"Super. How about tomorrow. I thought we could take in Tony Roma's in the West End. That's pretty close to you. I could pick you up at the Federal Building and we'd be there, like in two minutes, huh?"

"Sounds like a winner to me, Andy. Tomorrow's fine, but I have a session that probably won't be over until about twelve thirty or one o'clock."

"That'll work great, Chad. So I'll just—"

"Tell you what, Andy, suppose I just meet you there at one. I know that'll work."

"You got it."

∗ ∗ ∗

After work, Andy took off for the North Park Shopping Mall, still a little preoccupied with his conversation with the FBI man. As congenial as each of them obviously tried to make their warm phone chatter, it still came off a little formal. Whatever.

At the mall, Andy sprinted into Neiman Marcus like a man on a mission, which he was. He asked for help in the children's department and was led to some racks filled with dresses for eight-year-olds, who, as Andy had emphasized, are average in every way. The sales lady stood patiently, not pushing, while he browsed through them, frowning a little as he shoved along. "Er, I'm wanting something that's dressy and in a kind of soft yellow. You know what I mean, soft yellow?"

"Yes, sure, and that would be perfect for a dressy dress. Come over here with me," she said, looking over her shoulder as she strolled gracefully through the racks. "I know I saw ... oh, here it is." She pulled a long billowy dress from the rack and held it for Andy to peruse. "Now as you see, this has two, well actually three layers, but most important for you, the outer skirt is of clear, see-through chiffon—see, it's embroidered with patches of tiny red berries with green leaves, just kind of scattered all throughout and ..."

"It looks yellow," laughed Andy. "This just may be it."

"Well, It's sort of medium yellow, but this outer veil softens it, making it look like what I think you're after. It's called a Cinderella dress."

"Hey, that is absolutely perfect. I'll take it. Now I need some dressy shoes to go with it. I have no idea what color to get."

The sales lady picked out a pair of silver dress shoes and, at Andy's request, boxed everything up for mailing. Andy thanked her profusely and sailed away, whistling the tune to "Everything Is Beautiful."

At the florist back in Las Colinas, he picked out a spring bouquet with daisies, snapdragons, daylilies, verbenas, and some other stuff and asked the florist to wire them to Mildred Panacek in Baytown. For the note that would be tucked within the bouquet, he wrote simply: "To my friend."

Andy was nodding confidently as he drove toward The Lamp, convinced he had made the right decision about the kind of flowers to send his very dear, very precious friend. The thing is, he persuaded himself, Mildred is just not the dozen-red-roses type. Her personality is too all-encompassing for anything so specialized as that. *Yes, yes, yes*, he thought, still nodding, *this is what Mildred would want.* Thereupon he went back to his hauntingly beautiful whistling. He would mail Jenny's package in the morning.

Morning came, and Andrew Boone was still a very busy man. As hectic as it was with everybody competing for his time, he grinned through it all. At twelve twenty he headed for the West End and arrived about the same time as Chad Jarrigan, who was on the sidewalk when Andy pulled into a parking place. Inside Tony Roma's, they shook hands like long-time friends. Right!

"Chad, thanks for getting together with me. I thought I might could fill you in on what I know about the LeMay people and what I've done to try to find out ... and maybe you could give me anything you have that might work for me."

"Fair enough, Andy, and I want to ease your mind about something. What it all amounts to is that you win."

Andy twisted in his chair, tilted his head slightly, and pulled back a little. "I don't know what that means, Chad."

"It means I admire your dedication in your search for the little girl who's missing from your life. I mean—of course, she's a grown woman, now. Anyway, I think what you're doing is truly honorable. I apologize that our mission made it necessary to put you through any frustration. I'm truly sorry."

Andy stopped eating and pulled in a few thoughts before responding: *Is he really conceding, or is he just explaining their role in the world, hoping I'll shape up and be more cooperative in the future. Is this an apology or a threat. Well, he's due the benefit of the doubt.* "I accept your apology, Chad. In fact, that's very big and professional of you. I guess I should feel honored since I doubt y'all—in your mission—very rarely elect to apologize for anything you believe you have to do." *Damn me, why did I have to get in a dig like that?*

"Tell me, Andy, what exactly went on in your lives that drives you to search for the LeMay girl with such unshakable zeal?"

"Oh, please forgive me, Chad—that's the one thing I can't talk to you about. What does it matter now that you know I'm for real and don't have some clandestine motive pushing me?"

"Well, it's just ... OK, if I knew, there's a remote, very remote chance I might be able to explain some things that will ease your mind."

"I'm sorry. I just can't do it. I haven't even told my parents. I mean, no one."

Chad looked straight into Andy's eyes for a long time. Neither spoke. Chad's expression softened and seemed to reflect genuine concern, not just intellectual or ulterior interest. "Andy," he said, softly, "I respect you, and I just think maybe we owe you one."

"Well, maybe it's time I got it off my chest to someone. But Chad, you have to swear never to tell this to anyone."

The agent raised his right hand as if taking an oath in court. "I swear. You have my word. No one will know, not even anyone in my own agency will know what we talked about today."

"OK," said Andy taking a deep breath. "This isn't going to be easy, but … oh, before I start, it might help me relax a little if you mention what you said you have that might ease my mind."

"Oh, it was just what I already said, that we know you are legit and not collaborating with someone. That's all. Now, I believe when you called, you said you had something we might want to know."

"Oh yeah! OK, this is it. I have turned up all the stones in Baytown and on the Internet and everything else my simple mind can think of to get a trace on the LeMay family, and it has all come to absolutely nothing. I mean nothing. Chad, it's like they were never alive, not even here on the face of the earth. But I remember you saying to me one time that you were looking for a man who was trying to make contact with Charlotte LeMay. I think you said that man had violated a federal law or something like that. Well there's this one thing. I talked to a man who works at a car lot in Baytown, and he said he vaguely remembers that Charlotte might have testified in a drug trial, but he seems to know nothing else about it."

"OK, first, I can ease your mind here on at least one question. As far as I know, they are all three alive and well. Believe me, we have every reason to believe they are alive and well. That should ease …

oh, what the hell! Andy, here goes. I'm going to tell you something I'm not supposed to disclose to anyone. But as you required of me, you have to take an oath never to divulge this to anyone no matter how compelling the circumstances."

Andy raised his right hand and said, looking serious, "I so swear."

"OK, the fact is, this family is living under the Witness Protection Program. Charlotte LeMay had been an accomplice in a drug trafficking operation, and she and one of the other pushers got caught. As it turned out, on a plea bargaining deal, Charlotte LeMay testified at the man's trial, and her testimony sent him to prison. Now the third party is still on the loose, and you can bet he is after Charlotte, and we are after him. That's why we jumped on you when you started poking around in Baytown and asking questions. We thought you might be a hired flunky for this guy."

"That's it?"

"Pretty much. As you probably know, under the Witness Protection Program, every record about the parties in question is removed from its place and locked in a vault somewhere. Their identity is literally wiped out. They take on new names and move away for a new life under different names. Also, you must know this—we don't even know what names they chose or where they went. It's much easier that way."

Andy sat motionless for a long time as he tried to take this information in. Chad sat patiently, not pressing him to respond, apparently knowing what he was going through. Finally, Andy cleared his throat and mumbled, "OK, I need to keep my promise to you. Chad, please try not to ask too many questions, because I'll be reliving this as I tell it."

"I promise, and be assured, I do empathize with you."

"OK." He took some deep breaths and shuddered a few times as he started to talk, at first brokenly and then sort of getting into it. "One day in 1971, when Lorrie Dean LeMay and I were fifth graders—

we were sort of flirting friends, that type of thing—and we were at recess … OK, we were little infatuated kids, right? So I guess we were actually horsing around, laughing and teasing each other. Really we were flirting with each other but in a playful and sort of physical way. Lorrie Dean was laughing and jumping around, just drinking in all this sort of puppy-love thing we were having."

Andy had to stop at this point. He was breaking, and tears were soaking into his eyes. He brushed them away as quickly as he could. After all, he was man, a strong macho man. Then he tried to continue and let his faltering voice have its way. "Chad, that innocent, thoroughly delighted, sweet expression on her face will stick in my mind forever, whether I find her or not. Anyway, all of a sudden, it happened. Lorrie Dean rapped me on the shoulder and giggled and then I shoved her, I guess a lot harder than I realized, and she lost her balance, and fell backward and slammed into a bicycle rack. Then she fell to the ground, smashing her elbow on a steel brace. And, and, and … I'm sorry … the sweet expression was gone."

Chad nodded, his face filled with sympathy. "It's OK, Andy, I'm with you, buddy."

"All I can remember is how she looked as she tried to pull herself up, holding her elbow and crying from both a broken heart and what I found out later were shattered bones in her elbow. That picture will haunt me forever and ever and ever …"

"Oh boy, Andy. Oh my, I'm so sorry. Believe me, I understand your dedication completely. God bless you as you continue, if indeed there's anything else you can do."

When they left the restaurant the two newfound friends embraced and wished each other the very best.

Andy watched as Chad Jarrigan slowly drove away. Then he laughed outright, slapping his thigh, shaking his head, and jabbering to himself: "Andy, old Sport, you are one colossal liar. Wow, what a story. You should be voted fabricator of the year." Then the old guilt bogeyman hit him, and he sobered. He strolled to his car, settled into it, and rested his head on the steering wheel for a while. "What the heck—it was none of his damn business. He probably lied about not knowing where they went." Then Andy quit mumbling to himself, but he couldn't quit thinking. *One thing, though,* he thought, *the tears and broken voice were reflexes, not me acting. Even though the details of the story were fabrications, the memory of Lorrie Dean's expression at what really did happen will never, never go away—until I find her.*

Then, suddenly, it was back, the urge to down a couple of Manhattans straight up. Strange thing: he didn't particularly like the taste of booze, but at one time it had served him well as a relaxer when he was burning and churning to get ahead in his career and avoid calamity with women. He'd thought of himself only as a purely circumstantial drinker, not an alcoholic. No doubt, the circumstances were present now. Fortunately, he had to return to work, and by the time he got off, the temptation would be gone.

15

Andy was getting nervous about the conspicuous absence of his boss from his environment. Another mystery gnawing at his sense of well-being was the near civil attitude of his self-proclaimed rival, Kirk Daniels. Something just wasn't right in this picture.

Then things changed, as inevitably they do. His guys were getting testy with each other and bristling at the least little inconvenience. Proof of new times also emerged at midweek when he and Kirk chanced to pass in the hall and Kirk fired off one of his reliable barbs, followed by that silly little taunting snicker. Same to you, fellow.

So it went. Andy still had a full plate and no time to fret and worry. In the midst of his confusion, he so yearned for a night on the farm to restore his sense of balance. The solemn, warm friendliness of Dub Grimes stood in sharp contrast to the cool, patronizing attitude of his office crew. Dub smiled little, but his expression was genuine and supportive, while the office crew wore pasted smiles that betrayed their cliquish resentment.

Then came a break in the weather. One of his men, Morris Allgate, asked for an appointment, a nice contrast to Kirk's habit of just showing up in Andy's doorway. Morris was the older officer Andy originally identified, at least in his own mind, as his confidant.

"Come on in, Morris. You guys have been working hard. You deserve a break."

"Thanks, Andy. It's been exciting and a real pleasure until the last few days. I don't mean that against you, but that electric mood that we had seems to be slipping."

"Morris, I feel that here too."

"I was afraid maybe you had, and I really feel for you."

"Well, you know, Morris, one thing that's baffling me is the absence of any input from Wade and the unpredictable attitude of Kirk."

"I know, I know." Morris was fidgeting as he talked and pursing his lips. "I just think it's not right."

"What's not right?"

"The stuff that's going on."

Andy stiffened. "Morris, I'm sorry you're feeling that discomfort, and I want to help. Tell me what I can do that will support you personally."

"Oh Andy, I'm OK personally. I mean, I've been around a long time, and I know most all the games they play around here. So things don't bother me personally."

"Let's see, I think a few minutes ago, you said you feel for me. What do you mean?"

"OK, that's actually why I'm here. I mean I'm here for you, not for me." Now he pulled to the edge of his chair. "Andy, you're a good boss, a pro, and my principles won't let me stand idly by and watch injustice play out. I admire what you've done here. Dammit, you're putting us on the map. Before you came, if you asked someone about Employee Relations, they'd say 'who'?"

"Thanks for that, Morris," said Andy as he moved from behind his desk to take a seat near his visitor. I'm equally proud of your work. You, too, are a pro."

"OK, there's some history here that I think you have a right to know. We've all been put on notice not to leak certain specific stuff or suffer dire consequences, but dammit, I've had it! I'm pissed off. As I say, I'm not gonna sit idly and watch them destroy a good man. Besides, at my age and tenure, I dare them to try to fire me."

"By them I take it you mean, as a minimum, Wade Boliver."

"Right you are."

"Morris, why do you think Wade's lying low? Do you think he's plotting something?"

"Exactly! I know damn well he is. I have watched that man operate for ten years, and I know what he's doing. Believe me, he's posturing."

"Are you really OK with telling me this?"

"I couldn't be more OK. I mean I'm absolutely comfortable with what I'm doing. Here's the thing: Mr. Wade—Sneaky, as most of us call him—he is simply waiting for you to trap yourself. For one thing—and this is my opinion—he'll work things out so most of your innovations fail or disappear. That's why Kirk's so cooperative now. He is going to help you bomb."

Andy was shaking his head calmly as Morris talked. What he was hearing was even more ludicrous than he had imagined. Then he reached across and tapped Morris's shoulder and chortled, "Why am I not surprised?"

"Right," giggled Morris, shifting in his chair. "Well anyway— where was I? Oh yeah, be assured, Andy, when they calculate that their skullduggery has worked and they have enough stuff on you, they'll pull the rug. Mr. Sneaky will fire you for going outside channels, not keeping him informed personally, inaugurating something illegal under the union contract—stuff like that."

"Hmm. I've read the contract top to bottom. What are we doing that's illegal?"

"Nothing, but they'll twist it around, change the appearance of the results, and fabricate a foul somewhere."

"Wow! That leaves only one big, nagging question: why me?"

"Well, boss, here's where it gets really intriguing. *Why you* originates with Kirk. The hard-core villain here is that pathetic little imp. He has Mr. Sneaky over a barrel."

"Wow, this is getting interesting."

"Yeah, yeah, the whole thing is that Kirk knows something that implicates Wade in some illicit behavior. Let me try to make a long story short and say Wade had promised your job to Kirk and then suddenly headquarters—as they put it—forced you on them."

"You mean I'm a forced-on placement, a so-called mandatory selection?"

"That's the way they see it."

"Hoo boy. What are we into here? That explains so much. I still don't understand the inexplicable strength of Kirk's leverage over Wade. I mean, how can a little promise hold such power? You know what I mean—verbal promises, even those made in good faith, come and go all the time."

"It all started with an Equal Employment Opportunity case. As it happened, a woman filed a complaint of sexual harassment against our, at that time, squeaky-clean boss here at Clay Cutter. Actually, she filed a complaint of sexual harassment and sex discrimination."

"Who won?"

"Well, Kirk was to be the prime witness on the sexual harassment charge because he saw the event in question—if you know what I mean—and he was the only eyewitness. The fact that he was an eyewitness was not contested because some people near the scene witnessed him witnessing. You get the picture here?"

"Oh yeah, oh yeah. Son of a gun. Unbelievable!" Andy exclaimed, strumming on the arm of his chair and shaking his head.

"Well, I guess that about sums it up," said Morris through a long, deep, noisy breath.

"Whoa, wait a minute. How does that give Kirk the advantage all the way up to this day?"

"Oh, yeah. Right. Kirk never testified because Wade agreed to a no-fault settlement of the complaint in exchange for giving the woman what she wanted."

"And that was?"

"The company financed her relocation to the office in San Diego, issued her a fat bonus for, ahem, outstanding performance during the year, and gave her a promotion."

"Case closed."

"Right. The rest of the story is that Wade believes Kirk can bring him down by reopening the issue and threatening to testify. Yet at the same time, this has the connotation of unworthy motives, and that threatens Kirk's credibility. So they kind of have each other over a barrel."

"Can you do that, reopen an issue?"

"Well the regs are ambiguous on that matter, but the point is that they can try."

"Morris, you are my confidant, and I must say a very sharp one. And you're a gem. I owe you big time."

"Naw, you paid me already in advance."

The two stood up, shook hands, nodding and reflecting that natural, knowing look. Then Morris departed and Andy returned to his desk and dropped his head to rest in both hands. He held that posture for a while, then looked up, glaring out his window at nothing in particular and cogitating on his past, present, and future. Though Allgate's news was really no surprise in concept, having it confirmed with details was shocking. When he became aware of tensing in his neck and shoulders, he sought a few minutes under the calming influence of his hero, Paige Ivy.

"Andy, what's wrong?"

"Oh nothing, Paige, what makes you think anything's wrong?"

"It's all over your face, your posture, your walk, everything."

"Paige, you're amazing. Yes, I guess some things aren't completely comfortable in my bailiwick." There was no way he would ever hint at anything coming out of Allgate's disclosures. Still, he felt free to express his own perceptions about the strange things appearing in their shared environment. He managed a difficult smile at his friend and said, "I guess probably I'm just tired from struggling to know what my job is, what all I'm supposed to do, and the best way to do it."

Paige, in her inimitable way, tipped her head modestly and smiled. "Welcome to the club, Andy. I don't think any of us know what we're doing, really."

"I'm convinced you do."

"Well, if I was just efficient enough to get to it all ..."

Andy gazed around her office silently for a minute while she waited with patience. "Paige, what would you think if I sent one of my guys up to help with the backlog? Which categorically is not your doing. We could think of it as the rotation we discussed one time. It would be good cross-training for my guy and maybe help you to. Hunh, what do you think?"

"I'm perfectly comfortable with that if you think we have approval to work that out by ourselves."

"Glad you mentioned that point. First of all, I personally am fully confident that this is both proper, permissible, and accounted for within the principles of good management. But I can see where one might be a little concerned about that question, particularly in this strange environment we have here."

Andy narrated his perceptions and apprehensions about Wade Boliver's noticeable lack of involvement in his administration and Kirk Daniels's uncharacteristic behavior of late. He told her they still sparred from time to time but not as intensely. He also mentioned the resistance with which some of his people were starting to confront him. He ended by saying, "There's Wade, there's Kirk, there's scoffing among the troops, there's implicit disapprovals."

Paige nodded, saying nothing at first and then smiled and explained, "Well, you know, it's all in a day's work, and the pay is regular."

"I needed that." Neither said any more for a few minutes, both comfortable with the silence, for they accepted each other unconditionally. In time, Andy sighed and moaned, "Oh, Paige, why does life have to be such an argument?"

"Andy, my friend, don't sweat it so much. Life has a little drivel in one corner at its very best." She paused, starring blankly into the air, finally saying softly, "but that's OK ... that's OK ... gives us nerve, keeps our motor from dying." She giggled at that one.

"You sure have a way of cutting to the heart of things. And, by golly, you're right," said Andy resolutely. Paige just smiled, without a word. Then Andy rose from his chair. "Well, guess I better get out of your hair. Got a few things to tie up before I leave for the day. I'll send Calvin over next week. As you know, he has some background in Staffing."

"Thanks."

"Meanwhile, I have only one more thing to say, dear friend." Paige tilted her head like a little bird trying to catch a sound in the wind. "It's just this." said Andy, "Everybody should have a Paige Ivy in their lives."

"Thanks, Andy."

Andy nodded, strolled to the door, and was about to go through it when Paige called out. "Andy?"

"Yo."

She took a few steps toward him, looking humble and serious. "That was a very sweet compliment you paid me."

"It's true," he said and strolled out.

$$* * *$$

After he rested for a few moments in his trusty recliner back at The Lamp, Andy pushed up and said aloud, "It's Cylie Moe time." At the door he hesitated and then hurried back to the phone and dialed the number he had for Dub Grimes at the farm.

"Hello, this is Thelma Parker," a cheery voice sang out.

"Mom?"

"Yeah. Oh hi, Andy."

"Bless you, Mom, it sure is good to hear a friendly voice."

"Thanks, it's good to hear yours."

"Mom, please, I don't want to be a burden for y'all, but I sure would like to drop in this Saturday."

"Andy Boone, what do you mean, burden? Don't you ever talk that way. Never say that again, you hear?"

"Sure, Mom. It's just that I need you. I need to be around some people who have good sense and peace within themselves and don't have an ax to grind, like y'all."

"Andy, of course you come on. Get on down here. Believe me, it'll make our day."

"I'll wash dishes," chuckled Andy.

"Shoot."

"Excuse me?"

"No dishes. Besides, that's Kelly and Dub's job."

"Er, yeah, Kelly. Ah, how's she doing?"

"OK."

Andy waited, and when Mom didn't expand, he said, "Fine, I'll see y'all Saturday."

"That's great. Grandfather and Dub will be excited. See you then. Drive careful."

Andy replied, "Will do," and hung up. Hmm, Grandfather, excited. Dub, excited. Kelly—?

When Polly spotted Andy climbing onto the barstool, she lifted a finger in the air as if to query whether he wanted the usual. He smiled and nodded, and she had his drink in front of him in less than a minute.

"How you doin', Mr. Andy?"

"Fine. It's good to be here where I'm loved and to be greeted by the likes of you."

Polly winked and wobbled off to tend to business. She was looking pretty uncomfortable, thought Andy. Clearly, she was struggling to get around, and she looked very tired. In a few minutes, she came back to stand at a spot near him. There were only four or five other people in the bar at that time. Andy leaned toward her. "Polly?"

She strolled up, smiling, "Yeah, my man."

"How are you feeling? I mean, is it getting pretty hard for you?"

Polly nodded, started to speak, and then stopped and nodded. In a moment, she cleared her throat. "It's kind of you to ask. I'm really having a pretty tough time of it now. I don't know how much longer I can hold out here."

"I'm sorry, Polly. I really am. I wish you could just go home, rest, and have the baby."

"Me too," she said, as she ambled back down the bar.

After one more Turkey, Andy felt sleepy and decided to cut himself off.

Minutes later, at the foot of his bed, he prayed: "Dear God, thank you for now. Thank you for bringing me into this world and getting me to this point. Forgive me when I lose my temper and when I complain and when I pass judgment on others. It's not you, Lord. With all the breaks you've given me in my life, I should never complain about anything. Guide me and make me merciful to others. Praise Thee! Amen."

He slid into bed, exhaled loudly, and lay on his side. Good night, Lorrie Dean, wherever you are.

16

Thursday at Clay Cutter was the pits! The best part of Andy's day, even better than Cylie Moe's, was when Mom called back to encourage him to come on Friday so he'd wake up there on Saturday morning. She told him everybody had voted for that. Andy accepted gratefully.

Friday with the troops was no better than the day before. Didn't much matter. All Andy was interested in was getting through the day and dashing to the farm right after work, and he did.

He could feel his muscles start to relax as he got close to the Grimes's driveway. That made him think about the ice chest full of pork meats crammed in the trunk with his suitcase. He had reasoned that his farm friends never had to buy chicken and beef because they raised both. But he was pretty sure they had no hogs. So he loaded his ice chest with bacon, sausage, ham, pork loin, ribs, and chops. He smiled as he visualized Mom's likely reaction, fully animated at the sight of her unexpected inventory. Before he knew it, he was at the Grimes's drive.

As he expected, actually hoped, he was greeted at the front door by a pretty little charmer named Kelly Surrat. Andy said nothing for a moment as he took her in. There she stood in perfect pose in her bright red shirt, blue-and-white stripped overalls, and prim little bib cap. She smiled her trademark sweet smile and curtsied as she gracefully eased open the door. Like Andy, she said nothing. As their relationship stood, they both accepted that it wasn't necessary to fill the air with talk until the timing was just right. Finally, Andy decided it was time.

"Hi, ma'am. Have you been picking peas in those fresh starched clothes?"

"Oh, not really, I always dress up for special company—but it looks like we're not going to get any today, so I guess I might as well change into something comfortable."

"Isn't that comfortable?" blurted Andy as he doubled over laughing.

"Oh, yes, but I just don't want to get them wrinkled. Now get your giggling butt in here, Andy Boone."

"Kelly, if I might be serious for a moment," began Andy, solemnly, "it is an honor for me to be here … with probably the finest people in the world. I feel very, very privileged, and I thank you all from the bottom of my heart."

Kelly curtsied again, touched his shoulder, and said, "This way, sir," as she led toward the den.

When they strolled into the den, Mom popped out of her chair and sang out, "Andeee, get in here. Thanks for coming today—we wanted you to experience the dawning of a new day here. Come on, come on, come on!"

"How absolutely fantastic, Mom. Thank you a million times."

"Have you had supper?"

"Oh, that's OK, I'm really not hungry."

"Hey, we saved sandwich makings for you. I'm keeping the meat warm over there in that little toaster oven."

"Sounds great."

At once, Grandpa bound into the room from outside and shot straight toward Andy, his hand thrust out. They shook hands and rapped each other on the shoulder, and Grandpa whooped, "Welcome!"

"Thank you, Grandpa. This is super."

With that, Mom pointed a finger high in the air and sang out, "Here's our bellhop."

"Oh," said Andy, "that reminds me, I probably could use a little help with my ice chest."

"Let us hit it!" commanded Grandpa, grinning.

Andy and the resident bellhop toted in the laden chest and set it on the floor near the freezer. As he lifted the lid, Andy suggested that the goods inside probably should go directly to the freezer or refrigerator—including the two cartons of Coors that were wedged in around the other stuff. When Mom spied the stash of pork meat, she literally danced a jig, slapping her apron and singing praises. Abruptly, she scampered toward Andy, her arms outstretched, and hugged him vigorously.

Standing quietly nearby, Kelly started toward him also and then stopped short and stood, looking into him with the kindest expression. Somehow, she seemed unable to say anything. Minutes later when Andy sat down to have his sandwich, she sat across from him, smiling and bantering as usual. When he finished and reported how delicious it was, Kelly stretched her arms over the table toward him and said, "Glad you enjoyed, Mr. Andrew Boone … it is Andrew, isn't it?"

"Right you are. My full name is—now get this, see if you agree it's a really prestigious sounding name—Andrew Woodson Boone."

"Nice to meet you, most prestigious Mr. Andrew Woodson Boone." Kelly curled a finger under her chin and wrinkled her brow, "Wonder what I should call you? Andy Boone sounds too formal … maybe just Andy, like everybody else." Then she slapped the table and narrowed her eyes, "No, that's too easy."

"I'll be whoever you want me to be, my little friend."

"Come on, now, Andy Boone—this is big! You can't just rush through something like this."

"Oh, absolutely. Believe me, I don't take this lightly. It's serious, really serious."

"I know what," chimed Kelly, "what does your mother call you?"

"Andy Woo," said Andy, grinning.

"Hmm, sounds cool. Where does she get the Woo? Never mind, I know—it's from the Woodson, right?"

"Kelly, I never cease to be amazed at your …"

"Stuff it, Andy Woo," she interrupted. "Better still, I think I'll just call you Boone Woo."

"Then it's settled."

In a while, when the two self-styled comedians strolled onto the front porch, they came upon Dub sitting in a rocker, listening to music coming from a small cassette player. He looked up and said, "Howdy. I thought I'd leave you two to battle it out alone."

"What have you got tonight, Uncle Dub?" asked Kelly.

"Wagner."

Andy was speechless for a while. This cowboy—listens to Wagner, he mused. Guess that explodes another stereotype. When he recovered he asked, "What piece are you listening to?"

"Die Walkúre," said Dub, "I don't ever listen to the opera singin' part—just the orchestra. It's comin' up to the Magic Fire Music in a minute. That's my all-time favorite stretch of music."

"I'm impressed," said Andy. "I admire your taste. Don't let us interrupt."

"Oh, no problem. I can feel the music through the talkin'. Come on, let's talk."

"Let's do. I'm having fun getting to know the personalities of your—I started to say family, but it seems you don't all fit on the same family tree."

"True. We are all related in some kind of way, though not directly. Some of it's by marriage, which reminds me, I promised to give you a little rundown on everybody when you were here last time. Well, let's see, where shall we start?"

"Grandpa," said Kelly.

"Good place to start, Kelly, thanks. Well, let's see. First of all, Grandpa is Mom's uncle and, of course, Kelly's grandfather. See, Grandpa's son, Bailey, was married to my sister, which makes me the proud uncle of our dear Kelly. And Mom is the daughter of Grandpa's sister. Now, she's nobody's mom around here, but we call her Mom because we need somebody in that role and she's perfect in it. She's, like, you know, the resident mom. Also, both Mom and Grandpa are widowed.

"Then there's Aunt Leah. She comes in on the in-law side. You'll find her to be kind of shy—she don't say much, but she's very candid. As she puts it, she's happily divorced. But anyway, back to Grandpa, he's sort of the key figure here. Now you might not think it when you first meet him, but when you get to know him, you realize that Grandpa is a very sharp, well educated, philosophical old man. In fact our nickname for him is Professor."

"I could already tell he's very sharp, Dub," said Andy.

"Right. Now of late—and Kelly knows we pretty much keep this to ourselves—anyway, in the last couple of years, Grandpa kind of comes and goes mentally, and he does some very strange, mostly funny things. He doesn't go way off or stay there very long, but there are a few mild mental lapses here and there. As I say, nothing critical, just kind of weird. But mostly he's on the ball, very astute. Is that the right word, Kelly?"

"Uh huh. Tell him about Grandpa not ever using contractions in his speech."

"Oh yeah, it happens that Grandpa is a very big fan of the original *Star Trek*, and ever since—well, OK, there is a very shrewd character on there named Spock, and Grandpa admires him. So at some point, he noticed, or he found out somehow, that Mr. Spock never would say things like don't, or won't, or it'll, things like that."

"Contractions," reminded Kelly.

"Right. Now, Spock would always be very careful to say do not instead of don't and, it will, instead of it'll. So Grandpa took up the habit and obviously likes it."

"Well, I know this." began Andy, "Whatever all can be said of this family, one thing is clear. The people in it are extraordinary—admirable—and you all seem to be very dear to each other."

Kelly was nodding as Dub started to speak. "Yep, and mind you, nobody here has a spouse. OK? We've just sort of pieced together a family from available candidates. I guess you could say we're a collection of refugees. No matter, we are one big happy family. We just call ourselves the Singles Club, and we're proud of it."

"Yeah, the only bad news is that it takes so many bedrooms. Nobody sleeps together," chided Kelly.

Kelly went inside to get a glass of water, and Dub leaned toward Andy and said in a low voice, "I'll have to tell you about Kelly tomorrow when she's not hangin' on us every minute. Saturdays, she has little chores she does. But Andy, I'm so happy about the relationship you two have. It is beautiful to watch, and she needs you in her life. I'm so glad you came along and that the two of you understand each other perfectly after only just a tiny bit of time together. So, hers is a very touchin' story. It'll tug at your heart. And I think you'll come to understand what happened the last time you were here, when she went straight to her room without another word to anybody."

When Kelly returned, sipping water, the three buddies sat quietly, listening to Dub's music, occasionally offering but a brief comment. After a while, they all agreed that it was bedtime, that curfew had arrived. After bidding goodnight and pledging an early rousing the next morning, they scattered to their bedrooms.

Andy's room was perfect: comfortable and quiet with a double window facing the grazing fields. The view was beautiful, positively inspirational. Andy prayed and eased under the covers, thinking goodnight to all. I love you.

He arose before dawn, and though it was dark, he could make out the features of the fields and—as he was so prone to do—imagine life there, feasting on the calm surroundings. He decided he would watch the dawning over this peaceful land from the front porch.

When he emerged onto the porch, he at once saw Grandpa, rocking gently. "Good morning," said Andy.

"Good morning, Andy, my boy. You are up early. I am glad because I have been waiting for some company out here in this soothing air. Can you feel it healing?"

"I can indeed," said Andy, "and I'm glad you're here too, Grandpa."

They nodded to each other and rocked for a while without talking. In a few moments, when Andy looked at his wrist and discovered he had forgotten his watch, he turned to Grandpa. "What time is it, Grandpa?"

"It is morning!"

"Uh, but what … yeah, you're right. It is morning."

"Yep. On a farm, morning has a special place of honor."

"You know, Grandpa, that's fascinating. I have never thought of morning being anything but a section of the day."

"Most people look at it that way. Not I. To me, there is nothing in all of life as fine as morning. It is innocence, a chance to start clean. So you see, it can come at any time of the day or at any time in life. Morning has a sense apart from light and dark. It is warmth and coolness all at the same time … with a sort of special countenance. Even dulled senses can pick it up. Yep, it is just that clean and discernible."

"I see what you mean," said Andy. "Morning will be what you need it to be."

"Right."

Suddenly, Jenny hopped through the door and grabbed a rocker, "May I watch it with you guys?"

"Hey, Jenny, good morning," said Andy. "Sure, there's plenty for everybody. Rock away."

"Good one, Boone Woo."

Over the next fifteen minutes, Mom, Dub, and Aunt Leah ambled out one at a time and took up rockers. Now the household was all assembled. They rocked gently and nodded as faint murmurs trickled through this snug little group. Then, as the darkness started to fade, they all fell silent. Everybody seemed to be in tune. The gradual lighting of the day was a melody. The night and the day, each with its motif, blending, working together in easy counterpoint, one giving over, the other taking up, so easily, smoothly, no jousting for position or dominance. In a few minutes, a very narrow band of light started squeezing into the horizon. It was a glow, a hint of what was coming. The pitch black trees started to emerge out of the veil of night. Then all else started coming into view, as if everything was being reborn. Still it was dim, not yet ready.

At that moment, Grandpa stood up and lifted his arms toward heaven, and as he was easing back into his rocker, he started to speak. "You know, gang, as I have said before, it is altogether useless to get hung up on the technicalities of what is going on here. Heck, we know that technically the sun is not really rising. Sure, the world is spinning and each part is finding the sun at the right time. No matter, the sun is rising if that is what it looks like. It is the perception that counts, and most important of all, how it makes us feel. Of course, every day does not start out like this. Sometimes it is raining, even storming, but the changing of the guard still takes place."

Everybody was nodding and rocking as the Singles Club sage professor finished his soliloquy. Now the trees and the vast meadows, which had been almost hidden by night, were taking over. The woods were yawning and stretching, and a timid breeze awakened and started to whisper. They could hear the rustling of leaves in the trees and the crack of a fallen twig now and then. Now they could smell the grass warming up in the sun. Next came the early arrivals, birds sailing low over the fields, butterflies flitting above the tall grass. Then came the ground crew, rattling around, swishing, thumping, buzzing. Yet the feeling was soothing, healing—so very quiet and peaceful.

The sun that had been but a wink on the horizon now burst into the sky. It was morning!

After the applause faded, they all looked at each other and giggled and then turned to go inside for breakfast, which Mom had already started before the morning ritual. After breakfast, everybody seemed to go in different directions, their heads set firm, their strides determined, indicating they had something to do. Kelly was no exception as she sailed off to her bedroom to do her ironing. She explained to Andy that she did this chore in her bedroom where she could listen to the radio and not be bothered by the racket of others doing their thing.

In a moment, Dub was back and invited Andy to join him on a trek to the South corner of the ranch section because he needed to check out possible repairs for one of the gates there. Andy agreed, and they headed on out and into the pastures, cheerfully gabbing as they moseyed along. In a moment, Dub said, "Now, about Kelly."

"Yes, yes," said Andy, "after that brief preview you gave me yesterday, I've been very curious and anxious to hear about her situation."

"OK, I've cogitated on whether it was right or proper for me to tell you personal things about her life, and what I've come up with is that your regard for each other seems special, and for that reason, I think it'll be OK. I mean, I admire you both. So out of loyalty to each of you, I'm gonna tell you these things. Now, they're sort of like secrets to Kelly, so it'll be good if you don't let on that you've heard about them. I mean, don't change the way you relate to her and start actin' more sympathetic or somethin' because that little brain will catch it in a heartbeat. Believe me, for a seventeen-year-old, she is one bright youngun."

"Seventeen-year-old?"

"Right. So first of all ..."

"Wait a minute, Dub, I had figured her for about fourteen."

Dub laughed. "I know, everybody does at first. But she's seventeen, lookin' fourteen, and actin' forty."

At that moment, they came to a weathered old barn-wood gazebo. Dub motioned toward the bench. "Let's set down here for a few minutes." After they settled, Dub stared out across the field, then he began again.

"Anyway, Kelly's mother is my sister, and her dad is Grandpa's son. So far, so good, OK? So things seemed to go well, at least outwardly, until Kelly was about six years old. Then her mom and dad started bickerin' and it got to the point that it was scarin' Kelly to pieces. I heard this from Kelly herself right after she came here. To make a long story short, they divorced—and surprisingly got joint custody of the child. That didn't even work for six months. Dad gets the wanderlust and moves to Europe on some kind of rinky dink job and gives up his part of the custody in a legal way. It looked like he'd rather sail off to play overseas than to stay with his kid. Not too long after that, her mom—and this is my sister, Andy—she decides she don't want to have responsibility for the kid, and starts askin' around the family if anybody wants Kelly. Get that word, Andy, *wants*—you know what I mean?"

Andy's heart was in his throat, and he sat stone still, his face drawn solemn and sad. His voice cracked as he stammered, "Looked like nobody wanted her." Then, grown man though he was, he just dropped his face in both hands and wept.

Dub waited. After several minutes, when Andy raised his head, Dub continued. "Would you believe Grandpa at first didn' put out any effort to take her. Later, he relented. I think he really didn't know what was goin' on at first and just dismissed the whole affair as somethin' that would work itself out. When it didn', Grandpa set out to get her and adopt her, which turned out to be a problem, but with the help of some professional associates who knew him well, they finally legalized it—like he's a kind of guardian. Even though this worked out and the two of them love and adore each other, surely that whole thing has to stick in Kelly's mind, or I should say, her heart. It just seemed there was nobody who rushed forward to take her into their lives."

"Does she have a boyfriend or other peers who show they need her and want to be with her?"

"Yes, she has church friends and friendly school chums, and she has a boyfriend, sort of—I mean, they don't date hardly any, but they have a close relationship at school. Anyway, Kelly refers to him as her boyfriend. And from what we know, he is a nice young boy and very considerate of Kelly."

* * *

After lunch, Kelly chanted, "Raise your hands if you want to go to the cove for a bit." Andy's hand shot up instantly, and everybody else made excuses about "things to do." So the two little buddies strolled on side by side down the wooded pathway leading to what Andy now referred to as Kelly's Cove. As they bounced along bantering, their shoulders touched now and then, and they snickered in stride as it happened. Soon they were there, and Andy gasped with wonderment.

The cove was a shady inlet into the woods just off the pathway. It was about the size of a double garage and looked as if it had been carved out of the thicket of ancient trees with a plan in mind. The curve of it extended all the way around and opened briefly to the pathway along one side. It had a natural roof, given by age-old trees that completely engulfed it. Inside, there were two large seat-high stumps left by trees that had been cut down, probably on purpose to make room inside this cozy little chamber of enchantment. Each of the stump seats was cushioned with a feed sack stuffed with rags and hay.

"Pull up a stump and have a seat, Boone Woo," said Kelly cheerfully as she lowered onto a wooden bench nearby. "Does it feel good in here or what?"

"It does indeed. I think this would be the perfect place to escape to after a long day of stress and strain."

"Agree. And I can tell you that it works." Then they were silent for a moment as Andy glanced all around the little cave and surveyed the ceiling of vines and branches. Drinking it all in was the most gratifying experience he could remember having since he was a little boy. Then his banter-buddy broke the silence.

"Boone Woo, tell me. What happened that day that made your car crash into the fence?"

"Well … ah, something was on my mind as I passed the little schoolhouse in Tillman that morning. Remind me. I'll tell y'all about it some time."

"Tell me now!"

"You know, I haven't really talked to anybody about the details of it."

Kelly looked at him, waiting, wordless, letting her unpretentious, youthful countenance disarm him. As Andy met her gaze, he conceded in his mind that this precious human being was indeed irresistible and deserved an honest answer to a very reasonable question. Finally, he said, "I just lost control of my car."

"How?"

"Just took my mind off driving. I was thinking about something that happened years ago that the little school reminded me of."

Kelly shrugged. "Tell me, what happened all those years ago that you can't shake?"

"It's just so personal."

"But you've shared other things that are personal."

"What difference does it make? Why are you so interested?"

"'Cause you're my friend, and if I knew what it is that troubles you so much about it, I could understand better and be supportive."

"Yeah, maybe so, but I've never told anyone, not even my mother. Why should I tell you?"

"Because, Boone Woo, you need to hear it … hear yourself say it. It might give you closure or whatever."

"Wow, such astute wisdom for a fourteen-year-old."

"Seventeen."

"OK, seventeen. Still, extraordinary acumen for one so young."

Kelly huffed and thrust both hands to her hips. So, you gonna tell me or not?"

"Not."

They sat still for a while, staring at each other, silent, motionless. Finally, Kelly propped her chin on two fists and looked wide-eyed at her friend. Andy shifted, looked away, bowed his head, looked up through the trees, then eyed his little heckler. She looked so innocent, so sincere, and so downright caring. When he began to speak, it came out as a whisper, so he sucked in a deep breath and smacked his lips. "OK, Kelly, OK, OK, OK! Damn! This is a secret, understand?"

Kelly nodded. "What's acumen?"

"Don't be so cavalier."

"Boone Woo, I swear on my very life I will never tell anyone in the world what you confide to me."

"Well, here goes," he said reluctantly with another deep breath. "When I passed the little Tillman school on that rainy morning, I had a sudden flashback to something that happened at my elementary school when I was in the fifth grade. Keep in mind, I was only eleven years old then. Even so, an incident happened at recess one day that has plagued my mind ever since. Mostly it has stayed asleep in the way back of my mind as I burned and churned with my working career. I guess being so busy kept it from surfacing. So I was just thinking about that and took my eyes off the road and almost ran into the car ahead. When I braked suddenly, my car began to skid and finally wound up on your fence."

"What was it that happened? What was the incident?"

"Does that part matter?"

"It matters to you."

"Well, OK, there was this little girl, and she and I sort of flirted around like young school kids will do. I had the feeling we both thought we were sweethearts, but we never said that to each other." Andy felt he could not go on any further and fell silent. He was conscious of his young friend letting him deal with it in his own way, in silence, in his own time, and she appeared to wait forever for him to take the next step. He cleared his throat, now aware of a tear in a corner of his eye. Maybe Kelly was right, maybe he did need to hear himself confess it all.

Andy touched the lone tear, lifted his chin, and tried to sound self-assured as he began to speak again. "By the way, if it matters, this little girl's name was—I mean is—Lorrie Dean. She didn't deserve the way I treated her on that day. See, when I was a kid, I embarrassed easily. On this day at recess, she came up to me and handed me a folded note, and I took it. Just as I turned to open it, I saw two teachers watching, and I was sorely embarrassed. So I shoved the note back toward Lorrie Dean's hands, but she wouldn't take it. She kept backing away, and I kept pushing the note in her face."

Andy felt his shoulders shaking and his stomach beginning to quiver, the last signs before a complete crying breakdown, but he gritted his teeth and stifled it. "So, Kelly dear, she just kept backing away from me, and I was furiously trying to get the note back to her. All at once, she stumbled over something and fell backward, banging down to the ground. When she went down, she fell into some broken glass and it sliced her face all over on one side. After she started pushing herself up, she sort of stopped. She just hung there, half up, staring at me, shaking, and oh, looking so hurt and so shocked. But she never cried. I know she couldn't help but feel the blood running under her chin, but she wouldn't touch it. And she wouldn't cry. Oh, God, Kelly, why wouldn't she scream or just cry? Kelly, dear Kelly, I'm sorry to burden you with this, but why didn't she cry? Why?"

A few minutes passed, and Andy looked up at his dear friend; she seemed as overcome as he. They both simply nodded. No words were needed to explain what they were feeling—they were in tune, as always. After what seemed like a lifetime, Kelly sniffled softly and looked full at her friend and managed a faint smile. Then she cleared her throat and started to speak. "My Boone Woo, it hurt too much to cry. Even at that young age, it wasn't her torn face, it was the pain of rejection that tore into her very being, her life. But you know what, Boone Woo, that heals when you're young—it has to. And please, stop this disabling guilt trip right now! Today! You really are not guilty of anything uncommon among little children. You just have to dump those guilt feelings. Boone Woo, do this just for you, nobody else. I want that for you."

"Thanks, Kelly. You know, you're right. I needed to tell this, to hear it out loud."

"You're welcome."

Andy responded with a broad grin, but couldn't seem to go any further.

After awhile, Kelly said, "I'm sorry you crashed your car."

"I'm not. I'm glad I crashed."

"That's strange."

Andy was shaking his head as she spoke. "If I hadn't crashed into your fence, I wouldn't know you. I would never have met you—and the others. I can't even visualize my life without you in it."

She tilted her head and smiled faintly. Andy was aware that she could tell he wasn't jesting. Then the expression on her pretty face turned solemn, kind of sad looking, much like that day she abandoned their walk and went to her room without a word. Now she was gazing out through the cove toward the pathway. Soon, Andy raised up from his stump and glanced at his watch.

"It's getting late, isn't it?" noted Kelly, now standing.

"It is morning."

* * *

While Andy was repacking his suitcase, Dub dropped by to tell him everybody was gathering in the den for coffee and cake. As it developed, the babble at this mid-afternoon snack was a little subdued. When Andy started to speak of how very much he had enjoyed his visit, Mom interrupted.

"Andy, listen, why don't you stay over and go to church with us tomorrow and have some lunch, what do you say?"

"Really?" Andy asked, pitching for assurance.

"Really!" sang out the family clan in unison.

"Well—OK, I appreciate that. As a matter of fact, I brought along a necktie in case y'all would have me for that."

"Way to go," said Grandpa, and they all cheered.

Then Kelly squealed, "You brought a tie, Boone Woo?"

Andy nodded, and everybody got back to the matter at hand. When he finished his snack, he looked up and at once caught the face of his young friend. She was watching him and smiling—the sweetest, most radiant smile he'd ever seen on her or anyone else in his whole life. It was the smile of morning, of assurance, of life itself. Andy smiled back and hoped his had the same glow.

The rest of the day was relaxed and friendly, ending with another classical night concert, courtesy of Dub Grimes, on the front porch.

Sunday morning was busy but not frenzied as they all got themselves together and hustled off to church. When it was over, they returned to their nest and settled around the table for red beans and sausage—not your standard Sunday lunch of fried chicken and mashed potatoes. When lunch was done, Andy announced that he guessed he'd better ease on back to his apartment so he could get ready for the fireworks at Clay Cutter the next day. They all said good-bye and Andy pledged to return.

As he cruised along the two-lane highway, Andy began to take in his surroundings, and he was thinking of the fascinating contrast between the state's hill country and the roving woods and fields along this flat East Texas trail linking his two worlds. Each region was uniquely inspirational, and each had changed remarkably over the years.

The piney woods of East Texas anchored the southern end of Andy's route, but these softwoods ultimately gave way to the red oaks, sweet gums, dogwoods, and mesquite trees closer to Dallas. Some of the meadowlands along the route were actually clearings that had been carved out of the woods to make way for cotton fields. The other, more native fields, those brimming with lush tall grass, had served as cattle ranches.

Sadly, the cotton fields had been left to die years ago, the once thriving small farms were fading fast, and cattle no longer roamed the grazing fields. The little towns and communities that years ago had popped up in the fields and woods were still there, but now they were just quiet and peaceful—and lazy.

As he drew near his destination, Andy shook the visions from his head and started to think about the dear, genuine, unassuming people with whom he had just spent the weekend. His thoughts turned involuntarily to Kelly. She just burst into his mind. *I can't believe she got that out of me about Lorrie Dean. Still, she doesn't know about my search, which inexcusably has gone cold … got to build that fire again—Clay Cutter be damned.* Then he smiled and sped on.

<h1 style="text-align: center;">17</h1>

ireworks, indeed! How about Kirk Daniels for the first puny little pop pop? Woo hoo! In fact, Andy's nemesis was already standing in his office doorway when he arrived at work Monday morning. Andy sailed on past him and went straight to his desk while Kirk strutted in behind him, looking cocky and confident.

"Come on in, Kirk," said Andy, still standing behind his desk surveying the paperwork left there the previous Friday.

"Aren't you going to invite me to sit down?"

"Oh sure, have a seat on the floor." When Kirk's mouth popped open, Andy chuckled and said, "Just kidding. Have a seat. What brings you here so early?"

Kirk dragged a chair directly in front of Andy's desk, propped both elbows on it, and grumbled, "Why did you send Calvin to Staffing?"

"Come on, Kirk, that's part of the plan. Don't you remember— cross-training?"

"Well, fearless leader, that plan ain't goin' anywhere. For that matter, none of your so-called innovations are going to survive."

"Thanks for letting me in on the secret. Now I can be on alert for the early signs."

"Don't be so coy."

"What's your problem, Kirk? Is Calvin's brief rotation cheating you out of something?"

"Oh, boss, you're really cute." Andy didn't answer. He leaned back in his chair, folded his arms, and stared steadily at his agitator. Then Kirk began chiding his boss with whatever slime came to his mind. Every time he started to make a point of some nonsense, he pitched his head up and down like a rooster bobbing for rainwater caught in a tractor rut. When he finally ran out of taunts, he stopped talking and just grinned while he swayed. When Andy kept looking at him without responding, he said, "Come on, Sport, you owe me some answers. I ask. You have to answer."

Andy fixed his gaze on the pupils of Kirk's eyes and said, "Two things, Kirk. One, I never answer a baited question, and two, all I owe you is a fair chance to prove you're as good as you think you are. Right now, you're raising some serious doubts. So, old Sport, as you say, looks like you've got work to do."

"Now isn't that clever. I do believe you think you've got it made. You don't seem to appreciate that you have to deal with me." He stood up, apparently for a better position from which to feed off his own ranting. "Don't forget, I warned you right in the beginning. I, for one, am gonna be nipping at your heels at every turn."

"Thanks for letting me know who the enemy is, and by the way, since you're already standing, this meeting is adjourned."

"Whoa whoa—whoa whoa whoa! Are you throwing me out of your office?"

Andy stood up and started toward the door. "This office is company property. I'm not throwing you out of it. But I'm leaving it. If you want to stay in here and talk to yourself, be my guest." He looked back over his shoulder as he finished talking and then walked out of the room and closed the door. As it was swinging to, he heard some muffled words that sounded very much like, "We've got your ass."

In the company cafeteria, Andy was sulking over a cup of hot coffee, nitpicking his own behavior. Why do I try to be so smug with that little jerk? Soon he began nodding, now positive as to what Kirk's little game was all about. Kirk was just part of a larger strategy, the advance party of a planned siege of Andy's career. The handwriting was on the wall. Mr. Daniels's little sortie was a harbinger to an inevitable showdown. This would be phase two of their little concoction. The stage is set. Enter and exit ace tormentor Kirk Daniels. Now, Wade Boliver, you're on. Andy breathed a sigh of relief. He had all this argued out in his mind, and that meant he wouldn't have to think about it at Cylie Moe's.

✱ ✱ ✱

"Turkey and Coke, please."

"Hi, Andy. We missed you over the weekend."

"Yeah, I spent the weekend with friends down the country."

When Polly hurried away and returned with his drink, he asked, "Polly, how you feeling?"

"Don't ask."

"Is there anything we customers can do to make it easier for you—like you could bring us two drinks at once and then sit down?"

"You know, that's kind of you—I mean, to think of how I'm feeling, but it's OK. This is my decision to keep working right up to the last. But I thank you. I thank you very much. I'm OK."

"Well, you know, we're all friends."

Polly nodded and looked at Andy quizzically. "You know, Andy, I don't mean to get personal, but like you say, we're all friends here, and so—well, most of the times when you come in, it looks like maybe there's a weight hanging over you besides just being tired after a hard day's work. And like you said to me, I care about that."

"Thanks Polly. You're a jewel."

"If you ever want to talk about it—and I know it usually helps to talk about something—then I'm here to listen, not just from curiosity, but so maybe I will have helped somebody."

The place was nearly empty; there was only one other bar customer down at the far end, and he was lost in television. "Polly, maybe that would be a little catharsis for me. When I finish this Turkey, bring me two more, and I'll confide to you one really gnawing concern I have. The main problem is that I'm helpless." He chuckled, "I'm usually in control of everything, but I can't do anything about this deal."

Later, Polly came over with the two drinks, pulled up a bar stool, and sat in front of her customer, ready to listen. "Shoot."

"OK, the thing is—and this is really it, as simple as it may sound—there's someone missing from my life who I can't find. You know what I mean? She's a missing person. I mean really a missing person. Unfortunately, I'm at a total dead end. I've done literally everything possible to get a lead to her whereabouts, and it's like she has left the face of the earth. And I guess that's what confounds me so much. I apologize that it presents you with a glum customer."

"Hey, I don't mind at all. If I didn't care, I wouldn't even ask you about it. You know, personally, I don't accept dead ends. I mean, you just don't stop hoping and trying. You never know when you're just one step away from the truth—who was it said that?"

"I don't remember, but somebody famous, I bet. Anyway, thanks for that. You have indeed helped me. Maybe more than either of us can know right now. I'll keep you posted."

Tuesday morning at Clay Cutter was, as always, a laugh a minute. At his desk, Andy roused from his doldrums and spoke softly to himself, "Hey, it is morning. If indeed his majesty, the one and only, Wade Boliver, is poised to strike, I better get my own game planning in gear." Thereupon, Andy resolved that he would take the initiative himself and meet his boss face to face without further delay. Clearly, the quick-touchdown thing hadn't worked, but maybe he could at least avoid a sack in the backfield if he could mess up Boliver's timing. He would set about straight way to put his adversary on the defensive.

He asked Valorie to call Boliver's secretary, Edith, to arrange for an appointment that very morning, or at least that same day. Going through the two secretaries was protocol, and he certainly didn't want to foul up on a small point.

In two minutes, Valorie came in, looking puzzled. "Andy, Edith says Mr. Boliver is out of the office, and she's not sure of his calendar for the rest of the day."

"How convenient. So, let's see, what shall we do? Ah …"

Valorie was frowning and apparently couldn't resist interrupting her boss. "This kind of puzzles me, Andy, because I just came from the office next door to them and saw Mr. Boliver going into his office. That was, like, about one minute before I called," she said, shrugging and poking a finger at her temple.

"Hmm, see what you mean. Thanks for clueing me in. Tell you what, call her back and say I indicated to you that he really needs to see me. Tell her I have something important I think he would want to know about."

Momentarily, Andy answered the intercom, "Yeah, any luck, Valorie?"

"OK, Andy, Edith wants to talk to you. Can you pick up?"

"Sure, thanks, Valorie."

"Hello, Edith, how's it going?"

"Fine, Mr. Boone. Can you tell me what you want to talk to Mr. Boliver about, I mean, what the subject is?"

"Sales."

"Sales?"

"Uh huh, sales and profits."

"Sales and profits. Well, let me see if I can, uh, locate him. Give me a while, OK?"

"Sure, OK. However, tell you what, why don't I just come up there, and that way I'll already be there when he, er, returns, and that will also save you some time on the phone?"

"Well, that's entirely up to you, sir."

"Good. I'll drop by in a few minutes."

Andy was greeted warmly by his boss's secretary and, at her

invitation, took a seat in the adjoining conference room to wait. While he waited, Andy let his mind percolate on current events in his corporate life. It was a source of great anguish that he had not scored a quick touchdown in order to, as his man Willis Braley put it, quiet the crowd. Then, at once, a new insight sprang into his head. Even if you score a quick touchdown, you haven't won the hostile crowd's allegiance. You've only subdued them. Perhaps that was enough, thought Andy, for at least he had gotten their attention, and quite likely that had brought him a measure of respect among company rank and file.

The hours wore on and still no show for the high boss. Finally, Edith came in and said that Mr. Boliver had just called and advised he was in a meeting across town and would be going home straight from there. She said he indicated that the meeting would probably run late. Andy thanked her and left.

The days dragged on at Clay Cutter with the signs of doom growing ever stronger all the while. And it was obvious that Wade Boliver was not about to entertain a meeting with Andy Boone until he, himself, was ready to take the initiative. So the standoff continued.

On the brighter side, Andy did manage to write a letter, and happily he received one. Early in the week he had written to his farm family, thanking them for their hospitality and asking that they "please say hello to my humorless little accomplice."

The next day, he got a note from Mildred in Baytown that absolutely made his day, leading him to resolve, *Life is pretty darn good, period!* Mildred's message was simple but precious:

My dear Andy. What can I say? Just your friendship would have been enough, just realizing that you know me well and still love me was plenty. Still, dear friend, thank you from the bottom of my heart for the beautiful flowers and, well, just your thoughtfulness. Now, you should have been here when Jenny opened her box and found the beautiful Cinderella dress. Andy, she absolutely squealed with delight. She loves it. Thank you for making a little girl happy, not just by giving her a pretty dress, but just as much by walking along with her, as you two did that day, bouncing along side by side, jabbering and giggling and holding hands. That's priceless. Thanks again. Hope to see you soon. Love, Mildred

For the weekend, he had decided to stay in his apartment, do a little reading, listen to some music, and just rest up. Then Friday night, out of the blue, he got the weirdest phone call. The very instant he answered, the caller whooped into the phone.

"Heyyyy, is this Andy?"

"Yes it is."

"Of course you wouldn't recognize my voice, because it's been years since you heard it."

"Who is this?"

"Well, Andy, I'm sorry, I can't say my name on the phone, but I'd very much like a chance to meet with you in person and tell you why that is—plus we can catch up on all that time."

"I just don't know. I'm kind of baffled. Where are you?"

"I'm in Dallas for the weekend. I'm staying at the Adolphus. Want to meet for breakfast in the morning? Believe me, I think it will take a huge load off your mind and off mine too, 'cause I've also wondered about you since those days in school."

Andy's mind was racing so hard, his face and ears were burning, and he was breathing like he'd just finished a hundred-yard dash. "Uh … uh, OK, shall I join you in the Adolphus dining room at, say, eight thirty?"

"Super, I'll have a table for us when you arrive. I'll be wearing a pink silk blouse and will have a blue scarf around my neck. OK?"

"Good. I'll be there."

18

"Dear God above, please let it be Lorrie Dean," Andy pleaded aloud. He was speeding through morning traffic when suddenly he caught himself. Speeding was a reflex brought on by his anxiety. Actually, it was more like a dreadful fear that he was about to be disappointed, that it would be some weird character—not Lorrie Dean at all. Still there was no rational basis for speeding, so he slowed down, dropped back, and stayed patiently in his lane. He was way too early anyway. As it was, he'd have to kill some time somewhere after he parked downtown.

At eight twenty-five, Andy walked into the dining room and immediately spied a young woman in a pink top and blue scarf. Now his knees were getting weak, and he could feel the pulse pounding in his ears. The woman was reading a menu and hadn't noticed him. He sidled toward the wall and back a little from the entrance. Then he reached across to hold on to the edge of a foyer table and continued to study his subject. Nothing really hit him about this woman, nothing at all one way or the other, except possibly that her face didn't look very round, but perhaps that wasn't all that indicative. He was getting absolutely no definitive sensations about the woman. It could be Lorrie Dean, or it could be a foreigner. If indeed he had perceived instant promise in this situation, surely he would have rushed forward and embraced his obvious Lorrie Dean. But somehow he felt more like running away than running toward her.

In a few moments, Andy began to sway. He lost his grip on the table and almost fell. The hostess asked if he was OK, and when he smiled and nodded, the woman in pink/blue looked up. Now she was studying him and at once grinned broadly and looked right at him as he strode toward her table.

"Hi, I'm Andy Boone."

"Hi, I'm Teresa Aylor. People call me Terry."

"Nice meeting you, Terry."

They looked at each other for a while, both faces serious, swallowing now and then, neither glancing aside, until finally Terry broke the spell. "This is some day. I hardly know what to say, or do, or think."

"Same here," said Andy, still studying this purported long-time acquaintance with whom, just out of the blue, he was having breakfast.

Terry leaned across the table and whispered, "Of course, you know that's not my real name, but it's the one I have to go by. You know, Andy? Understand?"

"Yes, Terry, I understand fully. It's just that, well, I'm in shock. I guess what I'm hoping against hope about you is so totally unexpected and staggering that I'm just dumbfounded. I'm speechless. I'm thinkless. I'm not prepared for this moment like I thought I would be."

"Andy, dear Andy, what do you mean hope against hope? I am who you think I am, the one you've been looking for. Please, Andy, I am that person. I wouldn't expect you to recognize me on the street 'cause, you know, it's been about twenty years. Believe it, Andy, just know this is happening. I would have come sooner had I known, but I didn't know."

He didn't answer. Somehow he couldn't. He was frozen, sitting perfectly still, transfixed, every element of his being focused on this woman. Everything she said was seemingly credible, believable, relevant—so this had to be the girl—woman—he had longed to find. It was the only logical resolution for this unthinkable moment. Yet why wasn't he weeping? Why hadn't he sprung out of his chair and embraced her with all the fiber of his essence. At once, he decided he had better, as a minimum, perform some of this ritual, even if superficially. So he caused his lips to quiver, and then he blinked several times and slumped over the table holding his face in his hands, as if struggling to conquer an overwhelming urge to cry. After all, that's what he should be doing naturally. Why wasn't he? Why? Finally, he lifted his head and tried to create a sad-looking smile.

His woman companion smiled meekly and said nothing for a few moments. When she started to speak, there seemed to be sincere compassion in her voice. "I know. I know it's hard. It's OK, it's OK, take your time." Then simultaneously they picked up their menus and confidently spoke their order when queried by the server.

After breakfast, Andy asked Terry if they could walk around outside for a little while, and she agreed. Outside, they strolled along, Terry talking and laughing and slapping Andy's shoulder all the while. Andy tried to contribute but clearly was not the dominant figure in this partnership. However he did manage to steer their course so that, ultimately, they were walking alone with no one within at least fifty feet of them. Then Andy stopped, turned, grasped her shoulders so that they were face to face, and demanded, "Now say your name!"

"I'm Lorrie Dean."

The embrace was instant and lingering. When finally they eased apart, they continued to face each other and visit for a while, murmuring casually, and eventually resolving to spend the rest of the day together. They would have a fast-food lunch, take a tour of the arts district, and maybe spend a restful hour or two in a nice bar, all as a prelude to a leisurely dinner.

Still, some inexplicable, pestering little doubt hovered in

Andy's mind. This woman seemed all too exuberant. His Lorrie Dean was notably shy and reserved when she was eleven years old. To the best of his reckoning, he didn't believe basic personality ever changed so dramatically. He conceded that born introverts could train themselves to behave as extroverts in order to meet given situations, even career necessities. But this was not one of those situations. There was no reason to perform now, no reason to act unnaturally. Something simply didn't seem right about this Lorrie Dean. Moreover, it was inconceivable to him that the solemn little round face of his fifth-grade sweetheart would have elongated this much.

As they pulled into the tiny parking lot at Cylie Moe's, Terry—alias Lorrie Dean—asked, "What's wrong, Andy?"

At once he was aware of his frowning and answered quickly, "I'm sorry, Lorrie Dean, I banged my knee against a door facing this morning when I lost my balance, and it just bothers me a little when I drive, just certain movements of driving. No problem, Really." *Guess I'd better limp a little. Damn! It's too late now.*

"Oh, all right," allowed Lorrie Dean. "By the way, Andy, maybe this will ease your mind about something: my elbow is fine. In fact, it was a very tiny little fracture and healed in no time."

That did it! "That's good news. Let's go in. This is my place. It's orderly and peaceful. It's class."

When Polly saw Andy sitting at a table with his company, she apparently deputized herself as a floor server and, as much as her condition would permit, hurried toward their table. "Hey, Andy, welcome, and a hearty welcome to you, ma'am."

Both said thank you, and Andy introduced the two women to each other, being careful to refer to his date as Terry Aylor.

While they waited for their drinks, Andy couldn't seem to quit shifting around in his chair. He realized that it was probably arousing the curiosity of his date. But strangely, she pretended not to notice and said nothing about it. When the silence became noticeably awkward,

Terry remarked, "Your server looks as if she's getting pretty close to the happy event."

"Yeah. Indeed she is—really! Actually, she shouldn't be working right now. I don't know what the deal is, but she says she has to work as long as possible."

"Bless her! But that really isn't very wise."

"I know."

They sat fairly quiet through their first drink, except for an occasional matter-of-fact observation on some innocuous point. Then as they began their second drinks, they looked at each other as if on some kind of secret signal, smiled and nodded. They pursed their lips and nodded again in unison.

Terry was the first to speak. "It's not working, is it?"

"No, Terry, it isn't. Nice try."

"Are you angry?"

"Yes. Well, kind of."

"You had a premonition about it from the beginning didn't you?"

"I did indeed, even though, as I wrestled with it in my mind, I couldn't explain it to myself. I couldn't identify specifically what it was. I guess I so wanted you to be Lorrie Dean that I didn't question it overtly. Is Teresa Aylor really your name?"

"Yes." She was fidgeting with her fingers, clearly ill at ease. "Andy, we only wanted to help. Please. That's all we wanted to do."

"Who's we?"

"Chad and I—FBI."

"You work there?"

"Yes, I'm an agent. When Chad told me about all you had gone through, how committed you are, and how hard and, in fact, how ingeniously you had tried … and how it was tearing up your life, I thought maybe I could help, so I volunteered. You know, most everybody takes freedom for granted, not even realizing it when they don't have it fully. Freedom is precious, the strongest force in all of life, and forgive me, Andy, but you don't have it right now."

"I accept what you're saying, Terry, but you and Chad don't get it. Nobody does. I don't understand it myself. There's no way to communicate to anyone what this means to me. No way!"

"On the contrary, I'm convinced Chad understands. That's why he wanted to try this. He had nothing personally to gain from it, and certainly the agency wouldn't advocate it, but he was impressed with your dedication and your sincerity. I think Chad and I both have at least some inkling of what you're putting yourself through."

"You make it sound like I have a choice. See, that right there demonstrates that I can't communicate why I'm so driven." Terry nodded, and Andy smiled for the first time since the revelation began. "When we finish this round, what do you say we have dinner and forget about all this jazz."

"Right on! Andy, lay your hand on the table." When he did, she pressed her hand over his, leaned in a little, and said, "Could we meet a little while tomorrow, and if Chad's available, he can join? I really would like for the chance for us to explain some things that I think you will find helpful to know. We could meet in that park over near your apartment. Does this sound OK?"

"Sure." Terry patted his hand and leaned back, looking relieved.

"I hope your husband is OK with all this."

"Not to worry, we're not cohabiting right now. We're both hoping we'll work it all out, but for now, we're what you call—estranged."

"Terry, sincerely, I hope it does work out."

"Thanks. I'm optimistic."

When Polly returned to their table, they paid up and wished her good luck and an easy time of it for the rest of the way. At that, Polly clasped her hands and proclaimed confidently, "As a matter of fact, I'll be out of here in two weeks, well three for sure. Thanks for your good will."

Dinner was uneventful, particularly in that there were no new revelations or surprises. When they returned to the hotel, Terry remarked, "Surely by now you've figured out that I'm not really staying here, but my car is in their parking garage, so this is convenient." Then they bade good evening and wished each other a restful night.

Sunday morning was predictable. Not much going on, hardly anyone wandering around. Las Colinas was a lazy cat stretched out over the prairie floor with hardly a twitch of its head or tail. Life seemed comfortable, no evident competition going on in nature or anywhere else. It was a day that just seemed to be in a good mood. When Andy arrived at the park, Chad and Terry were already there and waved warmly to him as he approached. Somehow, whatever degree of anger Andy may have had at the sudden turn of events Saturday was gone now. He felt that these two people were human beings first and FBI agents second. They certainly deserved the benefit of the doubt, and he had convinced himself that they were sincere and really did have his interest at heart.

"We meet again," said Chad, standing and reaching to shake hands.

"Good morning, Terry," said Andy.

"Hey, Andy."

"Guess we might as well get right into it," said Chad. "You know, this is a strange thing—I guess, unprecedented. It's rare that FBI agents meet with a citizen to transact business mostly in the interest of the citizen. But, that's what we have here, and I hope, sincerely, Andy, that this turns out to be worth something to you."

"Thanks. And I thought I'd never be moved to say this, but I appreciate all that you've done, both of you, Chad and Terry."

"Good. Well, first of all, you remember we were looking for a suspect in a drug case when we first ruffled your feathers?" Chad sort of chuckled out the last few words.

"I do. I believe you indicated Lorrie Dean's mother had given incriminating testimony against him and the other guy that you caught. Right, I remember that."

"Well, guess what?" sang Terry, merrily. When Andy didn't respond, she said, "Don't you want to take a shot at it?"

"Ah—ahhh … you caught the suspect!"

"Good shot, Andy," she said. "We didn't actually catch him, but we know where he is and what he's doing. Tell him, Chad."

"OK. Well, that unfortunate bungling misfit is in a Florida prison. He's been there three weeks and five days."

"Super. Did this man find out where Lorrie Dean is living?"

"Get real, Andy. No way. There is no way anybody could know that."

"Chad, begging your pardon, but someday I'll know where she is, and someday I'll hold her hand."

At that, Terry jerked back, stretched her eyes wide, and dropped her chin, fixing Chad with a stare. "So there!" she said.

Chad chuckled and slapped his head. "Andy, you are a dreamer."

"You're telling me you positively don't know where the LeMay family is?"

"Exactly."

"OK, you say they're in the witness protection thing, so how can you protect them if you don't even know where they are?"

"The Witness Protection Program gives them the opportunity to protect themselves. We don't provide guards, but we do round up all the records and lock them away."

Terry held a hand up as if calling for a truce and explained, "Andy, we aid them in entering the program, losing their identity, and going into hiding, but all the big choices are theirs—where to go, what names to choose, how they'll connect with the community they flee to, and so on."

"OK, what else did y'all want to tell me?" Andy felt himself getting testy again, so he smiled as warmly as he knew how and pledged to himself to settle down and be congenial.

"All right," began Chad, "what we have left is to present you with three or four questions to answer to yourself. We don't want to know the answers, but we think they will guide you in coming to grips with your situation. What can you say, Terry?"

"Right," said Terry, looking straight at Andy. "If indeed by some miracle you found your Lorrie Dean, could you protect her? How could you, at that point? I mean, what steps would you take to assure her contact with you didn't jeopardize her security? Don't answer— just think about it."

Andy squirmed, nodded, and tried to think of something. Then it occurred to him that under the circumstances it was probably better for him to just listen. "OK, what else?"

"If, by some collusion with Lorrie Dean, you managed to isolate her from her family, what could the two of you do to assure the safety of her mom and dad?"

Andy looked toward Terry and remarked calmly, "Lorrie Dean is a grown woman. It's doubtful she's still living with her parents."

"True," said Chad, "but they're still a bonded family. They still have ties. Presumably they would be in touch, even visit from time to time."

"I see what you mean," conceded Andy, nodding.

"One final point. If you keep stirring around, calling attention to the question of this family's whereabouts, and turning up stuff, would that not make them more vulnerable to discovery by the wrong element? Just the fact that you're calling attention to their status, you know, keeping the whole thing hot, not letting it just vanish as it should. And suppose there's another drug runner or two out there who'd like to find this group? Again, don't answer except to yourself."

"Well, y'all, I appreciate this. Really. You've given me a lot to think about, and you were not obligated to do so. And you're right. Those are challenging, relevant questions. Thanks for your guidance. I respect it, and I agree it will be useful to me."

"Our pleasure," said Terry.

"Well, I guess that about wraps it up," said Chad.

"Guess so," began Andy, trying to collect his thoughts in a hurry. Then he smiled. "Oh, just one thing—and this is not intended to be a dig, but I was wondering, are all you, all FBI agents, comfortable with the role you play sometimes, I mean like setting up impostors, fabricating accounts of things, posing as taxi drivers, I guess outright lying. Are y'all OK with that?"

"No, we're not comfortable with those roles," said Chad, "but it's the only way we can operate. If we were completely and categorically honest all the time, we'd never catch a crook. That's the way intelligence works. Think about it, Andy. You probably have occasions where it serves your purpose to use strategies like that." Chad laughed unexpectedly, then raised a finger in the air as if to make a point. "For example, what about the story you gave me about the little incident with your Lorrie Dean in grade school?"

Before Andy could answer, Terry laughed amiably and added, "And what about it, Andy. Did you really hurt your knee on a door jamb?"

"Touché!"

At that, Chad began rubbing his chin and looking pretty serious. "You know, guys, if our bosses ever find out we capitulated to you, we'll get fired straight away."

"If they ask me, I'll lie about it," said Andy, "and I'll do so in good conscience, believing that's my role—because, well you know, I owe you one."

And so it went. The three players gallantly strutted out of the park and never looked back.

19

He sat quietly by a window.

Andy Boone had decided to take some time out and let his feelings have full sway—no reasoning, no wrestling with logic, no heavy thinking or calculating, deciphering or gaming. He wanted to see how he was feeling, to give his feelings some priority, and let something besides his brain do the talking. So he just breathed deeply for a few moments, let his shoulders relax, and then yielded to whatever would be.

Through the window, he could see far out toward the horizon. He was beginning to nod off when faintly there came into focus a band of little children playing way, way off in some faraway place. They seemed so happy as they frolicked and played in their dreamland. They looked so tiny, way out there, as though they were in another world. Now the dreamer was pleading, for he so longed to be with them, if but to hear their innocent, genuine laughter and sing whoops of delight with them—and be among consummate friends who just savor life and have no ax to grind.

Then it started to rain on the little gala, and all the children lifted their arms up toward the sky, tilted their heads back, and let the rain bathe them and tickle their faces. Now the dreamer could hear a motor growling, and all at once a yellow bus rolled into the scene. One by one, the children scampered aboard, still giggling and waving their arms merrily. As the bus pulled away, the dreamer's eyes fluttered, his head bobbed, and he heard a car clamoring out on The Lamp driveway.

He rose and wandered around his small living room for a while, round and round, his hands clasped behind his back, deep in thought. *If those are my feelings, what do they mean?* Why did a bus come along and take the happy children away before he could figure out a way to get there? Were the children simply symbols of innocence? Why were they so far away? Possibly his life was the farthest thing from such innocence. Maybe it meant his obsessive search for Lorrie Dean was wrought with selfishness, and maybe he seized on that mission only to cover his extraordinary sense of guilt.

After a while he dropped into his recliner and heaved a deep, nervous breath. He was struggling to understand his feelings of guilt, where they came from, what they meant, and what reasonably could be done about them. Andy was getting a sense that the guilt was a purely selfish disposition, that in truth it was a matter of being inconsiderate rather than sympathetic. One thought led to another but never strayed far from his perception that a sense of guilt was not so much compassion for the victim's misfortune as it was injury to the perpetrator's self-esteem.

Too bad he couldn't bounce this issue off the erudite Grandpa at the farm, or possibly even better, his little sidekick, young Kelly. She'd been through some very difficult times and made it through with a clear head. Not only that, she was the brightest little star he'd been around in many years. Truly, this needed a day at the farm. But that would have to wait. First he needed to spend some time with his mom and dad, and before he could do that, he had to get through another exciting week at the infamous Clay Cutter playgrounds.

Early Monday, Andy decided not to press his initiative with the boss, Wade Boliver. He had put the ball in his court, and he would just wait him out. And wait he did. Nothing emanated from the venerated front office. Throughout the week he mainly kept his eyes and ears tuned in, paid attention to everything that developed around him, and otherwise tried to go with the flow. At one point, an idea started brewing in his mind. By week's end, he had not exactly perfected it, but it was still there and seemed to be sprouting a little. So Andy decided he would leave it alone for now and let it ferment for a few days.

With nothing much going on, he had time to think back on his strange weekend with the dubious pair of FBI agents. As he mulled over this affair, something suddenly hit him, the ever-popular lightbulb. This was not a feeling. He had finished with that business; this was purely intellectual. It occurred to Andy that the very questions the agents tossed out for his consideration were revealing of something they clearly had not intended. The questions showed that the agents, contrary to their claims, had not completely dismissed the idea that Lorrie Dean could somehow be found. The questions they asked him to think about showed that they could see the potential for someone as dedicated as he finding this family. What else could lead them to formulate such questions? Heh heh, he giggled, *I think my dedication has them worried.*

A couple of nights during the week at Cylie Moe's easily provided the intermittent R&R he needed. After Friday's visit, he went straight to bed so he could arise early Saturday morning and head for Diboll to spend the weekend with Mom and Dad. He had already packed his ice chest with groceries and had his clothes hanging on a doorknob.

When he arrived, Mom and Dad were waiting on the front porch, and they welcomed him with hugs and genuine smiles, the kind only devoted parents can give. *And what a priceless gift they are,* thought Andy. The three of them played hard and gabbed cheerfully throughout the day. After dinner Saturday evening, Andy confessed to his parents the complete, unabridged story of his mission regarding Lorrie Dean LeMay, including the precise details of that memorable incident with this grade school classmate for whom he was searching. Mom cried and Dad patted his shoulder.

When Andy brought up the issue of guilt feelings, his mom picked up the ball. Clearly, she wanted him to quit punishing himself, a classic maternal instinct. "There's no reason for you to feel the least bit guilty," she said, very forcefully. "All kids do things. We all did something like that or worse. Plus, kids heal quickly. And stop this obsessive search for her. That's not going to do a thing for either of you. Quit it, now, Andy Woo!"

As he cruised along the highway to Dallas Sunday afternoon, Andy thought deeply and respectfully about his mother's admonition. Reflecting on her words, he could not deny the logic of them. They did make sense. They were real world. This stuck in his mind as he traveled on, and he hardly noticed it when he passed through Tillman and alongside the little school that had mercilessly thrust him into his mission. At the moment he passed the driveway to the Grimes farm, he was questioning in his mind whether maybe he should indeed call off the search for Lorrie Dean.

Really now, what would he say if he found her tomorrow? "Hi, how are you? I want to apologize for getting embarrassed twenty years ago. I'm sorry I wouldn't take your note. Did the fall hurt much? Is your face okay now? Are you okay?" *That's all I can think of to say to Lorrie Dean. Do you have anything else?* How could he justify a defiant, relentless search that would lead to such mundane comments as that?

Still, no matter how predictable and realistic that picture of the ending was, Andy knew in his heart that such an eventuality as that would not offer the conclusive resolution it seemed to reflect. First of all, he could not picture himself asking those silly questions even though their answers seemed to be all that his mission sought. Something inside him was screaming, No, that's not all of it! But what else could it be? He had no inkling of an answer to that formidable question. Andy Boone, you're crazy—smart, but crazy! He grinned at his own self-assessment. Something very mysterious was going on in his smart but crazy world.

20

The search would go on! That meant Andy would have to shift his priorities. His resolve demanded that he arrange his job involvement so that his search would become the primary focus of his life. This brought to mind the idea he had recorded in his brain the week before. If implemented, that as yet unperfected plan would create just such a division of his personal and career life.

Monday is not a good day to spring new strategies on a corporate organization, so Andy decided to wait until Tuesday. Early that morning, he called the one and only, the heel nipper, Kirk Daniels. Andy was about to send up a test balloon.

"What's up, Andy?" giggled Kirk.

Andy couldn't figure out what was funny, but he didn't let that affect his mood. "Yeah, Kirk, thanks for coming down. I think I have something that you'll be very interested in. It could change everything for you, and I mean for the better."

"Awesome, Andy. Really now?"

"This is real, Kirk. Don't prejudge it. This is a proposition that's in your own best interest. You don't want to dismiss it a priori."

"Gosh. Boy. I'm all ears. Let 'er roll."

"OK, here's a question for you, Kirk. How would you like to have my job?"

"You goin' somewhere, Andy?"

"Well, among other things, it would mean I'd be calling you boss."

"What is this? Do you think I'm a fool?"

"On the contrary, I know you to be very sharp and capable and well qualified to take this job—if you don't mind the headache of supervising others."

"Andy, I didn't just fall out of a tree! Something here ain't right. Don't be insulting. Quit talking down to me."

"I understand this is shocking and probably a little puzzling at first blush, but hear me out. You'll be glad you did."

"Well, I'm just curious enough to hear what kind of concoction you've been scheming, so fire away."

"OK. Obviously, this would require Wade's support, but if you and I went to him united on this proposal, I think he would bless it. He seems to have a lot of respect for you."

"So what are we gonna do, trade jobs?"

"That's pretty much what it amounts to. In actuality, it would require a couple of separate actions, but there's no reason why those wouldn't work. When we go to Wade, I'll have all the mechanics worked out for his consideration."

"OK, Mr. Andy, that's a nice fairytale. But, Old Sport, you have underestimated me, as you are prone to do."

"I don't underestimate you at all, Kirk. I wouldn't have you in here if this wasn't completely aboveboard."

"Please, Andy. My job doesn't require me to listen to insulting bullshit. I know you're bound to have an ulterior motive. You got snot in your nose just like everybody else."

"Well, that's obviously true, Kirk," said Andy, coolly. "Nobody can deny that, but that's a rather crude analogy, and I'm just surprised that a man of your class would stoop to such base talk as that."

"Is that all, Sport?"

"That's all."

As Kirk started for the door, Andy called out, "Don't ever say I didn't give you a chance." Kirk didn't even look around. He just marched on out. As he was leaving, Andy swatted at his forehead, disgusted with himself. *Dammit, why did I let him sucker me into that smart-ass retort that I made about his stupid snot comment? Boy, do I ever need a farm—no, not a farm, the farm. I'm sorry, Grandpa, but it is not morning right now.*

So, OK, pop goes the balloon! Before he sailed off to Cylie Moe's, Andy called the farm, and Mom answered. "Mom, I need you all. Would it be … I, ah, was wondering … please be honest with me now. I don't want to—"

"Andrew Boone, get yourself to this farm-ranch on the next bus," said Mom in her dependably indulging voice.

"Oh, Mom, thank you a hundred times. Is this Friday night all right, or would it be more convenient if I wait until Saturday?"

"No, no, Andy, Friday's great. Everybody will be excited. But there's just one thing, Andy."

"Oh sure."

"Are you listening?"

"I am indeed."

"OK, now get this—no groceries! Understand that, Andy, no groceries, OK?"

"Well OK, if you say so."

"Good, now be assured the tub full of meat you brought is greatly appreciated, and believe me, it really helped, but I just don't want you feeling obliged to bring something every time."

"OK, Mom, thanks again, and I'll do as you say." It was still early, time enough for a quick dinner and then on to Cylie Moe's.

After a very satisfactory meal at the cafeteria, Andy rushed to his favorite bar and ordered two Turkeys when Polly struggled over to his stool, smiling. She had his drinks in no time. The place was unusually busy, so she didn't have time to tarry. "Looks like this is going to be my last week," she said over her shoulder as she made her way down the counter to serve another customer.

When she returned, Andy slid off his stool, stood straight and tall, held his drink high in the air, and said, "Here's to you, Momma Polly!"

Others in the club apparently witnessed Andy's little private toast, for it was followed by a little round of applause. Then, spontaneously, others raised their glasses to their very highly respected hostess.

"See what you started, Andy?"

"Polly, dear Polly, they love you."

She smiled shyly, pressed her lips together, and nodded. Then she drifted down the bar, held both arms in the air, and said, "Thanks, gang." Everyone applauded again.

This all-out participation of club patrons fascinated Andy, and he started to think about how private he had kept himself during his visits. Clearly, most of the drinkers came there to relax, inhibit their cares, and enjoy the company of others. Most of the lounge patrons gravitated toward the back, not necessarily to be near the rest rooms but most likely to get as far away as they could from the frenzy of the world outside.

Andy picked the same barstool every time he came in. Luckily, nobody else ever attempted to claim it. It sat midway into the curved end of the bar, near the entrance but out of the way of its draft. The club had only one window, a high, narrow pane of tinted glass that overlooked Andy's spot at the bar. The soft glimmer of electric lanterns hanging from the ceiling was enchanting and gave the club a sense of seclusion and comfort. Oddly, there was no jukebox.

After a while, Polly came back to Andy, smiling broadly, and said, "I wish you well, Mr. Clay Cutter."

"And you, Polly. You're special. I wish you and yours the very best."

"Thanks. You too."

"Do they have a replacement for you yet?"

"Gosh, I don't think they have. You know, Cylie and his wife work the lounge on weekends, but I haven't heard anything about anybody coming in." Then she turned away at the beckoning of customers. Andy finished his second drink and left for The Lamp.

He had a nondescript Wednesday at Clay Cutter. After work, he dashed to the mall, picked up a yellow layette set, and had it wrapped. He stopped off at his favorite cafeteria, then spent the evening trying to relax in his apartment before bedtime. His last visit to the bar for the week came Thursday evening, when he presented Polly his present for the baby.

"Andy, you rascal," whooped Polly. She cradled the neat present to her chest and looked teary-eyed at her special guest. "Thank you, my sweet friend. You are top shelf."

"Thanks for everything, Polly. I'm going out of town for the weekend. God bless you!"

"Oh, by the way, Andy, they have now hired someone to work in my place. I'm sure you'll like her. She seems kind of quiet, like me—don't laugh, you know I really am fairly quiet compared to most barmaids. So anyway, she's pretty, and she seems sweet."

"We'll try not to be too rowdy with her," teased Andy.

When it was time, Andy and Polly parted with good-natured smiles, and very soon after he was saying his prayers at the foot of his bed. Friday at work was about as exciting as an onramp at rush hour. It didn't matter, though, because at quitting time, Andy sailed away to his favorite place on earth.

21

As Andy rounded the gradual turn in the farm driveway, he spied a sign just ahead that read:

singles club welcomes andy boone

At the front door, there was another smaller sign that read: members only. He was met by an engaging little girl, and before she had time to say anything, he looked up at her, pitifully, and said, "'Scuse me, ma'am—I was just passin' by, and I was wonderin' if y'all are takin' applications for—I mean …"

The young lady opened her mouth to speak, but Andy rattled on, "What I'm sayin' is, ahem, I'd like to apply …"

"OK, excuse me, sir …"

"Like I mean, you know, I saw the sign about that guy and …"

"Sir, OK, hold on, let—"

"You know, if I was the guy, I wouldn't—"

"All right already, now—"

"But you know, since I ain't him, I'll have to—"

"Sir, excuse me—"

"But it's not—"

"Sir, do you mind!?"

Andy looked up, feeling the unabated glee in his face, and paused for her.

"So, you want to know about the qualifications?"

"Yes, ma'am, if you could."

"OK, hold it right there. Do you have a necktie?"

Andy turned instantly and dropped full force into the nearest rocker, holding his sides and doubled over with laughter as Kelly pressed two fingers against her lips, trying, with little success, to choke her expanding smile.

All the Singles seemed genuinely glad to see Andy. Even Aunt Leah hugged him. They had waited dinner for his arrival, so without further ado, they all scooted, pell-mell, up to the big round table and bowed for Grandpa's prayer. The chatter during their meal was festive and funny with a lot of teasing. Somehow, Andy thought, Kelly looked a little down throughout the dinner, not way down, but at least a little pensive. She laughed along with the rest of them, but her voice didn't have the customary twinkle in it and she didn't join in the teasing as much as usual.

When they finished and Andy had been soundly defeated in his campaign to help with the dishes, he turned to Kelly, who was still seated at the table with him. "You OK?"

Kelly nodded and smiled and appeared to be trying to think of something to say. At that moment, Aunt Leah pulled up a chair beside her and put her arm around her. "Can I tell him, Kelly dear?"

"Sure, if you want. But really, y'all, I'm OK."

Aunt Leah looked at Andy and said, "Kelly is afraid she's hurt her boyfriend's feelings."

Nobody said anything for an awkward period of time. Finally, Kelly cleared her throat and said, "He's OK with everything, but I can tell he's disappointed, and, like Boone Woo, I don't like to hurt anybody. See, Andy, originally we had planned to take in a movie tonight, but I told him we had company coming and that the family liked for everybody to be here when company comes."

"I think I understand that, Kelly. It's a compliment to both of you."

"How do you figure that?"

"Your boyfriend's disappointment means he cares about you, and your remorse about hurting his feelings means you care about him."

"Well, we do get along pretty good. He reminds me of you a lot, but he hasn't learned how to tease. He's kind of serious."

"That's good. That way you complement each other."

"Touché, Boone Woo! Now I'm feeling better."

"Tell you what, Kelly. Call him tomorrow, just out of the blue, and tell him you miss him."

Kelly smiled instantly and gave Andy a vigorous thumbs-up. "Shall we all retire to our favorite meeting place?"

The front porch was full of Singles. The talk was mainly about the last time they had all gathered there and watched the dawning of a new day. Grandpa had been unusually quiet throughout the evening, congenial but seemingly a little depressed. Dub had also seemed to be preoccupied as he sat in his own world, shuffling through a big stack of audio CDs. Andy thought, *This must be down day on the farm, or maybe it's some kind of periodic observance I don't know about, unique to farms and ranches. In any event, a good night's sleep will probably restore everybody.*

After breakfast the next morning, they all lingered at the table a while. Later, as they started to scatter, Andy said, "Why don't we all slip on down to Kelly's Cove for a little tranquility?"

"Great," chimed in Kelly.

"You two run along on down there, and we'll join you in a little bit," said Mom.

So the two buddies set out, with Kelly lagging a couple of steps behind. Andy was looking at the sky as he started down the back porch steps and stumbled over something on the landing.

"Watch my cat," warned Kelly, matter-of-factly and way too late.

Andy glanced back over his shoulder as he regained his footing and spotted a grungy gray, raggedy, bobbed-tail, slicked-skin critter camped on the bottom step. "What's his name?" he asked as Kelly caught up to him.

"It's not a his, it's a her, and her name is Fuzz because she doesn't have any—fuzz, that is."

"Why didn't you name her Spot? She doesn't have any of them either."

Kelly shrugged. "Spot's a boy's name."

Pausing to look back at the lifeless glob on the porch step, Andy said, "On second thought, maybe you should have named her Lightning."

"Come on, Boone Woo, get serious. She works the barns. She's on her break right now."

"Works the barns?"

"Yeah, you know, catches rats and mice."

"Hmmm."

"Well, she does! She does a good job, too. Grandpa's hoping she'll eventually catch all the mother rats and we won't have any more mice at all."

"Good deal."

"No, it's not." When Andy looked curiously at her, she continued, "No, if she ate up all the rats and mice, there never would be any more. She'd be a pretty unhappy cat."

"And considerably undernourished, I guess," said Andy.

"Exactly. It amazes me how quickly you catch on, Boone Woo."

At Kelly's Cove, they both opted for the bench, sitting side by side a little apart. They alternately took deep breaths and glanced all around the cove. Andy was the first to speak. "It's so serene in here."

"It really is." murmured Kelly, "That's the whole point." They fell silent again, clearly soaking it all in. After a while, Kelly twisted around to look directly at Andy. She smiled lightly and spoke softly. "Boon Woo, now you're down."

"Come on, my Kelly, that's not what you say. You don't say to someone, 'You're down.' You're supposed to say, 'You look down.' Then you say, 'I'm so sorry, my dear Boone Woo—is there anything I can do?'"

Kelly leaned over across the space between them and whispered in his ear, "Boone Woo, pee on you."

"Good one. As a matter of fact, there's no reason I should ever feel down around here, where I'm in the most peaceful spot in the world with the finest people on earth all around me, and where I'm seated beside my little morning light—the sweetest, brightest, most adorable human I've ever known. And Kelly, just in case you don't understand that … I love you."

Kelly bounced to Andy's side and wrapped her arms around him, squeezing tight as he eagerly hugged her in return. They sat quietly for a long time, still embracing, which was a little difficult because they were seated side by side. It didn't seem to matter how awkward it might be or how much effort it required, nor did it lessen the fulfilling grace of that unexpected moment. After a while, as Kelly pulled away, tears bathing her pretty face, she spoke to her friend in a voice that was barely audible. "I love you too."

By and by, the two chance friends, devoted beyond imagination, regained their composure and babbled through a little banter about ranch life. Then Kelly's expression turned serious, and she said to her Boone Woo, "Tell me more about your little grade school incident."

"Strange you should ask. That subject is rarely off my mind. It seems so big, and on those rare occasions when I try to analyze it, the whole thing seems so irrational. But, sadly, my academic reasoning has no impact on the hold this thing has on me. By the way, I told my mom and dad about it—finally."

"Thank God. I'll be honest with you, Boone Woo, that really

worried me that you wouldn't confide in them about something so large in your life."

"You're entirely right. There's no excuse for that, none at all, and I feel guilty about it, as well I should."

"Well, you've told them now, and that's what matters."

Now Andy was thoroughly distracted from everything else and, for that matter, from every other subject. Still, he managed a genuine smile at his little buddy and asked calmly, "Did I tell you I've been searching for the girl, for Lorrie Dean?"

"Not exactly."

"Well I have. I've put forth a pretty determined effort to locate her, but at this point, I don't have a clue. Everything I've done has only led to a dead end. But I swear I'm going to rejuvenate my effort. I will not let this die!"

"Go, Boone Woo! I've never heard you talk with such resolve."

"Well, I'm going to go back over my trail and dig up more people to talk to in my hometown, anyone who might have any remote chance of knowing where she and her family went."

"I guess I understand all that—I guess, I'm not sure. I just wonder, my dear friend, what's really driving you on this."

"You know, lately I've tried to face that question myself, and honestly, I always find a way to dodge it. I never come to grips with anything other than that I want to assure myself that she's all right, and to apologize."

"You're feeling guilty."

"Yes. Now that you've used the word, I have to own up to reality. I am really overwhelmed with feelings of guilt."

"So when you find out she's OK, that will end your guilt feelings?"

"I'll still feel guilty that I did it, you know, that I hurt her one time in her life."

"But if you see she's well and flourishing and so forth, would there be any reason to feel guilty anymore?"

"What else could it be?"

"Let me ask you this. Did you two have some feelings for each other?"

"Well, yeah, of course, but we were kids."

"Love?"

"Excuse me?"

"Boone Woo, listen to me. Quit trying to evade the real issue here. Those feelings we're talking about, no matter how young you were, were real. Get it? They were not false feelings. And feelings of love, or whatever it is, can last even into adult years, even for a lifetime. Think about it—some people have married their childhood sweethearts and really made a go of it."

"Oh, my."

"Boone Woo, you're giving me the strangest look."

"My little morning light, until this instant I have not thought of that. I mean, not at all, not even a hint of it, at least not in my conscious mind—love?"

"Now, do I have acumen or what?"

They hugged again, and just as they broke up and scooted apart from each other on the bench, the rest of the Singles Club drifted in.

Three hours later, everybody was gathering for their most popular activity, lunch. As they sauntered one by one around the big table, Mom said, "Where is the Professor?"

Aunt Leah answered immediately. "I don't know where Grandpa might be right now, but the last time I saw him, he was in the henhouse giving the finger to the chickens—just standing there, shootin' the finger."

Kelly, sporting a mischievous grin, waved a finger around in the air, and said, "I think Grandpa's been drinking out of the creek again."

Ten seconds later, Grandpa strolled in, seemingly sane, grinning, and apologizing for being late. His incidental depression was clearly on the wane. During lunch, he asked Andy if he could stay over again and join them for church.

"Yes I can," replied Andy. "Thanks for asking. Honestly, I've been looking forward to that possibility." Then he nodded toward his buddy and said, "Kelly has already checked me out on the necktie question."

Kelly winked and, in a falsetto, sophisticated voice, wheezed, "Why yes, most worthy associates of the Grand Order of Singles, I have reviewed Mr. Woodson Boone's credentials, and he checks out on all points, including the delicate factor of dress, particularly the matter of a proper necktie—although, mind you, I haven't actually seen the tie."

Before she finished, everybody was applauding and watching as Andy laughed himself practically out of his chair. Then his smile faded, for it was during moments like this one that his love for this incomparable family welled up inside him, almost to the point of making this grown man cry.

In a moment, Kelly excused herself, saying, "Pardon me, everyone. I have a phone call to make." When she returned, she was grinning broadly. She paused at Andy's side and punched the air with a perky thumbs-up, and her Boone Woo returned the gesture.

Hours later on the front porch, someone asked Grandpa if he knew what the Sunday sermon was going to be about and what the scripture reference was.

"Of course," barked Grandpa. "It was in the bulletin. The sermon is on creation, and the scripture is Psalm 8."

There followed a discussion of the controversy over the source of creation, including the views and opinions of scientists, philosophers, and theologians. At some point, Andy asked Grandpa what he thought God's greatest creation was.

"Girls," insisted Grandpa without hesitation.

"OK, what do you think mankind's greatest creation is?"

"Biscuits." He paused while a little titter ran through the crowd. Then, without cracking a smile, he said, "I like girls and biscuits."

"Good choices," said Kelly. "Right, Boone Woo?"

"Right on."

* * *

Sunday was fulfilling. Church services were inspirational, lunch visitation was leisurely and friendly, and the parting moments for Andy were warm and promising. A few minutes before the ceremonial good-byes, Kelly buttonholed Andy and offered to help in his search for Lorrie Dean. "Boone Woo, can I help you in any kind of way that you can think of? I'm pretty good with the Internet."

"Kelly, you're so thoughtful, dear, precious friend. Thank you. The problem with the Internet is that there are no records to input from. They've all been confiscated and locked away somewhere. Thank you, though. I'll keep thinking about it to see if there might be some things you can do. One thing is for sure—you can help me think. You are good at that."

"OK. Well, just let me know."

As he was turning to get in his car, as everyone watched, Andy reached for his little buddy, took her gently into his arms, and hugged her. When they parted, she smiled and whispered, "There's something else I can't get off my mind. I just wonder what was in that folded note your Lorrie Dean tried to give you."

22

Something happened at Clay Cutter early Monday morning that defied the laws of nature: Mr. Daniels called politely and requested an appointment with his boss instead of just showing up unannounced. If that wasn't enough to boggle the mind and destroy all manner of theory about fundamental personality, Kirk also apologized for his "snotty" comment of the week before.

The tide is turning, thought Andy. It was entirely mystifying to see Kirk sitting somewhat away from the edge of the desk and wearing a cordial smile instead of his usual smirk. Andy returned the smile, trying his best to look equally contrite.

"Boss, I've been thinking about the deal you offered last week. Honestly, I was sure you had an ulterior motive in proposing such an unprecedented move, but then I got to thinking, so what if you do have such motives? Why should that bother me."

"Good point, Kirk, and you're right, I do have an ulterior motive. It's not a negative one for anybody, but I certainly have a selfish interest in the matter, in that I feel it would help me out of an untenable situation I've gotten myself into. I guess we always have an ulterior motive in the choices we make and the things we do. It's a matter of survival, a case of the ego doing its job."

"OK now, do I understand you are willing to give up your position as department head and take something less, such as my job—no strings attached?"

"Yes. A positive, unequivocal yes."

"So what's involved?"

"I would voluntarily relinquish my position in exchange for one not involving supervision. You could then compete for the resulting vacancy. Odds weigh heavily in your favor because of your tenure, your experience, and Wade Boliver's strong impression of your potential and capabilities."

"What if headquarters doesn't buy it?"

"Wade has advised me in no uncertain terms that headquarters doesn't work here."

"Why do you want to do this, Boss? Surely you know that all of us will think it highly irregular—you know, strange."

"No question about it. But Kirk, I'll confess to you, the strain of supervising is threatening my health. Obviously I can't afford to be unemployed, but economically speaking, I can live well with less."

"You know what? I believe you. I'll have to admit, personally, to me you seem always to be on the edge, defensive, sometimes downright insulting, as if we are a threat to you."

Andy nodded. "So, shall we give it a shot?"

"Let's go for it," replied Kirk with an uncharacteristically civil tongue. "Are you going to set up a meeting with Wade?"

"Yes, assuming he'll return my phone calls."

Kirk winked and pushed out of his chair. "Well on that point, let me know if you need some leverage."

"Gotcha." After Kirk left, Andy drew up the final plan, complete with every detail, for Wade Boliver's consideration.

✳ ✳ ✳

At the end of the day, he was so exhilarated that he wanted to run all the way to the farm and hug Kelly. He phoned his mom and dad just to let them hear their son sounding carefree and happy—for a change. He was fully aware that he had not presented them with a picture like that in the last several weeks. He didn't tell them specifically about the very promising matter he was working on, but he did let them know, if only by the sound of his voice, that a burden had lifted. He could tell his parents clearly recognized this because they sounded every bit as excited as he was.

Afterward, Andy treated himself to pizza at Campisi's and then headed straight for one of his favorite sanctuaries, Cylie Moe's— second only to Kelly's Cove. Happily, his barstool was in place, unoccupied, and apparently waiting just for him.

Only seconds after he sat down, he glanced up, saw his server on her way, and then did a quick double-take. In all his excitement, he had forgotten that Polly had left the premises to have her baby. At once, the new girl was standing squarely in front of him. She smiled when he looked up, and so did he. "Hello," she said, "I'm Kimberly. May I get you a drink?"

Andy nodded, momentarily forgetting that he needed to open his mouth and speak real words to this polite lady so she would have some idea what drink he wanted. He had unconsciously neglected this point while he was absorbing the presence of this extraordinarily good-looking, perfectly composed young lady. She, on the other hand, seemed unruffled by the situation and waited patiently for Andy to regain his senses. Suddenly, he did. "Oh, yeah, I'm sorry. I just wasn't thinking. Forgive me, I don't know where my mind is today."

"Oh, that's all right. No one should feel rushed when they're ordering a drink." She smiled again, sweetly, and as before, Andy smiled back.

"Oh, by the way, Kimberly, I'm Andy—Andy Boone, actually." Why am I so nervous? This has been a wonderful day and everything is going right. I just don't get me. "And ah, I'd like a Wild Turkey and Coke highball, thank you, thank you very much."

"Very good," she said and walked away.

Andy watched as Kimberly eased along the bar to get his drink and again as she returned. Every step she took was perfectly measured, like a model. She just seemed to glide along, holding her head straight and letting her natural poise do the communicating. *Anyone with that much composure doesn't have to talk a lot*, thought Andy. As she served his drink, she smiled again. "There you are. Anything else right now?"

Andy shook his head and then once again realized he needed to speak to this gracious lady. "Oh, no, not right now. This is great—thanks again."

While Andy tried hard to get into some ardent drinking, somehow his mind kept going back to this new barmaid's unusual countenance. *Polly was right*, he thought, *she is pretty and quiet.* She appeared so resolute, yet her easy smiles seemed to say that she was genuinely happy to be sharing a piece of the world with those around her. She was the epitome of neatness, average in height, and just on the plus side of slender, and all the features of her pretty, winsome face were in perfect harmony. Her tailored, midnight-blue dress traced the contours of her shapely figure without exaggerating anything, and it was a perfect companion to the short, black hair that just brushed the tops of her shoulders and drew attention to a tidy row of slightly curled bangs above one eye.

Soon Andy began to settle down and was savoring his Turkey and Coke. He knew his nervousness was fading because he had quit fidgeting with his highball glass and was just peering into it. And with that, he began reliving his unusually satisfying day and letting those peaceful thoughts take him wherever they would. As he gazed hypnotically into the rapidly disappearing liquid tranquilizer, he was gently aroused by softly spoken words.

"Would you like another, Andy?"

A few minutes after she delivered his second drink, Andy caught himself frowning. Why? He didn't know why. He just seemed to be immersed in some kind of mystery. He couldn't figure out what was different about this evening compared to all the others, except, of course, for the new barmaid. That certainly was not something that should upset his mental equilibrium. If anything, that incidental change was more fascinating than anything else, certainly not mysterious. In any event, he decided to shake that pestering diversion, dismiss his curiosity about himself, and get back to the business of drinking.

Just as he took the last sip of his second drink, Kimberly was there, smiling. Her timing was remarkable. This time he didn't wait for her to speak. He smiled resolutely and said, "I'll have one more, Kimberly."

"Very well," she said, and she was gone.

When he was done drinking for the evening, Andy paid up, tipped generously, and strolled out of the club, frowning and shaking his head and trying to think.

* * *

You picked a fine time to leave the field, Wade Boliver. Andy learned Tuesday afternoon that his boss had taken a three-day "hiatus," as his secretary called it. Word was that he'd be back on Friday, but his plate would be so full, he would be busy with so-called high-priority items. Damn!

So Andy muddled through the day, reading job sheets and company statistics, and spending a little while with Paige Ivy. In that brief visit with her, she proved to be the truest friend anyone could ever hope to have. As they talked candidly, she confronted Andy with some pretty hard-hitting observations about himself. While such frankness invariably has a sting to it, in this case, it was clear to Andy that his friend was being honest and trying to be helpful. After all, what are friends for? It started when Andy confided in Paige concerning his failed quick-touchdown play.

"I really had confidence I could pull it off, Paige. The first couple of weeks, everyone affected by the program innovations seemed enthused about them. I mean, they seemed to be really into it. Then it all started to sour. I don't understand."

"Andy, we're friends, right?"

"We are indeed."

"I want you to know I have the highest regard for you, both professionally and as a person."

"As I have for you, Paige, and here's a little secret it's probably OK to reveal to you. When I'm thinking about you from time to time, in my thoughts I call you my company hero."

"Thanks, Andy. I'm honored." There was a brief pause, and then Paige took a deep breath and spoke firmly to her associate and friend. "Andy I want to tell you what I think about your ever-loving innovations, if I may refer to them that way."

"Let it roll. I'm all ears."

"Before I do, I want you to understand that I'm doing this in order to contribute to your life and for no other reason. You don't know it, but one time you contributed to mine in a way that has lifted my confidence and the professional regard I have for myself. I'll never forget the first time you said to me, 'Paige, you've got a good point.' Andy, that was the one and only time a man at Clay Cutter ever said that kind of thing to me. And another time, after we had talked about the subjects of specialization and generalization, when you left this office I could tell that you were going to adopt something in your operation that I had suggested—and, in fact, you did."

"Oh, yeah, I remember that. Hey, and it's working too."

Paige Ivy smiled and took another deep breath. "OK, here we go. Andy, my friend, you are not a politician. Oh, I'm fully aware of the popular rank-and-file belief that holds it is degrading to concede to whatever is politically correct. Hogwash! You can get ahead without doing and saying politically correct things, but you reach a point where, in order to get further ahead—and if you're really smart—

you'll practice a little politics. And if you can't bring yourself to do that, fine, be happy where you are, and that's perfectly all right. Andy, you're at that point now. You're at that plateau. It's going to take something more than brains, skill, and creativity to get you to that next level or even to get you on a good footing where you are." She paused, apparently to let it soak in and maybe even let him express a little understandable anger if needed.

"Paige, I think I need this. What can I say? You've got my full attention."

"The point is—well, OK, you are an artist, an extraordinary one, by far the most imaginative artisan I've ever known, personally. But you are not a politician. You're not a good organization man. Really. Let's face it."

"But—"

"You took that spectacular path from trainee to department head based on skill, diligence, and brains. But from here on, and especially in this particular environment, it's going to take something else."

"You know, you're right. Now that I'm forced to confront my own behavior, I'm aware that I've handled Kirk Daniels all wrong. I mean, I'm sure that's just one example. But I have enjoyed putting Kirk in his place intellectually, to get the better of him in his crudest moments. I've unwittingly allowed Kirk to force me into a contest over his personality and self-styled conquest. So even though I always trump with some brilliant comment or move, that very situation proves he keeps me on the defensive."

"I think you're probably right, there, Andy. I'm just glad it's not me trying to figure out how to relate to Mr. Daniels. Anyway, your innovations were very creative and seemed to have the potential to work. But really, Andy, you don't have a market for them around here. Please, Andy, the market comes first and the innovations second. You can't just sit around dreaming up better ways to do things, even if they would revolutionize the company's competitive leverage. I'm not saying this is the right way for things to be, but the fact is they are that way, and if you're smart, you'll fit into them. And after you do, then you'll find ways to improve them."

She paused, fixed Andy with her gaze, and rested her chin on one fist as if to indicate she was finished with her lecture. They looked at each other for a few moments, and then Andy started nodding. He kept it up, finally settling on something to say. "Paige, you got me on that one."

"I wasn't trying to get you. I just wanted to be both a colleague and a friend, simply because I like you, I respect you, and you have helped my self-esteem immensely."

"I have the same regard for you, and believe me, I take to heart all you've said. I absolutely cannot argue against any of it." Then he took a deep breath and added, "I can assure you that I will go back and do some earnest soul searching. Thank you—thank you."

When they both sensed that they needed to get back to their duties, Paige followed Andy to the door. As he reached for the knob, she said, "Well, I guess, Andy, I guess I pretty much let you have the full load."

Andy turned to face her and took her shoulders gently in his hands, "My very dear friend, my company hero, I love you for it, and I owe you big time."

At the end of the day, he decided to have dinner at his cafeteria, stay in his apartment, perfect his Baytown search plan, and go to bed early.

* * *

For the rest of the week, Andy mulled over the very forthright counsel of Paige Ivy and began in earnest to study the unwritten policies of his employer. His pending rotation plan with Kirk Daniels already had him conceding the death of his existing innovations and any he might propose in the foreseeable future.

He made it to Cylie Moe's only one more time that week, Thursday evening after dinner. The second he saw Kimberly, his new barmaid, he felt a little catch in his throat, maybe even a tiny flutter of his heart. "What is this?" he asked himself aloud under his breath. Before he could deal with that question, she was there. It was amazing that she traversed that distance so fast without appearing to hurry.

"Turkey and Coke, Andy?"

"Sure, Kimberly. Thanks for remembering. How's your day going?"

"Oh fine, just fine, thank you." She started to step away, then hesitated, glanced back at Andy, and said, "And how was your day?"

"Pretty good."

Kimberly smiled, nodded, and resumed her course. She returned shortly with the drink and, using both hands, eased it down in front of him, like putting a little baby kitten to bed. They peered thoughtfully at each other and for a moment, it looked as if Kimberly would tarry there for a bit, but suddenly a call from down the counter stole her attention and she left.

Cylie Moe's was unusually busy, and the tall, lank, grumpy-looking guy who served the tables seemed to be getting somewhat frustrated. He was having trouble pleasing four rowdy young men who were talking and laughing loudly and slapping the table after every supposedly clever quip. They seemed to labor at the task of convincing themselves they were having a good time and had not a care in the world. This had been going on since Andy arrived, and there appeared to be no end in sight.

As Andy was finishing his second drink, he pondered whether to cut himself off and head for the rack. The unabated noise from the rowdy table was getting pretty nerve-racking. When he saw Kimberly, he relented and ordered a third drink. At about that same moment, the four rowdy rascals wobbled out of the club, still reveling. When they were gone, the sight of Kimberly flowing along the bar recaptured Andy's attention.

Midway through his third and last drink, Kimberly came to stand in front of Andy and, looking very serious, asked, "Is something wrong, Andy?"

"Oh, not at all, Kimberly. Everything's fine."

"Good. I noticed you were shaking your head, and I thought maybe there was a problem with your drink or something."

"Oh, no, not at all. I was just ... well, do you have a second? I'd like to explain the head-shaking thing."

"Sure."

"I know that shaking your head usually indicates disapproval—but it can also mean the opposite. Know what I mean?"

Kimberly nodded. "I think so. Yes, I think I know what you mean. Sometimes we're just touched."

"Right. Impressed or fascinated. So it just seems natural that our heads rock gently as we take it in, like maybe when you hear a pretty strain of music."

"I understand. I bet you were remembering pretty music in your head when I noticed."

Andy squirmed a little on his stool and raked his hand along the bar rail, cleared his throat—twice—and opened his mouth to speak. "Ah, Kimberly, at the time you noticed, I was ... honestly, I was marveling at your presence."

"Presence?"

"Yes, the grace of you, your poise, your bearing. Putting it bluntly, Kimberly, you're all class, and I guess I was just instinctively shaking my head because I was impressed."

Kimberly looked into his eyes as he explained. She placed a hand over her lips and started shaking her own head, caught herself, snickered, and said, "I see what you mean about natural head-shaking."

They laughed, then, turning to answer a call, Kimberly rested her hand for a second on the counter in front of Andy and said, "Thanks."

As she drifted away, Andy began talking to himself, "I can't believe we two devoted introverts actually had a conversation that long." Then he chuckled and hoisted his drink playfully and indulged in a whopping big gulp.

Then Kimberly was back, her graceful, endearing smile lighting her pretty face. "Andy, I just want to say that was a very sweet compliment. Really, I'm touched by it, and thank you so much." As she finished, her eyes were glistening and her expression was softly thoughtful.

"It's all true," said Andy. "I guess I would never have said anything about it if you hadn't caught me."

They laughed together, and that was Thursday evening.

23

The trip to Baytown stank! So did Monday at Clay Cutter. However, there was one bright spot: namely, Andy and Kirk were united in their expectations. Both were getting restless waiting for Wade Boliver to return their calls. Certainly, each of them had a personal, self-serving interest in the matter, which, remarkably, each of them acknowledged and accepted. With nothing much else to do, Andy took the time to reflect upon Paige Ivy's frank counsel of the week before. As he thought realistically about it, he discovered that he pretty much agreed with her in every respect. And for sure, he sorely needed the tough good will she had offered. He needed it—critically needed it—and Paige Ivy recognized that. Only a bona fide friend would make the effort to do what she did. He wasn't absolutely certain he was ready to subscribe to her notion of market before innovation as a general, infallible rule, but he conceded that, given his specific situation, that needed to be the order.

The timing of Paige's advice was amazing, coming when, hopefully, Andy was about to meet with his boss, the eminent director of Human Resources, to pursue a delicate proposal. He certainly needed to play it right this time or forever after forget it. So he began to think in terms of being politic with Wade Boliver, thinking of the kinds of things to say that would be politically correct. With that thought process, it was at once clear to Andy what his boss wanted him to do: be subservient, don't argue, don't try to be smarter than he, and agree with him on things that don't really matter, such as anything that doesn't relate to the proposal Andy was bringing for his approval.

Then there was morning—well, almost. The long-awaited tripartite hearing did get underway. So far, so good. They were all in Wade Boliver's office, the three master gamesters, each wearing a politically correct smile. Let the games begin!

"OK," began Wade enthusiastically, "who wants to go first?"

Kirk pointed toward Andy at the same time Andy was raising his hand. "OK, Andy, take it away," said Wade.

"All right, thanks," began Andy. "I have a proposal that I offer in good faith, and that I believe will be productive for all three of us. The plan is detailed in the paper I left with your secretary last Friday. In a nutshell, I am willing to acknowledge that my efforts to make a positive impact and thereby serve your expectations have suffered because I was determined to be of value quickly. However, in my zeal to do that, I have not used my skills in a way you have a right to expect of a supervisor. I have not created the harmony we all need, because I have unwittingly concentrated on innovations instead of supervision. In addition to not serving you well and not giving Kirk the support he has every right to expect, I have let the stress of this tenuous situation threaten my well-being. So, simply stated, I propose that, in effect, Kirk and I trade jobs, according to the mechanics outlined in my written plan."

Wade turned to Kirk, nodded, and said, "What do you think?"

"I'm in favor of it," said Kirk, dryly. "I felt I was a strong candidate for the director job before Andy got it. And, obviously, I have been frustrated and actually disheartened by that development. So in that regard, I probably haven't felt a strong enough obligation to give Andy the support he needed in his job as supervisor."

"OK, you two. Here's what I think. The idea is reasonable, and the plan is workable. I understand where you two are coming from, and certainly, Kirk, there's no question as to your basis. Clearly you have the greatest stake in this, and there's absolutely no doubt that you would be selected in the competition. But Andy, your motivation baffles me. Surely you can understand that."

"You're entirely right, sir. I grant you that, but I'm willing to risk that this might be misinterpreted. I think the prospect for harmony in the organization is worth the price."

"All right, you guys. I buy the idea and am ready to lend it my support with some adjustment in the plan." Wade Boliver shifted in his chair and looked only at Andy, making it clear by that gesture that he was about to place the full weight of the matter squarely with him. "Boone, I will adopt your proposal with one change. Namely, I will accept your request for a nonsupervisory position, but not Kirk's job. I would not approve of your dropping only one level to the senior officer level."

Andy raised in his chair. "Well, sir, that is not my—"

"Hold on. Hear me out. The whole point is I will go along with this basic concept here, but I will not ignore the careers and aspirations of your three junior-level officers who've been sitting there for years without an opportunity for promotion. No, I want them to have an opportunity to compete for the position Kirk will leave vacant."

"Boss, I genuinely respect your thinking there, and I think it is responsible of you to consider those other variables. However, I'm stunned by the idea of going down two whole levels in pay status. Honestly, I just don't believe it's in my interest to accept those conditions."

"OK, so be it. Think it over for a couple of days and get back to me."

"I can pretty well give you my answer now."

"Boone, look at me. Think. It. Over! While you're thinking, keep in mind that you have raised the question of your competence to perform in your present position. You did that yourself. No one else has brought forth this issue."

"Clearly," said Andy, confidently. "But I have not filed a signed written request for another assignment. So it's all hypothetical until I do."

"Get real, Boone. Your signed, written plan is tantamount to a formal request."

"Sir, I only signed a transmittal slip for a set of procedures for carrying out any such proposition that would affect an employee seeking alternate placement. Note the plan itself is written in the third person."

"Come on, Boone, let's not let this collapse into a case of strategies and counterstrategies. Really, now, give me some credit here. These are not generic papers you have filed with me. They are the work of your hands, and by virtue of your stated purpose in this meeting today, you've established that they apply to you personally. And, finally and most importantly, you have confessed that you are doubtful you can carry out supervisory duties."

"OK. As you said, let me think it over."

"As you do, keep this central point in mind. By raising doubt about yourself, you have given me cause to question your placement and take appropriate corrective action. Let's face it—that would be the only responsible action for me to take."

"Sure, but boy, what a process that would be."

"Yeah, well, like I say, think it over. Let me know your decision by Friday."

On that note, the three stood and prepared to leave. Andy was struck by Kirk Daniels's ability to keep quiet during the debate. By doing that, he'd played his best card. He had to give the guy credit.

Back at his desk, Andy was still thinking. It occurred to him that Wade Boliver's failure to categorically implement his own idea in this matter meant he had some reservations as to his authority to remove Andy from his position. Otherwise, why give him time to think? With that in mind, Andy decided he would let the time pass, and for that matter, he would deliberately miss the Friday deadline.

Hopefully, this strategy would lead Boliver to speculate that Andy may have an ace in the hole. With that uncertainty, perhaps he would sweeten his counter proposal a bit. He was also counting on Kirk to put some pressure on Boliver. After all, the old man owed him a little hush perk now and then. Andy was prepared to make his adversaries think while he was thinking. His strategy was to keep a poker face and know when to hold and when to fold.

Friday came, and Andy took no steps to respond to his boss's counteroffer. He was, of course, a bit nervous—OK, scared—over the matter. He may very well think of himself as a master strategist in corporate matters, but he was, after all, a human being.

* * *

As he moved onto his stool at Cylie Moe's, Andy glanced down the bar—and there she was. Kimberly was in motion toward him and then stopped short and made the sign of a T with her hands, poised gracefully in the air, leaning a little toward him like a ballerina about to go into a twirl—or whatever. Andy gave her an instant thumbs-up, and she did indeed twirl away and glide toward the drink station.

When she returned and placed his drink before him, she tilted her head with a curious twinkle in her eye and said, "Andy, I think you look a little down. You don't have to tell me, but I do care how you're feeling."

"Kimberly, your sentiment has already lifted the mood of my day. Believe me, it's worth plowing through a few dismal days to get into your presence. Thank you for that comment, and yes, your observation is very perceptive. The fact is, I just had a disappointing weekend going back to my hometown. Sorry it shows—it shouldn't be your problem. In any event, it's good to be where you are."

"Disappointing?"

"Yeah, since last April I've been trying to find someone who's missing from my hometown. I've done a lot of things trying to trace her, but everything leads to a dead end. It's all so mysterious. There are no records, and no one knows anything about it. It utterly amazes me that neighbors in Baytown don't really know anything about each other these days. Of course, that's true everywhere nowadays. I was already gone from there when she and her family moved away. But be assured, I will never quit trying to find her."

"She's important to you?"

"Very. When we were in the fifth grade, we sort of flirted around, and I guess it was tacitly understood that we were sweethearts. I know positively that I had feelings for her, or I wouldn't care so much now. But, anyway, I did something cruel to her one day at recess, and I can't get over it. Kimberly, please, I just want to find her, see if she's OK, be good to her, find out if she needs anything, hold her hand, and tell her I'm sorry. Dammit, why can't I find her?

"Oh my goodness, Kimberly, I'm sorry. What am I doing? Why in the world should I burden you? You didn't ask for all this. But you, with your typical grace, have stood there listening while I rattled on, looking very serious about it. Thanks, dear friend."

"Know this, Andy, that is no burden on me. On the contrary, I recognize it as something very personal to you and I'm honored that you trust me enough to share it with me. Oops, sorry, Hank is motioning for me—gotta run. We'll talk more."

Kimberly had his next drink in front of him precisely at the right moment. *How does she do these things? Does she have me timed out?*

"Honestly, Andy, I can't picture you doing anything cruel, even as a little boy."

"Well I did. We were at recess, and my little friend passed a folded note to me, and I wouldn't take it—or rather, I shoved it back at her when I discovered two teachers were watching."

"That's not all that bad, we … you were just kids then."

"Well, something else happened in the course of it that I caused, but I don't want to talk about that."

"And you sure don't have to. But Andy, I don't want you to be down on yourself like this." They smiled at each other, knowingly, and Kimberly was away.

A few minutes later as business began to dwindle, Andy looked down the bar and saw Kimberly strolling toward him.

"I see your drink is still holding out."

"Yeah, I don't like to rush it. If I did, I might wind up drinking too much and get drunk."

"My guess is you're the type who, if they ever did get drunk, would give away the ranch."

Andy chuckled. "I think you pretty well have me pegged, Kimberly." Neither said more. There was really nothing to follow up on in this little conversation, and these two souls felt neither the temptation nor the obligation to just fill the air with talk. Their budding friendship was not built on it, and it did not depend on it. Finally, Andy was moved to ask Kimberly about herself. "Kimberly, have you always lived in Dallas?"

She shook her head, looking determined. "No, in fact, I've never lived here. I'm only here for the summer."

That unexpected revelation, for some reason, came as a shocking disappointment to Andy. It probably showed, because although his mouth was open in readiness to speak, nothing came out of it. Finally, he said, "I see."

That was all he could muster for another few moments while he continued trying to reckon with this profound moment. Predictably, his innately patient, unpretentious friend let him have his time, never once either urging him for more or interrupting his thoughts with questions or saying anything at all. She just stood still, composed, looking at him kindly. Suddenly, Andy was back. "Kimberly, I have to tell you that comes as a huge disappointment to me."

"Oh?

"Yes, you're rare, Kimberly. Is that OK? May I just say that and leave it there?"

"If you want."

"Thanks. Oh, I was wondering … what, uh, what days do you get off around here, if ever?"

"Sunday. That's it. I could use another, but they need me six."

"Guess you're pretty busy on that one day."

"Not really. I do laundry and other maintenance duties before I come on every day. See, I don't start till three thirty. On Sundays, I go to church."

"Where?"

"First Methodist in Irving."

"I guess I'm ready for my third shot, you know, my limit."

"Right away."

Andy finished his drink as the lounge got really busy, and that was it for Friday.

24

Nothing much happened at Clay Cutter Monday. To Andy's disappointment, there was no word from his boss concerning his momentous proposal. So goes another day, thought Andy as he wrapped up the day's work early and stopped in to pay his respects to Paige Ivy and thank her for being a very special friend. He described to her the meeting with Kirk and Wade and indicated he had followed her advice, and that he tried to act more like a politician. She looked genuinely thrilled when he said to her, "And it worked, Paige. Thank you a million times."

After work, Andy felt discouraged and was not motivated to do anything, not even go to Cylie Moe's. He so wanted to get on with finding Lorrie Dean, which now loomed as the single most important thing in his life. So he watched TV, but paid no attention to it, and went to bed early.

Then it happened Tuesday morning! Wade Boliver called him directly and very cheerfully invited him to meet in his office as soon as was convenient. He indicated Kirk was already there.

"Come in, Andy, and pull up a sandbag, as we used to say in the Army," said Wade, chuckling awkwardly.

"Thanks, boss."

"Well, I didn't hear from you last Friday, so I figured you were still thinking."

"I was. I still needed a little more time to work out some things in my mind."

"Oh, no problem, no problem at all. Anyway, I've kept thinking too, and I have something I think you'll like. Here's what I'm willing to do. If you will accept an assignment to a junior position right there in your own shop, the company will grant you saved pay for two years from the date of the placement. That means you will retain your present salary for two years."

Andy's response was instant. "Mr. Boliver, that's a deal. I accept, with no reservations."

"Then it's done!"

Andy was absolutely euphoric as he left work that day, mumbling to himself, "Clay Cutter, from this moment forward, you are on the back burner. Lorrie Dean, take the front."

Kimberly must have seen it in his eyes when she brought his drink that same evening, for the first words out of her mouth were, "Boy, do I feel better about the way you look today."

"Gosh, it really shows, I guess. It's true, I had a very good day, and something happened that is going to relieve me of certain hindrances in my search."

"Oh." She studied him for a moment. "Will that take you out of town often?"

"It may very well. I'm not giving up on Baytown yet. There has to be a stone that I haven't turned—someone they did business with, a feed store, veterinarian, a barber shop, the laundry, a mailman, a schoolteacher—you know, somebody, something."

"Sure."

"First, I want to make a trip this weekend to visit my very dear farm friends and let them know about this turning point. See, they know the basic things about it that I told you. They'll be glad, especially my little girlfriend there."

"Girlfriend?"

"Yeah, I have a little banter pal there. I guess she could be my daughter, and if so, I would be exceedingly proud of her. Anyway, they're all like best friends to me, and we get together every couple of weeks or so. They're so very good to me. Don't ask me why."

"Oh, I know why."

"You do?"

"Sure. I'll just repeat to you something you said to me one day. You're very rare."

"Hey, I'll buy rare. I like rare."

They laughed together, and then business began to pick up, which was good if you accept that it was good to see the four rowdy men back at their table. Oh well, that's business. Andy continued to nurse his Turkey, and Kimberly got very busy. Now the four uninhibited loudmouths were getting really repulsive. Other customers were frowning and cringing and looking uneasy about the invasion of their happy hour. Hank, their server, frowned too, but apparently it was too much for him to handle.

Then something very unexpected happened. Kimberly walked to the point along the counter nearest the rowdy table. She held her hand about shoulder high and said, ever so calmly, to the men, "Guys?" There was no change. They didn't even look at her. Then she said, again in a perfectly calm but determined tone, "Guys—hey guys?" They paused to listen, and she said to them, "Hold it down a little!" Then she turned away.

And the men? They settled down.

Andy? He was grinning proudly and shaking his head.

So went the evening, and two days later Andy was back. While he was on his first drink, the rumble of a thunderstorm and spatter of loud rain caught everybody's attention. After about a half hour, it subsided and soon afterward apparently had moved on. When Kimberly came with his second drink, she stroked her brow and said, "That's a relief. My windshield wipers quit working the other day. I should have already taken care of that." She turned to walk away.

"Kimberly, please, can you hold just a second? You say you don't have windshield wipers?"

"Right, but the storm seems to have passed on through."

"What time do you get off?"

"Usually around twelve thirty."

After his usual three-drink pattern, Andy headed for The Lamp, feeling uneasy, and went to bed. But he couldn't sleep. Later he heard the rain sweeping around his window and lay on his back, staring into the dark like a hoot owl. The rain continued to crash down, harder and harder.

Now Andy was out of bed and getting dressed. It was eleven forty-five.

When he walked into Cylie Moe's, he stood in front of the bar between two empty stools. There were only three customers left. Kimberly came up to him, smiled nervously and asked, "Did you come back to get drunk, Andy?"

"I want to drive you home. You just can't get out there without windshield wipers."

"I'll be all right. You have to go to work in the morning. You need to sleep."

"I won't sleep a wink knowing you're out there in danger."

After a long pause, Kimberly sighed and said, "Well, OK."

"Good. I'll just sit at one of the tables till you get off."

"Want something to drink?"

"Maybe a glass of water."

When she brought his water, Kimberly said it looked as though she would get out early. She did, and they left together, with Kimberly holding the extra umbrella her devoted customer had brought along for her.

As they drove through the rain to Kimberly's apartment, they were mostly silent. These two didn't need to talk a lot in order to communicate. The silence said respect. Love? At one point, Andy said, "I'll pick you up in the morning and we'll take your car to the garage and get the wipers fixed. You can take my car and do whatever you need, and I'll wait with yours. When it's done, I'll drive it to your apartment or job, depending on the time, and we'll trade cars."

"Andy, you have to work."

"No problem. I have flexible hours. I'll explain that some time. Remind me."

"You sure?"

"Yes, dear friend, I'm positive."

Soon they were at Kimberly's place. Andy escorted her to the door and told her to keep the umbrella for tomorrow. Then she took his hand, squeezed it, looked deep into his eyes and said, "Thanks." They bade goodnight, and it was done.

The car plan came off like clockwork the next morning, and they were able to trade cars by two PM. When it was done, there seemed to be nothing to say beyond what they already knew about how each other felt. They stood facing one another in silence, and finally said, "Thanks," and "You're welcome."

Early Saturday morning, Andy took off for the farm, his little respite island of enduring friendship. At the door, he was met by the dependable little charmer, his morning light, who opened the door only a crack, and peeping around the edge of it said, "Yes?"

"Right," said Andy in an artificially contrite tone, as he held up a cup that he had just whirled around from behind his back. "I was wondering if I could borrow a cup of sugar. I just live down the way here."

"Well, I'll have to get someone higher up to approve that. I don't recognize you, and I know most everybody from, as you say, down the way. So, what is your name?"

"Andrew Woodson Boone, affectionately—I hope affectionately—referred to as Boone Woo. Here's my driver's license. When you go to get approval, will you tell them I can drive?"

On that one, Kelly could no longer hold a straight face. She laughed heartily and said, "Your score! Now get your butt in here, Boone Woo!"

Everybody was a babble of good cheer, teasing, and fun for Andy's two days with this remarkable family of friends. Sunday morning, Andy, in full dress, tie and coat, accompanied them to church. Later he broke the good news about the pleasant turn of events in his job situation and the renewed freedom to resume his search for Lorrie Dean.

Before he left, Andy spent some private time chatting with Dub. Then the whole family retreated to Kelly's Cove and visited peacefully with subdued, reflective conversation, some of which was about Kelly's boyfriend and the promising trend in their relationship.

Everything went well, and Andy returned to Las Colinas early Sunday evening.

25

Something was amiss. Andy seemed off course in trying to get himself ready to sail off to Cylie Moe's. He couldn't figure out why he was panting and why he was struggling just to get his pants on—one leg at a time. He made several passes at each leg, stumbling around, stepping on the cuffs while trying to yank them up, and just all around having a tough time of it. He finally danced his way into them and headed for the door. He stumbled as he was fumbling his way through it, a sequence that is normally instinctive, that this man, though still young, had negotiated flawlessly for more than twenty-five years. When he got to the parking lot, he dropped his car keys—twice—then as he steered away from his apartment, he uttered some unintelligible things to himself, finally mumbling, "Hope I can find my way there."

At the club, Andy fidgeted his way to the bar stool. When finally he was safely docked there, he pounded the counter with a fist and said under his breath, "I gotta do this!" Then he stiffened his back and got himself ready, just as Kimberly approached. Before she could open her mouth, he blurted, "May I take you to church Sunday?"

Without hesitation, Kimberly accepted, in the only way this lady did anything, graciously. "Yes, Andy, I'd like that. Thank you, dear." She lingered there for a bit, leaned close to him, beaming, and whispered, "I'll get your Turkey."

It was pretty quiet in Cylie Moe's. What few customers there were seemed to be pacing themselves so that there were wide gaps in demands for service. Now Kimberly stood before her pending date, lifting a curious eye. "Tell me, Andy, what is your missing schoolmate's name?"

"I don't think I'm supposed to reveal that, because, you know ... well, OK, I understand that the family may be sort of in hiding. That's another challenge I face. I have to try to find them without anyone knowing when, where, or how I do it. Guess that sounds like a lot of double talk."

"I must say, it is strange, kind of ... what would you say, confounding?" She giggled, recovered quickly, and said, "But that's fine. Don't tell me any more, and don't worry about it that you can't. I understand."

"You know, Kimberly, you're all class."

"Thanks. Do you have a picture of her?"

"No, I don't. I haven't even seen a picture of her since she was eighteen. I did see her picture in the high school yearbook for her graduating class. That was last April on my second visit to Baytown."

"So you have a good idea of what she probably looks like now."

"Well, darn it, I don't. I'm not that intuitive or something. I mean, I don't think I have the perception or vision or whatever it takes to age someone in my mind's eye. I probably wouldn't recognize her if I saw her on the street."

"Bet you would. Tell me about her picture."

"First of all, she was just plain pretty, and she was a little shy, pretty reserved. Kimberly, this little doll seemed so serious for her age, but when she smiled, you wanted to bow to her. Know what? It's that same way with you. Anyway, when she was solemn, which she was most of the time, her face was the picture of a winsome little girl.

Then when she smiled, it was aglow, and her beautiful dark eyes just swept you into her graces. And she was so sweet and adorable, and oh, she had perfect posture. Now that I've said all that, I guess that's basically my memory rather than the picture."

"Well, the picture probably sharpened your memory."

"Right. Exactly. That's it. The picture brought her into focus for me. Let's see, what else do I remember from it?" Andy was looked into Kimberly's attentive face as he talked. "The picture showed she had shoulder-length, dark black hair and deep dark brown eyes, and she had soft, very feminine features. Every feature was in the right proportion—her ears, her nose and mouth, and those full, perfectly formed lips, and her face was sort of rounded ..." Suddenly, Andy stopped talking, unable to go on. As he studied the face of the extraordinary lady listening patiently before him, he saw her lips move but could barely hear what she was saying. He felt in a trance. He jostled his head vigorously a couple of times and then heard Kimberly talking.

"It seems you really cared about her."

"Who wouldn't?"

After Kimberly left to fix some drinks, Andy sighed and glanced all around, trying to make sure he was still there. Just testing. Then his mind leapt ahead to the coming Sunday when he would actually sit beside the chance acquaintance who had so charmed him since their first, low-key, bashful meeting.

* * *

Andy picked up his date at her apartment late Sunday morning, and they headed for eleven o'clock worship services at First Methodist. They talked church the whole way, and it felt pleasant and right. Inside, they took seats near the front, perused the program, and book-marked the hymns that were announced in it.

Speaking of hymns, something unexpected happened, something

neither of them had even thought about. While they were singing the first hymn in their normal quiet voices, Kimberly glanced at Andy and smiled, a sort of note of approval. Andy returned the gesture, then without skipping a beat, Kimberly dropped her voice to the alto part and the two sang in harmony. Clearly, it wasn't your ordinary, standard mechanical blending of voices. Andy felt it, and he could tell that Kimberly did also. There was something special about their particular voices in harmony that caught the attention of people nearby, and they turned to smile at the young couple and nod approval. After they were seated, Andy felt the friendly taps on his shoulder of people behind him, and he saw them acknowledge Kimberly in the same way. As things settling down, she reached to Andy, smiled, and squeezed his hand, sending through him an indescribable feeling. There were times when their shoulders brushed as they stood up or reached for a hymnal or moved around, and each time it sent a cozy little tingle chasing through Andy's body.

Near the end of the services, Andy and Kimberly again harmonized as the congregation sang "Bless Be The Tie That Binds." Afterward, the people around them complimented their singing and urged them to join the choir. Later, at Sunday lunch, Andy and Kimberly talked about their singing and agreed that, although neither had intended for any such thing to occur, it had been a lot of fun.

The following Sunday they went back to church and enjoyed the inspiration of the services and again marveled at their own singing. Then they decided to spend the rest of the day together. Between lunch and dinner, at Andy's suggestion, they drove around in the country for a while, down some quaint old roads. It all went well, and it felt good. At one point, Kimberly suggested they sing a little while they poked along the country roads. The first song she picked out was "My Bonnie Lies Over the Ocean." They really lived it up on that one, bouncing with the rhythm and singing right out like young school kids. Clearly they were having a big time. As they rode along, Andy was suddenly startled by Kimberly's voice.

"Andy, why such a puzzled look? What's up?"

"Oh, I didn't realize it showed. What I was thinking about was … Well, what made you pick out 'My Bonnie Lies Over the Ocean'?"

"Nothing special. I remember we sang it a lot in grade school. Everybody liked to sing it. I guess. I don't know—it's just a song that sticks in my mind from the early years. We sang it a lot."

"Hmm. So did we."

They had an early dinner after their relaxing country drive and then decided to call it a day. At Kimberly's apartment door, they mumbled a few sweet words to each other, hugged, and said goodnight. It was just your basic, regulation hug. It was clear to Andy that they both were being careful, unpretentious, and making a point to show respect for each other. In his car, he leaned into the steering wheel for a few moments before taking off. He thought, *Oh, but how, someday, I'd like to embrace that precious girl and just let the passion and magic surge.*

During the following week, Andy was at the club most every evening, but he felt something brewing inside that was making him nervous, maybe outright scared, as though he was worrying about some impending disappointment. Kimberly apparently could see it in his countenance because when he came in Friday, she asked him point blank, "Andy, what's wrong, sweetheart? What's going on?"

"Kimberly, please forgive me for being terse—but my dear, dear friend, this is it!"

"This is it. What does that mean, this is it?"

"I hope I can get through this, Kimberly, but I have to do it—I just have to do it." Kimberly raised her eyes as if to say, "Go on."

"I'm just not going to treat you this way any longer. I'm being a total selfish jerk."

"Whatever are you talking about, Andy Boone?"

"Falling in love with you, that's what." Kimberly gasped, and Andy jumped ahead, "Yes, yes, maybe you can tell, or maybe you haven't picked up on it yet, but I am rapidly falling in love with you.

And you see, I simply can't do that to you when I'm so fully given to finding a certain other girl to see if I can love her." He stopped there to let Kimberly respond. After a moment, he said, "Why are you smiling?"

"What would you have me say? What would you have me do?"

"Yeah, you're right. I see your point. There's nothing to say when …"

"I didn't mean that in a cavalier way. Sure, it hurts, but you know, I'm a big girl." Andy nodded, and Kimberly, looking ill at ease for the very first time since he had met her, said meekly, "I guess it wouldn't hurt, except that I …"

She didn't seem to want to finish, and Andy didn't ask her to.

26

What have you got for an encore, Andy Boone? This was the all-consuming thought in Andy's mind as he sat brooding by his window. In one shattering moment, he had reduced his life to one overriding question: Now what? This was the essence of him. As perplexing as it was, this spell left him with barely enough clarity in his thinking to recognize that he had to see Kimberly—and see her soon. He literally ached to see her. He couldn't shake it. Strange thing, in times like these the corporate mind-set has no power. "How many times in my life is God going to permit me to be a fool?"

He was the first customer at Cylie Moe's the next afternoon. When he walked in, Kimberly looked toward him and smiled. Then he moved to the bar to stand beside his stool and waited for Kimberly, who was already in motion toward him.

"Hi, Andy."

"Kimberly, I don't want to be a bother to you." She shook her head, and Andy continued, "I'm sorry, I hate to do this in here, but … well, it just can't wait." He managed a thoroughly awkward grin, so stupid, in fact, that he could feel the shame of it stretching his lips. So he tossed his head about a couple of times, trying to shake the disgust out of it. Kimberly, meanwhile, waited patiently. Andy resolved to remain standing. If this grand lady had to stand, he was going to stand with her. In any event, they both allowed a few moments for him to regain his composure. Then he sighed, looked squarely at Kimberly, and exclaimed, "OK here it is—I'm calling off the search!"

"Andy?"

"Yes, It's over."

Kimberly swayed backward, stiffened her neck, and glared at him in disbelief. She remained speechless.

Andy left it there for a moment, and Kimberly's countenance softened as the two stood perfectly still, letting the silence speak for itself. Then Andy went on. "I don't expect you to say anything, and I don't expect anything from you. But you had to know!"

"Andy, right now I don't think I can say anything. I'm shocked and not at all in control of my feelings."

"That's OK—that's OK, perfectly understandable. All I ask is that you let me come around you. This is big for me, and I just want to be near you as much as you'll put up with. I want a chance to try to win your heart."

"I'm sorry you're going through this, Andy."

He nodded and, as the two held each other's gaze, Andy lifted his eyes to a place above Kimberly's left shoulder as he spoke very softly, plaintively. "I'm sorry, Lorrie Dean, my sweet, wherever you are. May God forever bless you!"

"Lorrie Dean?"

"Yes, but we can't say her name very much, not where people can hear."

"Andy, would you like to sit down?"

"Sure. Bring me a big one. I think I'll get drunk." They giggled, and Kimberly whirled away.

Though he still felt in the grips of physical strain, Andy had a sense of mental peace that hadn't been with him since that rainy day in April when he passed the little schoolyard in Tillman. Contrary to his earlier comment, which he made in jest, he had no intention of getting drunk.

Now the place was getting busy, but Kimberly continued to drop by from time to time to check on his drink, even though her knowledge of his past drinking patterns should have told her he wouldn't be ready at those particular intervals. Still, she kept coming to him frequently, and he liked that. There was just one thing that bothered him about it. Whenever she came around, she was biting her lower lip, although lightly.

Finally, it was time for his second drink, and Kimberly was right there ready to serve. She was sweet to him, but her normally radiant smile was looking a little strained. Andy loved this fine lady, and he wasn't about to make her uncomfortable by asking questions. Everybody is entitled to their moments and their moods.

When he was about half through his third drink, Kimberly said, "Before you go tonight, I have something for you, so if I'm not right here when you're ready, don't leave without it. Wait for me."

"Oh, sure. I won't dare leave without you're knowing it."

A while later, Kimberly returned, and after she determined that Andy would be finished for the night, she said, "I'll get what I have for you now. Be right back."

She was not exactly right back. In fact, it seemed a while before she strolled up to him. When she stood before him, she smiled, and this time, she seemed more relaxed, more Kimberly. Then, methodically she slid a small folded paper underneath his fingers as they rested on the counter. Then she pressed her hand gently over his and held them there. "Andy, my boy, this is a folded note, obviously, but please don't look at it in here. Would you just slip it in your pocket and leave it there until you get to your apartment? Then you can read it whenever you want. In fact, since it's near your bedtime, you may want to wait until tomorrow."

"All right, my dear Kimberly, I'll do as you say."

27

onight or tomorrow? That is the question. With that quandary in his head, Andy reflected back to the counsel of the farm's erudite "professor," Grandpa. According to him, the spirit of morning is wherever you need it to be and when you want it. So tonight can be morning, thought Andy. Yet it troubled him that the note's message might keep him awake through the night, so he decided to wait until the morning.

The next day, he went to work with the unopened note still in his pocket. At his desk, he tried to anticipate what the note possibly could say. Kimberly had made such an extraordinary point of it and staged it with such unusual ritual that surely it must contain life-changing instructions. He reached in his pocket, felt it, and left it there. He decided to let the flow of office routine neutralize his situation until break time.

In the course of his morning activity, Andy heard the good news of Kirk's promotion to his own former position, so he took a few minutes to drop by and congratulate him. To his disappointment, Kirk Daniels was back to being his usual sarcastic, smart-ass self. Bad things never change.

At mid-morning, Andy sat alone in the company cafeteria,

savoring the aroma of hazelnut-flavored coffee, his hand touching the note still in his pocket. Then he sighed, nodded to himself, and brought out the note. He stared at it a moment, then gently unfolded it, turned it right side up, and read: Andy will you sit by me in music class?

* * *

At Cylie Moe's, Andy walked quickly to his spot along the counter. As before, he would remain standing. He would stand in tribute to this fine woman, who was now walking slowly to him—elegantly, proudly, bashfully. Now she was before him, looking directly at him, her lips lightly pursed, a tear in the corner of each eye. She dropped her arms down by her sides, leveled her head, and looked at him as if to say, "OK, I'm ready."

Andy felt his own tears as he leaned in as far as he could toward this woman he called Kimberly. Then he looked humbly into her knowing eyes and whispered, "Lorrie Dean?"

When she nodded, he reached across the counter for her hands, and she gave them freely. As he squeezed them gently, he took her in, absorbing the essence of this lady fully into his heart and soul. Solemnly he said, "I love you with all my heart, whoever you are."

"I love you too." They held on and quietly cried it out together. After a while, they released their hands and Lorrie Dean said, "Andy, there are some things I have to tell you. It'll take a little while, because they're, ah, well, a bit complicated. When do you want to do it?"

"Shall I join you in your apartment tomorrow morning, say, after we have breakfast together?"

"Good, yes, that sounds great."

Andy looked all around the lounge and chuckled. "Wow! Notice how quiet it is in here?"

"It sure is. Shall we take a bow?"

"We could. Hope they know we weren't acting."

"Really. Hmm, I seemed to have forgotten my watch today. Andy, dear, what time is it?"

Andy just smiled mischievously and said, "It is morning."

"Smarty," chortled Lorrie Dean as she turned to answer a call.

After she left, Andy scanned the club and said to himself, "OK, drink up, folks!"

* * *

At breakfast, Andy and Lorrie Dean merrily chatted about their grade school days, naming their teachers, trying to remember classmates, and reminiscing about that great time in their lives twenty years before.

"Your note said it all," remarked Andy. "Is that what the real note said?"

"Yes. You could have saved us a lot of time if you had accepted it then, you rascal."

"Yeah, guess you're right. In all my speculation about the note, it never occurred to me that it would relate to music class. As I remember we only had music two or three times a week."

"It was two, Tuesdays and Fridays, and remember, we always had to leave our regular classroom and go to another room, sometimes that little auditorium? And it was always right after recess."

"You're right. It all comes back to me now." Suddenly Andy stopped eating. He leaned over to examine the right side of Lorrie Dean's face. His voice cracked when he asked her about the lacerations.

"Oh, Andy, it really was nothing. A couple of tiny little cuts. You know, any time you get the slightest cut on your face or head, it bleeds profusely. But it was nothing, and honestly, I don't remember any serious pain."

"Praise God!"

"Amen! Well, I guess we might as well push on. We've got a lot to talk about."

Andy was impressed by Lorrie Dean's apartment. Even though it was a prefurnished unit, it clearly reflected her touch—the arrangement of things and the simplicity of decorations. The small sitting room with painted walls and ceiling reminded Andy of his own rooms at The Lamp, except this one had the feel of feminine pride and good taste. There was only one plush chair, tan, and a small matching couch. As they walked in, Lorrie Dean motioned Andy to the chair, then she took the couch. She was the first to speak. "Not exactly a luxury suite, but it works."

"It's the same as I have. As you say, it's all we need."

Lorrie Dean held her hands in her lap and stared at them for a moment, then took a deep breath and said diffidently, "Where to begin?"

"Yeah, that would be a tough question for me. You probably have already guessed this, but I can't help wondering why you waited so long to tell me you're Lorrie Dean."

"No, Andy. Don't you see? You had to find me. I could have told you the first day you came in the club, but you needed to find me."

"I see."

"Well, the FBI guy, what's his name—Clyde, ah …"

"Chad."

"Chad. Right, well he thought I should tell you right away and, as he put it, get you out of your misery. But Andy, I didn't think that would give you a sense of fulfillment. I was afraid you would always feel you fell short on your part."

"You know, that's true. I probably would have felt let down with myself, that I hadn't put enough into it."

"Well, I was honored when I found out you were looking for me, and I confess my heart did palpitate a little at the thought of it."

"Had you thought about me any in all those years?"

"In the years immediately after grade school, I would think about you in brief moments. I mean, at first, right after the recess incident, I thought about you a lot. I wondered what made you act that way.

I couldn't figure it out, because I thought you liked me, as we kids used to say. Then later, as time passed, I really didn't think of you or anybody else from our school years. So, you know, I hadn't been thinking about you, but I remembered you the instant that Chad guy mentioned it. By the way, he was really taken by your resolve and sincerity and the nobleness of your efforts. He said he'd never seen anyone in all his life so committed to a cause as you, to the point where he felt he just had to help you."

"I guess that sort of brings us up to now," said Andy.

"Yeah, in a really fast-track way. I know it skips a lot." She sighed and continued, "But here we are—and Andy, my dear, beautiful, sweet man, where we are is very complicated, and that's what we have to talk about."

"I understand, sweetheart. I won't interrupt anymore."

"Oh, I don't mean you have to just sit there and listen and say nothing. Please, do say frankly the things that come to your mind."

"All right."

"First, I understand you already know we're living fictitiously under the Witness Protection Program."

"Yes. In fact, I've been pretty well briefed on that and what it entails."

"Frankly, Andy, I'd just about as soon serve a prison term and get it over with. It has a very, very high price. Your life doesn't just change artificially. You die!" She began to cry and fought it as she struggled to talk. "Oh my, how I'd love to be Lorrie Dean LeMay again, and know you, and know all my friends from the past, and know my aunts and uncles and cousins." Now she was sobbing heavily and stammering.

Andy came over to sit beside her on the couch. He put his arms around her and nestled her gently to his side. "My dear wonder girl, just rest for a while. Don't feel you have to finish this in any particular time. There's no deadline here. I'll be beside you for as long as you want."

Lorrie Dean raised her head to look at him, her sad face awash with tears. Then she nodded and sniffled a few times, managing a little conciliatory smile, and murmured, "Thanks."

"Want me to get you some water?" asked Andy. I know I haven't been checked out on your kitchen, but I bet I can figure it out."

"Yes," she said, visibly distressed. "Glasses are on the second shelf, cabinet to the left."

Andy brought a glass of water for each of them, and as he sat down, he said, "I admire how you're handling this, Lorrie Dean. I don't know how I would ever deal with losing my freedom like that."

"You hit square on the point—freedom!"

"So can't you just come out from it?"

"Possibly you can walk away, but you'll still have to be somebody else, some dumb alias, and you still can't lead your regular life."

"I see, so you really can't come out?"

"Not at all. They have warned us with heavy word never to surface, and they told examples of a few who tried it and met with tragedy."

"I hear you. I see where you're coming from."

Lorrie Dean stared blankly across the room. "But I wonder how many have come out and made it OK. Personally, I'm willing to gamble, but I have my mom and dad to consider. I can't afford to jeopardize them."

"OK, could I come in?"

"Oh, Andy, you're not understanding at all!" She threw her hands up at him, then doubled over and buried her face in them and bawled, her trim body shaking violently. After a few moments, she straightened and began rocking and slapping her knees. "You're just not getting it. You're not." Still gasping for breath, she tried to gain control, and in a while, she did. Then she looked up at Andy as tears streamed down her face and into her trembling mouth. "Oh, Andy, my Andy, I'm so sorry. Can you forgive me? You didn't deserve that. Oh, oh, oh, I'm so sorry."

Andy was at her side before she finished the last "sorry," wrapping her in his arms and snuggling their heads together. When finally they eased apart, he said, "Lorrie Dean, you of all people in the world don't have to be sorry for anything. I love you, and I understand."

"Thanks, Andy. Thanks for everything. And by the way, the answer to your question about joining me in hiding is no. I would never, ever let you come into this kind of jeopardy ... never, never, Andy.... But, let me go on, ah, with this ... there's just a little more I need to bring out about this—this whole thing."

"Take your time," said Andy as they turned to face each other. "And just know that it's all going to be OK."

"No, it's not going to be OK, not at all. My time is about up here, and ... soon I'll be going back to my prison, back into living in isolation, if you will. That's no life for two lovers like us. As I said, I will not have you live in that kind of misery."

"But—"

"Wait. I'm so very honored that you wanted to find me. I love you for that, and I love you because you are my connection with the freedom I once had." With a little snicker, she said, "I wish we could be kids again, little innocent, naive people sitting in that cramped, hot, scrubby little fifth-grade classroom."

Andy tried to laugh with her, sad as he was, "That's a beautiful dream. We had it all and didn't know it. Who could have predicted that twenty years later we'd be sitting here like this, anguishing over our love for each other."

"How true. That's kind of what I wanted to tell you. I guess, mainly, that we can't go on together. It is not to be."

"That seems so blunt, so final. I'm trying to understand it. I think I'd rather still be searching for you, anticipating that day when I would find you. I know that's selfish of me, but I love you more than I could ever express to anybody—including myself. I guess my love for you means I have to understand and accept the situation—for your sake. And, Lorrie Dean, I do want whatever is best for you. But I pray that some day, you'll be free. I want that just for you."

At that, Lorrie Dean took his hand, and as Andy looked into her pretty face he went on with some things he felt he had to get out. His thoughts were just what they were—how he felt. "So I won't miss the search, but I'll miss the humble thrill of hearing you say in your kind, enduring voice, Hi, Andy, and watching you turn away so gracefully to fetch my Turkey. I'll miss just marveling at your style, your class, seeing you hush a table of rowdy campers, watching you smile at people as if you're really glad they're in your world, just seeing you flow along the counter, admiring your every step. Feeling the faint touch of your arm beside me in church, hearing your pretty voice singing into mine, seeing your eyes lift up to me, and shivering at that gentle sensation of falling in love with you. I will always look back and say, These were the days. Then, when—"

"Andy, please!"

"You're right. My word! What am I doing? I'm sorry, I was just feeling sorry for myself."

"Sadly, it almost worked."

"I wasn't trying to work something. But I must confess I was being very, very selfish. Please forgive me."

"Sure, but there's nothing to forgive, sweetheart. I'm going through the same things."

Andy heaved a big, deep breath and began to lament. "I guess I've sort of lived my life in dreams and fantasies. But Lorrie Dean, this is real!"

"For me too."

"There's one request I would have of you."

"OK."

"Will you go to the farm with me Sunday? We can leave early and spend the entire day there. I want you and these dear friends to meet each other. And, my Lorrie Dean, I want them to see what you are, to be comforted, like me, to know the world has people in it like you."

"I'll go. I want to go. But Andy, do you understand this situation, all that I've been saying? Do you understand this is what has to be? I abhor hiding myself, being denied the right to be me. I don't want to be Kimberly Malveaux. I want to be Lorrie Dean LeMay."

"Sweetheart! I fell in love with Kimberly Malveaux."

28

Two solemn lovers were mostly quiet as they cruised toward Andy's farm, only now and then breaking the melancholy silence with a subdued remark about the day or the countryside. Their backseat was filled with fruits and vegetables, a gesture that Lorrie Dean noted was admirable of her escort. Andy had pointed out that he had chosen things they didn't raise on the farm, which was devoted mostly to soy beans, melons, sweet potatoes, peas, and grain crops. So he was bringing squash, green beans, Irish potatoes, strawberries, and tomatoes. He was under no orders this time not to bring groceries—only because Mom hadn't had a chance to get to him.

It was a pretty decent day. Truthfully, in the eyes of an impartial observer, it would be regarded as an absolutely wonderful day. But nothing seemed remotely cheerful on this day for these two denied lovers, caught by a cruel villain bent on demolishing their world. But the day itself was clear, cool, restful-looking, the kind of day you could see all the way through. It seemed so tranquil out across the fields and meadows. The day was everything it could be, a sweet song, a peaceful melody—for those who are free. *How inconsiderate,* thought Andy. *How dare the day try to be perfect?* How could it be so glorious under such heartbreaking conditions? It was as if the world was taunting them, thumbing its nose at them. *Damn the day! Oh, my, oh God, please forgive me—I didn't meant it.* In that moment, the two travelers glanced at each other and nodded as though each knew they were thinking about the same thing.

When they turned up the driveway to the farm, they looked at each other and smiled, still wordless. Now the air was raked with the smell of pine sap, and somehow the sight of the great house with its special magic stirred them out of their doldrums.

"Wow!" said Lorrie Dean. "What a grand home!"

"It is indeed." said Andy. "Everything around here is grand, including the people who live and work here. I fully expect we'll be met by Kelly, my little girl, my morning light, as I call her. If she's true to form, she'll lure us into a precious little game of role playing, her special brand of teasing. On the other hand, she could be more reserved out of respect for someone she hasn't met. Guess we'll see. Here we are."

Predictably, Andy's morning light opened the door wide and looked straight at Lorrie Dean. "Hello, ma'am. It's so good of you to drop by, but do I see you found a stray along the way?"

Lorrie Dean looked at Andy meekly and then confidently raised her chin to Kelly and said, "Ma'am, it's hard to get transportation these days, so, you know, you take pretty much whatever you can get for a chauffeur."

Kelly clapped her hands and doubled over with unbridled laughter. When she brought herself under control, she thrust a thumbs-up into the air and sang out, "Good one, Lorrie Dean. So how do I know you're Lorrie Dean? Well, from Boone Woo's captivating descriptions, you just couldn't be anyone else."

Lorrie Dean, now smiling broadly, bowed and said, "And the same I can say of you, Kelly. And thanks, you make me feel so welcome by being yourself, which my old stray here staunchly admires."

"Well, do please come on in, you and your, er, gentleman friend, assuming you can get him awake."

The mood had changed completely. Andy and Lorrie Dean winked at each other and walked into a different world. Whatever kind of day it was outside no longer mattered—they were under a new spell. As they trailed along behind their hostess, Andy flailed the air with his arms and mumbled gibberish at Kelly, saying, "You never laughed like that at my good ones. I feel so insulted, like, you never ever doubled over for me."

Kelly looked wide-eyed at Lorrie Dean and said, "Bless his heart."

Everybody hugged Lorrie Dean, and then the hearty welcome spilled over into a din of chattering and laughter. Mom was in her element and simply having fun, although she did have to scold Andy good-naturedly for bringing groceries. Aunt Leah tried to monopolize Lorrie Dean but Grandpa wouldn't let her. Dub seemed a little bashful but genuinely thrilled by their new friend. Kelly sat stoically yet smiled at everything and didn't try to interfere too much with the others clamoring for Lorrie Dean's attention. Andy was sure that Kelly was patiently plotting her own time with their guest. Andy's two girls made eye contact often, and it seemed natural and sincere. It was somehow evident that these two were going to hit it off well.

After church and a scrumptious lunch, Andy and his two girls headed for Kelly's Cove while the others promised to join them later. Lorrie Dean was obviously taken with the wonder of the cove. She walked casually around the interior of it, graceful as always, pausing often to look up into the limbs of each tree and then bending low to see through the dense underbrush. Clearly, she was fascinated and was feeling the peace of it. Andy took his trusty stump chair as Lorrie Dean strolled over to sit with Kelly on the bench. They turned to face each other. Then they smiled and squeezed each other's hands. Yes, it was clear they were going to be buddies before the day was out.

Andy was shaking his head. Momentarily he heard Lorrie Dean whisper to Kelly, "I'm sure you know what it means when he grins and shakes his head like that."

"Uh, like he's sittin' on a cocklebur?"

"Close enough."

"Yeah, I know what it means when the rascal acts like that—it means he loves you."

Then Andy chimed in, "I guess this is basically a two-way conversation. I mean, that's OK. I'll just play like I'm one of the trees here."

"You don't qualify," said Kelly, and at once Lorrie Dean high-fived her.

The two girls rattled on while Andy's mind drifted back to the dilemma he and his sweetheart were in. He hated himself for that because this was supposed to be a respite trip. So he punched his way out of that dread and decided to simply listen to the girls pleasantly visiting with each other. At one point, Kelly tucked her head low and chortled over to him, "Just jump in any time, Boone Woo. That is, if you have anything important to say—which, that'll be the day."

Andy waved to her, and she turned back to Lorrie Dean. In a while, he heard the girls talking about the ranch part of the acreage. When Kelly tilted her head and looked at him, trying to appear puzzled, Andy picked that up as his cue, or permission, and said, "I would join in on that but I don't know anything about cows."

"Not a lot to know," said Kelly. She paused, and the girls looked goggle-eyed at each other and then turned to look at Andy as if expecting a little more from him. When he only grinned, Lorrie Dean said to Kelly, "Well, I imagine you get along with cows all right, don't you, Kelly?"

"Sure," said Kelly. "I like cows."

"That's nice of you," chimed in Andy.

"Wey yuhl. Thank you so much for that tremendous support, Boone Woo."

"So, I mean, if you like them, that's proof enough for me that they're OK."

"Oh my, what a vote of confidence for the cows. But you know, I feel sorry for them. They don't have anything to do. They just wander around and graze, and chew—"

"And moo," said Lorrie Dean, nodding.

"Right, and moo," said Kelly.

"Well, I just want both of you to know," said Andy, "that in all my thirty-two years, I've never hurt a cow, not one, not one single cow have I ever harmed."

Kelly ignored him and said to Lorrie Dean, "Do you see what I have to put up with when he's around?"

"You have my sympathy."

After a while, Andy excused himself and said he was going to mosey down to the fields and look around while his girls talked. Just outside the cove, on the pathway and presumably out of earshot, he heard Lorrie Dean say, "… yeah, and he calls you his morning light."

✶ ✶ ✶

When Andy returned from his cursory review of the fields, his girls were still deep into girl talk, so he sauntered around at the edge of the woods opposite the cove. After a while, he peeped in on his girls, seeking permission to leave them. "Will it be OK with y'all if I mosey back up to the house? I want to visit with Dub and Grandpa if I can catch them there." He was met instantly with resounding approval.

Happily, Dub was rocking on the front porch, and not long after Andy got there, Grandpa showed up. Andy considered Dub the best male friend he'd ever had, chiefly because the man was constant, unpretentious, and fiercely loyal to the people in his life.

"You know what, Dub?" said Andy. "This porch is the place! This is were life happens. I perfectly understand why you come out here at night and listen to music."

"Agreed. Also, I like to sit out here when it's rainin'. I guess …

well, I don't know of anything as relaxin' and reassurin' as to be under a porch roof in the rain."

"You are right, my boy," said Grandpa. "This is security—which is the reason we are all here on this farm." With that, he turned toward Andy. "You see what it is all about out here, don't you? I can tell you do." When Andy nodded, Grandpa said, "This land we are sittin' on here is not something any of us individually has great rapture for, but it is a tangible thing that we can share, a part of our common bond."

"Right, Grandpa," said Dub, leaning forward to gaze out across the porch. "This is where you can touch reality, where you can reckon with things. I mean, I sit out here at night and listen to classical music and pine for Kelly's early life because it seemed nobody anywhere wanted her. And I pine for this whole severed family, because each has lost something, yet we cling to this forsaken plot of land."

Andy nodded that he understood. "I don't think it's only the land holding you all together. I think it's you, all of you, your spunk, and I salute you all."

"Yeah," interjected Grandpa, "and I guess it is OK, the pain each of us had. It is the contrast of pain and triumph that moves life. Sometimes I think it is not love that makes the world turn, but rather pain."

"I think I'm agreein' with you, Grandpa," said Dub. "You know, it seems every piece of really good music has its sad part, its happy part, and its triumphant part. I think we're that way here—we have sad times and times of great joy." Dub chuckled at that point, saying, "I guess we're still waiting for the triumphant part."

"Every day is a triumph," sang out Grandpa.

"Guess so," said Dub. "On the really bright side, Andy, as I think I mentioned to you before, you've been a big boost to Kelly's life. God bless you! And I think your influence has helped her and her boyfriend sort of polish their relationship."

"Well, Dub, I care for Kelly and I want her in my life for as long as I live."

As the three candid, gentle friends fell silent, two young women bounded onto the porch. "OK, wake up, everybody," whooped Kelly.

Lorrie Dean drifted over to Andy's rocker, leaned down, placed a hand on his shoulder, and held her face to his for a moment. Then she found a rocker for herself and eased into it, gazing out across the meadows. Now it was Kelly's turn to indulge Andy. She came over to him, leaned real close to his ear, and whispered, "That's quite a lady you have there."

By and by, Andy and Lorrie Dean were to leave, and that turned out to be a little harder than anyone anticipated. The whole family was scattered out across the yard between the porch and Andy's car. The good-byes had become routine because they all knew they would gather again. Still, something was in the air this time.

For Kelly and Lorrie Dean, it was a little poignant. They departed teary-eyed and were still waving to each other as Andy pulled away. In a few moments, as Andy turned onto the highway, Lorrie Dean patted his knee and said, "That's quite a little lady you have back there."

"Amazing! That's absolutely amazing. Kelly came to me on the porch and whispered that exact same thing about you."

"I've known her less than a day, but I already know I'm going to miss her. When someone like her enters your life, you know you've stumbled onto a treasure. Actually, we'll miss each other." Now she was quietly crying. She looked at Andy and sobbed, "But she'll still have you."

Through his own tears, Andy said, "How ironic. Just think. My communion with that blessed family back there all started when I crashed into their fence—thinking about you."

They looked at each other in amazement and fell silent again. After a while, Lorrie Dean said, "I'm glad we made this little journey. It was precious. And I got to see a new side of you, Boone Woo, the playful side. Always before, you've been so serious."

With a cheerful smile, Andy said, "And I got to see a whole new social dimension in you, Lorrie Dean."

"All in all, I guess we needed this."

"Yes, indeed. Thanks for coming along."

Now Lorrie Dean raised a finger to her chin and held it there. Andy waited. Then she glanced at him and asked, "If Kelly is your morning light, what am I?"

"My symphony." And they said no more until they arrived at Lorrie Dean's apartment.

At the door, Andy asked, "May I step inside for a moment?"

"Sure."

As he closed the door, Andy said, "I didn't want to be a spectacle at your front door, but I do want to hold you for a moment."

"Yes, Andy," she said, and stepped forward. Slowly, ever so slowly, she tipped her head back to look at him, her eyes pleading meekly, surrendering.

Andy squeezed her shoulders, rocked her gently, and then stopped and gazed at her face. He tried to imagine how it was possible for anyone to be so beautiful, so unassuming and gracious, and so resolute in her own self-image. He pondered how much gold it would take, what kind of sacrifices he could make to buy her freedom—and his. Now he was beginning to sway, and as he did he reached around her soft body and curled her fully into his arms. They kissed and they squeezed, and they nestled their heads together, and they held on for an eternity.

The two resigned lovers were, for the moment, oblivious to all else. Andy felt as though he was standing at the end of a pier that had wandered far out over the waters—just himself, the sky, the sea, and his soul mate. He wanted to sail away and ride the wind with her in his arms, just calmly holding her without a care. Suddenly, he was conscious of the warmth of her body overtaking his own. All at once, he felt the surge of raw passion completely take him over. He was enveloped in it, rapidly losing self-control. Then the tides of sexual desire were washing over him, soaking into his will. He wanted this woman, this living jewel, more than life itself. He wanted to take her wholly into himself, to pet her and kiss her and caress her everywhere.

Andy so longed to give in, to toss everything, to have Lorrie Dean, to absorb the profound feminine essence of her. Trembling, he fought, and the frenzy marched on. Finally, the stubborn power of pure love began to give him a hand, and then all at once, within the frenzy of his sexual passion for Lorrie Dean, Andy felt the throbbing of deep, steadfast caring for this, the girl in his heart, the sweetheart of his dreams.

29

M oments to remember. That's what they would try to build into their lives in the short time they had left together— little accents they could store away for a song in their hearts. The two steadfast lovers set about to spend all the time they could together: quiet time in church, dining out at cafeterias and West End restaurants, morning strolls in the park, meandering down country roads in the Cutlass, singing their "Bonnie" song, Saturday matinees, forcing laughter at so-called funny movies, pizza to go, morning TV and music in Andy's apartment, pancakes and an occasional bed at Lorrie Dean's, and reliving old times at Cylie Moe's, holding drinks to only three because this was no time to get silly.

Andy continued to give Clay Cutter a responsible day's work and to patronize his new boss, Kirk Daniels, who, in his own butthead way, tried to return the favor. As far as giving anything extraordinary or creative to his job, Andy couldn't care less anymore. His strength had always been in his imagination. But of late, he saw it as his weakness. In his work, his creative talent had been both his triumph and his downfall.

He called Mildred in Baytown to let her know he had found Lorrie Dean. She sounded genuinely pleased and congratulated him on ending his search. When he asked about Mildred's little buddy, she said Jenny was a live wire and doing well in school and everything else. His mom and dad also seemed excited that he had, as they put it, "Found closure in his life."

By mutual agreement, Andy and Lorrie Dean never talked about their imminent separation, and they tried deliberately to avoid subjects that might remind them of that eventuality. And their love grew and mellowed: there was no stopping it. Their bond was forever, and it was natural and genuine and clean, and that was one thing they could smile about.

Through the weekdays, Andy camped at Cylie Moe's in the late afternoons. He drank his Turkey as if nothing had changed, and he continued to grin and shake his head at the grace and sheer presence of his lady. He found both comfort and sadness in the sensation that she was no less an angel than ever. She was Kimberly Malveaux, and she was Lorrie Dean LeMay, and she was just one dream. Her classic "Hi, Andy" was one of those spine-tingling moments he would always remember.

Then one afternoon, he walked into Cylie Moe's and she was gone. This was prearranged. They had agreed that this would be the way they would separate. They would spare themselves the unbearable anguish of having to say good-bye, of walking away and then looking back for as long as they could hold each other in sight.

Andy wept at the bar, and the new server seemed anxious to console him. But she was discrete about it, and mercifully, she didn't press the matter. The world held nothing that had any power to console him. Now he questioned in his mind whether they had chosen the right way to part. Is it remotely possible that facing each other in their customary loving way and saying good-bye could be any more staggering than this was? He felt a calling to get sot drunk, to drown himself in his Turkey. Then he thought of Lorrie Dean, who would be sorely disappointed in him for such a reaction. He owed her more than that. He felt he owed her everything. He still had to be her man. He would always have her near him, and he had the consolation of knowing he would be able to close his eyes and let the girl of his dreams, his little symphony, ease his pain. He had one more drink and left.

Andy struggled with a dilemma about when to call his friends at the farm. He didn't feel strong enough to do it just yet, but on the other hand, he owed them the courtesy of timely news. Still, he had no idea how he was going to do it. What exactly would he say? But ultimately, all that jazz didn't matter; they were his friends. He knew that Kelly would be disappointed, but her character was solid enough that this would be one time she would withhold the teasing and banter. So he flexed his muscles and called. Mom answered, and he broke the news at once. Then he asked to be excused from talking to the others until he could gain some composure.

From that point on, it was a matter of methodically transacting each day and each night, carrying out the rudiments of living. He avoided Cylie Moe's and every other self-indulgence except sleeping, eating, and tending to his assigned duties at Clay Cutter. Then on a Friday evening at the end of a notably routine week, the phone rang as he was coming in from the cafeteria. He was so surprised to hear the voice on the other end that he fell into his chair, gasping, and almost dropped the phone. It was his morning light, pleading urgently.

"Please, Boone Woo, please, please, please, can you come here at once, right now, tonight? Please, Boone Woo."

"Sweetheart, I'll be right there. I won't do anything else here—I'll leave now. But what's wrong? Is somebody hurt?"

Oddly, there was a long silence. Finally, Kelly said, very nervously, "No. Everybody's kind of all right." Then there was silence again before she continued. "But we do have a serious matter that can't wait another day. Oh, Boone Woo, just please come—I can't explain it over the phone. Could you just please come?"

"My Kelly, I'm practically out the door. I should be there by eight twenty. Bye!"

Andy decided to talk his way to the farm to distract himself, to take his mind off the intense worry that something terrible had happened to his farm friends. "I'll just try to think about esoteric things," he said to the steering wheel. "Like infinity or what's the meaning of the universe. Hmm, that makes me think of my two planets, my corporate world and my farm world. We need both. Without that balance, the universal engine wouldn't run. And by golly, we need Dub Grimes and, as much as it pains me to say so, we need Kirk Daniels. It takes this oscillation, this rhythm to keep the world on course. And we need heaven and earth, and night and day, and Cylie Moe's and Kelly's Cove." Suddenly a lump hopped into his throat, and he stopped jabbering as he spied his turn, the ever-welcome driveway to the farmhouse. His knuckles were white on the steering wheel as he lurched to a stop at the top of the drive.

Andy bounded up to the porch and shot to the front door just as Kelly opened it wide and motioned him in. "Go on in, Boone Woo and say hello to the others while I run to my room for a second."

When he came into the family room, his friends didn't look all that distraught. He hurried through the hugs and handshakes and then started to speak. "What's—"

"Kelly'll tell you all about it, Andy," said Dub. "But don't worry. Everything's gonna be OK. We just needed to see you."

Before much else could be said or done, Kelly was back. She marched straight toward Andy, holding out her arms for what would be the first greeting hug he'd ever had with her.

"Boone Woo, I need you privately for a few minutes. Don't worry, everybody understands."

Andy thought if one more person told him not to worry he would drop dead from worry over not needing to worry. But he joined Kelly as she headed for the back door. He would simply do what she asked. After all, when his morning light was around, she was in charge.

As they headed out and down the pathway, Andy knew better than to make conversation. It was clear that the folks now in his environment would let him know when it was time for him to speak. Meanwhile, it seemed that he and Kelly were scooting along at a noticeably faster pace than usual. When they were within site of the cove, Kelly took his arm and stopped them both.

"Boone Woo, you go on. I forgot something at the house. I'll hurry."

"Can I get it for you or run back with you?" asked Andy.

"No. You just go on. I'll be right back."

"Well, that's OK. I'll just wait here for you."

"Boone Woo, go!"

"Yes ma'am." *Goodness, what does a guy have to do to get along around here?*

Andy moseyed on toward the cove, pausing now and then to look back. As he neared the entrance, there was just enough daylight left to cast a faint glow inside, lending it an air of enchantment. He stopped at the entrance, turned and took a couple of steps back toward the house, then, remembering his orders, relented and strolled straight into the cove.

Then he stopped abruptly, rolling up on his toes to keep from tumbling. A woman was sitting sideways on the bench. She turned to face her intruder, and then slowly, calmly, actually very gracefully, rose from her seat and stood in place, still and quiet.

Andy, too, stood speechless, motionless as he stared through the dim veil of light at the most beautiful, most adorable woman he had ever known. He dropped to his knees, lifted his hands prayerfully, and whispered, "Thank you, Lord."

While the woman stood stoically, clearly waiting, Andy eased a step toward her, and in a moment, another. He paused as he felt unadulterated joy race through his body. He started again toward her, and she in turn moved toward him. When they were only a couple of steps from each other, she paused, smiled sweetly, and said his name in the kindest way anyone had ever referred to him, "Hi, Andy."

He felt completely born again, and the gratitude welling in his heart sent tears to his eyes. Now they were both crying soundlessly. Andy reached toward her and walked into her arms, and they embraced lovingly and for a long time. When finally they eased back a little, sniffling—and giggling about that—their hands naturally trailed down their arms to join. They rested that way for a while, at arm's length, holding hands, and let their profound caring for each other settle around them. All at once, life seemed so tranquil, so peaceful, so utterly right.

Andy was the first to speak. "Are we free?"

"Yes, my Andy. Love has set us free."

"I guess I'll never be skillful enough to find a way to tell you how very much I love you, my Lorrie Dean. But oh my darling, I do so love you, and I will forever."

Lorrie Dean again reached for her man. They embraced tenderly as she whispered, "I love you too, and so will I love you for the rest of my life."

After some time, they sat on the bench and sorted out what had happened. "How did you get here?" asked Andy.

"I drove. My car is hidden down behind the tractor shed." Then she snickered and said, "When Mom and Dad found out about us, they kicked me out, saying 'To hell with protection—you go to that man!' They said they were tired of that kind of life also and weren't going to worry about it anymore. So I called my dear, new-found friend, your morning light, and she squealed with delight and said, 'Get on down here!'"

Andy stood and then knelt in front of his Lorrie Dean. "Will you let me be your husband, and will you be my wife?"

"Yes."

There being nothing further to say, they strolled hand in hand out of Kelly's Cove and on up toward the house. Soon they were met by Kelly, who came skipping along, swinging her arms, and smiling to the heavens. When she reached the two lovebirds, she fell in behind them and then wedged in between them and put an around each.

Each of them brought an arm around her, and the three marched merrily on toward the house.

As they drew near, they saw the others waiting at the head of the path. In that moment, a full moon popped up over the housetop and bathed them all in moonbeams. The three, still locked arm in arm, strolled on as the others started toward them. At once, Grandpa called out, "What time is it, Andy?"

The three bosom friends sang out in unison:

"It is morning."